THE
WANDERING
SWORD

The Last Eternal
Book One

By

JACOB PEPPERS

Visit the author's website:
www.JacobPeppersAuthor.com

To my wonderful and wonderfully wild children,
To my incredibly patient wife,
And to our hectic, running late, mismatched socks, stepping on
toys in the morning and stifling cuss words sort of life.
If there's another way to live, I don't want to know it.

Sign up for the author's mailing list and, for a limited time, receive a free copy of *The Silent Blade: A Seven Virtues Novella*.
Go to JacobPeppersAuthor.com to claim your free book!

CHAPTER ONE

He came with the dawn.

A lone figure covered in dust, wearing a tattered brown cloak that looked ready to fall apart in a strong wind. Despite the earliness of the hour, the day was already hot—it always was, here in the south—yet the stranger walked with his hood pulled up, concealing his features from view.

Claude frowned from his hiding spot in the roadside bushes as he studied the approaching figure's shabby appearance, thinking it unlikely that the bastard would have enough coin to make robbing him worth it—not that such a thought would keep him from doing it, of course. After all, a little coin—or a little food—was far better than none. That he knew from hard experience.

He continued to study the figure as the stranger moved calmly down the road, his frown deepening as he took in the unmistakable shape of a scabbard strapped across the stranger's back. And also hanging from the stranger's back was a long bundle, wrapped in a dusty cloth that hid whatever it contained from view.

Claude licked his dry lips at the sight of that, his frown slowly turning into a smile. Whatever was in the bundle, the stranger didn't want it visible, that much was clear, and that could only be a good thing. After all, men tended to hide things they considered valuable.

"What are you thinkin', Claude?"

A whispered voice beside him, sounding like the low rumble of a thunderstorm, and Claude turned to regard Earl, his second. A monster of a man was Earl, with arms the size of tree-trunks and hands that could crush rocks, if he took it in mind to do so. Unfortunately, the man also happened to be a complete fool.

"I'm thinking, Earl," Claude said, "that I'd give quite a bit to know what that fella is carryin' on his back."

The big man's eyebrows drew down in concentration. "But...that's a sword, ain't it, Claude?"

Claude held back the sigh that threatened to come. A fool and no mistake. Zane had been a far better second, that much was sure, though since he'd caught an arrow through the throat, Zane wasn't good for all that much. Except feeding the worms, maybe, and Claude thought that those bastards, at least, never had to worry about going hungry.

"I don't think we should do this, Claude," said another voice, a young man's—a boy's really. Claude turned to his nephew, Jessun, not bothering to suppress the sneer that always came to his face when he looked at his sister's son. For the hundredth time in as many days, he inwardly cursed himself for letting his sister talk him into bringing the nineteen-year-old along. "I got a bad feeling about this one," the boy said.

"How about you keep your mouth shut, or I show you what a bad feelin' really is?" Claude countered. Then he turned to Earl. "Listen, this is how we're going to do this. You and—"

"He's got a sword, Claude," his nephew said quietly.

Claude gritted his teeth, turning back to the boy. "And just what do you think you've got strapped in your belt there, boy? A candleholder?"

His nephew glanced down at the crude blade in its moldy leather sheath strapped to his waist, frowning. "I don't know how to use it, though...what if he does?"

"And what if he don't?" Claude demanded. "Heed me, boy, a man can starve to death wonderin' over the 'what if's.' We're doin' this, so keep your mouth shut and do as you're told, or, nephew or not, I swear by the Eternals, I'll—"

He cut off at the sound of a low whistle from Earl, spinning on the man. "Quiet, damnit," he hissed. The big man didn't seem to notice, though, too busy staring in the direction of the lone traveler.

Frowning, Claude followed his gaze and felt his own breath catch in his throat as a pure-white horse—the largest horse he'd ever seen—trotted over the rise in the road where the man had appeared moments ago. The man turned and said something, though too low for Claude to hear, and the horse gave its head a shake as it moved up and began to walk beside him.

"Damn," Claude found himself saying.

"That's a big horse," Earl offered.

Even his fool second's useless observation couldn't sour Claude's increasingly good mood, not now. The prospect of robbing the man, after all, had just gone from hoping to find a few hunks of stale bread and a few coins to quite a bit more. He didn't know how much a horse that size would sell for, but he expected it would be a damn sight more than whatever the traveler hid in the bundle at his back.

But it wasn't just the beast's size; Claude didn't know much about horses, never had been able to afford one himself, but even he could tell that the horse had been well taken care of, far better, it seemed, than its owner. For while the stranger looked one step—a very small one—removed from being a beggar, the giant horse was a far different matter. Its coat shone in the early morning sun, and it gazed forward with eyes bright with vigor, its body seeming to be made up entirely of muscles that shifted as it walked, as if it might explode into a gallop at any moment.

"H-how much you reckon we could sell that for, Claude?" Earl asked. *"A horse like that?"*

"How the fuck should I know?" Claude countered, still smiling.

"But who would we even sell it to?" Jessun said. *"A horse like that, once we steal it, word's likely to get around about it—there ain't no mistaking it. Besides, horse that size, people'll ask questions. It won't do to just say we found it."*

Claude felt a bit of his mood souring after all as he noticed Earl frowning. *"Might be he's right, Claude,"* the big man said. *"Maybe we ought to let this one pass. After all, the lad says he's got a bad feelin'."*

"You ever known him to have a good one?" Claude snapped, telling himself that he would have to have a long talk with his nephew. Soon. Maybe the kind of talk only one of them walked away from—after all, being family didn't give the bastard any right to screw with Claude's livelihood. *"Besides, if we can't sell the horse, or if it's too risky, then...well,"* he said, glancing back, *"horse that big...that'd feed us for a while."*

"*You mean you'd eat it?*" Earl said, a childlike expression of disgust on his face, "*a horse?*"

"*You ever starved, Earl?*" Claude asked.

"*No, Claude, but—*"

"*Well, I have. Went to bed with my guts achin' like there were rats in there gnawin' at me. You're damn right I'd eat that big bastard before feelin' that again. Shit, Earl, came to it, I'd eat you and the lad both. Now, can you all shut the fuck up and focus on the task at hand?*"

The big man paled, swallowing hard. "*O-of course. Sorry, Claude.*"

"*Now then,*" Claude said, satisfied, "*you take Dell and Brent, you go on up in front of the bastard, come out in the road. Carl still hidin' up in the trees?*"

"*Don't know, boss,*" Earl said. "*Can't see him. You know, on account of he's hidin'.*"

Claude stared at the man, once again regretting his choice of second. Still, he told himself, even big bastards had to sleep. That was a guarantee. What *wasn't* was that they'd wake up again. Might be time to clean house, Earl and his nephew both. Fact was, likelier than not, the thing was overdue. "*Just take Dell and Brent and go out in front. Me and the lad here'll come up behind him.*"

The big man nodded. "Okay, Claude."

Claude watched him trying to sneak away through the bushes, walking like he had to take a shit, making just about as much noise, Claude figured, as a rutting pig might. The big man made his way toward where Dell and Brent waited, and Claude watched as he relayed his instructions, watched as Dell gave a curt nod. According to him, Dell used to be a soldier, and while Claude didn't know that to be true—mostly on account of he didn't give a shit either way—there was no arguing that the man knew his business. Liked to drink a bit more than was good for him, but then who didn't? What mattered was that the man was steady when steady was called for.

Brent, on the other hand, didn't nod as Earl spoke. Instead, he grinned, a grin that grew wider by the moment until it looked as if the corners of his mouth meant to meet on the backside of his head. Claude winced even from where he crouched. Brent was damned good in a fight, fastest with a blade Claude had ever seen and that among no small amount of competition. The man might have made a fine second except for that he enjoyed showing that particular talent off a bit too much and sometimes took it in mind to stab—or kill—someone without any apparent reason. Not the type of man Claude wanted watching his back. After all, that'd just make it easier to stick a knife in it, if he took it in mind to do so.

He glanced up at the trees, looking for Carl, his scout. In truth, the man was a pickpocket turned mugger turned bandit and not particularly good at any of them, but bad pickpockets often made for good hiders, or so Claude had learned. If the man was up there in the trees, he was damned sure keeping out of sight, but just in case Claude raised one finger, signaling for him to hold his shot.

"Come on, lad," he said then as he saw the other three in the distance preparing to step into the road. "Let's get it done."

"Claude, I—

"I know, I know you got a bad feeling," Claude said, rising from his crouch. "As bad as it is, boy, it ain't so bad as starvin'—you can take my word on that. Now stay behind me and keep your damned mouth shut."

He rose and grunted at a crick in his back, knuckled it as he gave a stretch. Then he tugged at his sword belt in a vain effort to tighten it. It had fit once, but that time was years gone now, and those in between had been damned lean. Too damned lean.

"Don't even look like he's got nothin' on him worth stealin'," the boy said, sulking now.

Claude glanced at him, wanting to cuff him over the head but knowing if he did the boy'd cry out and give away their position. The man would know they were there soon enough, but Claude just as soon he didn't know until Claude was *ready* for him to. "Maybe he don't," he answered. "There's only one way to know for sure—now, quit your whinin' and come on."

And with that, he suited action to words, timing it so that he stepped out of the trees the same time as Earl and the boys, or at least near enough as to make no difference.

The stranger didn't cry out, which was good—some did, and while there was no one nearby to hear, that being one of the primary reasons Claude had picked the spot in the first place, he'd just as soon get the thing done quiet, if he could. All that shouting and begging had a way of giving him a headache. The stranger didn't cry out, but he *did* stop, he and his horse both, and Claude frowned as he noted that the two moved in unison far better than he and his lads.

The stranger seemed to regard Earl and the other two silently from beneath his hood before slowly turning his head to the side, looking over his shoulder at Claude and his nephew. Or, at least, he thought he was—wasn't no way to tell for sure, not with the tattered hood hiding his features.

"Mornin'!" Claude called out, grinning, not drawing his sword, not yet, but walking forward with his hands up as if he meant to give the man a hug maybe. The stranger said nothing, didn't even seem to so much as move, continuing to watch him from over his shoulder.

"I said mornin'!" Claude tried again.

"I heard you."

Claude found himself frowning. He'd been in the game for a while, had long since forgotten how many such people he'd robbed, how many such roadsides he'd waited beside. He'd seen plenty of reactions from those whose coin purses he'd helped lighten, fear chief among them, but anger there too. This man, though, didn't seem angry, and he damned sure didn't seem scared. Claude's frown deepened. It was that Eternals-blasted hood the man wore, that's what it was, no doubt hiding his terrified expression.

"Well," Claude said, forcing a grin. "Ain't you gonna say it back?"

The man said nothing, only watching him, and Claude sighed, shaking his head as if with regret. "Don't know what the world's comin' to, a man can't wish another a good mornin' and hear as much in return."

The stranger said nothing, was so still it was hard to tell if he was even breathing. Claude glanced at the lad, saw him watching the man nervously as if he weren't a lone man at all but a contingent of town guard come to escort him to his execution. Claude promised himself he would deal with the youth later, maybe permanently, tell his sister he tripped or got attacked by a wolf. Why, in the woods, anything might happen, and what she didn't know wouldn't hurt her. That was for later, though. For now, there was the dusty son of a bitch standing in front of him.

"Well," Claude said, trying a different tack as he turned back to the man, "ain't you gonna at least take your hood off? Or are you some famous king, afraid we'll ask you for an audience? Or maybe..."

He paused, his eyes going wide. "Are you some infamous criminal, fearin' we might recognize you?" Earl and the others laughed at that, even the youth gave a nervous chuckle, and Claude found himself feeling better.

"There are those who would."

The stranger slowly turned to fully face him, and the horse turned with him, like the damned thing was trained, and Claude felt better yet. Horse flesh was all well and good, but a beast in fine condition like the one with the stranger, and one trained too, well that'd fetch a pretty price. "That right?" Claude said, not having to fake the smile as much now. "And who are you then? King or criminal?"

The man said nothing, standing there casually as if he didn't have a care in the world.

Claude sighed. "Well, I s'pose that puts paid to the niceties, eh?"

"Suppose it does."

"I guess you know why we stopped you?"

The man moved then, so abruptly that Claude found himself reaching for his sword, suddenly sure that the man meant to attack and never mind that it would be suicide considering that he was outnumbered six to one. The stranger didn't attack, though. Instead, he only lifted his eyes, staring up at the canopy of the trees overhead. Or, more precisely, at one specific tree. Claude followed his gaze, seeing nothing but the branches of the trees, and the leaves adorning them. "Sorry, friend," he said, annoyed, "but are you distracted?"

"Just wondering if your man means to join us."

Claude frowned. "Just who the fuck are you?" he demanded, dropping the pretense of civility.

"Does it matter?"

Before he knew it, Claude's fingers were tightened around his sword hilt. There was something about the man he didn't like, something about the whole damn situation he didn't like. He told himself it was nothing, just age. The truth was he was getting too old for this. The *bald* truth was that he'd been too old for the last ten years or more. He needed a break, needed to retire, in fact, but then selling the horse standing beside the man might go a long way toward making that more than just a dream. "Well," he said, "best get to it then." He drew his sword and started forward, pausing when he noticed the youth hesitating.

He turned, shooting an angry glance at the boy who swallowed. "S-sorry, Claude."

Claude hocked and spat then started toward the hooded stranger, the youth shuffling after. "Now, you don't give my friend another thought, except to know that Carl is a damned fine shot with that bow he carries." A bit overselling it maybe, as that even when he was sober—which was pretty much never—Carl wasn't capable of hitting a deer unless maybe the deer walked up and stuck the arrow in itself. Still, this bastard didn't need to know that. "A *damned* fine shot," Claude said again, "fine enough to stick an arrow through that pretty face of yours if you do anything stupid." He shrugged. "Or maybe it's an ugly face. No way to know, I suppose, with that hood of yours, and I don't much care in any case. All I care about is that you toss your coin purse over. Now."

"And then I'll be free to go?" Asked in a calm tone, one that almost sounded slightly amused, and Claude silently cursed his nephew for making him nervous as if he hadn't done this a hundred times or more.

"Well," he said, forcing a grin on his face, "I wouldn't say *free.* But maybe you'll settle for alive, how'd that be?"

The stranger didn't move for several seconds, only stood regarding him from the shadows of the hood he wore, and for a moment, Claude was possessed of the wild notion that the man was considering charging him. Crazy, of course. There were five of them, six counting Carl in the trees. Not as many as there once had been, maybe, but plenty enough to handle one dusty bastard in a tattered cloak, plenty enough to get the job done if it came to a scrap. But then, in that moment, Claude didn't feel much like getting in a scrap. Felt, in fact, like calling the whole thing off, like turning around and leaving the strange son of a bitch to it, finding someone else, someone who didn't wear their hood in the middle of damned summer.

He realized something then—he was afraid. *He,* who in his younger, wilder years had been known as Claude the Cruel. And on the tail end of that realization came another emotion, one with which he was far more familiar: anger. Anger at himself, at the stranger, and anger at the boy standing beside him. That was it then.

The youth was going to have an accident—that was all there was to it. His sister was still young enough to pop out another squalling brat or two. "The purse," Claude growled. "Now."

The stranger only stood there again, watching him, and Claude's hand began to sweat where it gripped the handle of his sword.

The stranger finally did move then, reaching one hand underneath his cloak. He moved slowly, yet Claude found himself tensing, gripping the handle of his sword so hard his fingers ached. But when the man withdrew his hand, he held no weapon. Instead, he held a small, leather coin purse which he tossed at Claude's feet.

Claude glanced at the tiny purse then raised an eyebrow, looking back at the man. "Don't look like much of a fortune sittin' there, does it?"

"Maybe not," the stranger said. "But it's all I have."

"Oh, don't sell yourself short," Claude said, feeling better now, feeling more in control. "Why, I'm sure you've got somethin' worth more than that. I don't mean to quibble, understand, but after all, well, there's six of us, ain't there? Six mouths to feed—I'm sure you understand."

"It's all I have," the stranger said again, and though the man seemed to speak the same as before, Claude thought he heard what might have been a warning in his tone. That made him worried, and *that* made him angry.

"No, fella," he said, "it sure as shit ain't. Why, seems to me you've got yourself a mighty fine bit of horseflesh there. Sell for a damn sight more'n what you could fit in that little purse, I shouldn't wonder."

The man glanced at the horse, or at least he seemed to, then he turned back to Claude. "No."

"No?" Claude asked, frowning now. "What do you mean 'no'?"

The stranger's shoulders lifted in a slight shrug. "The same thing most people mean, I expect."

"Listen here, stranger," Claude said, "you see that fella there, the big one behind you?"

The cloaked man turned slowly regarding Earl and the rest. He took his time, as if he was in no hurry and, after a moment, he turned back to Claude. "Yes."

"Now see," Claude said, "that there's Earl. Earl, well, he ain't as patient of a man as me. Not as kind, neither. Bigger though, in case you hadn't noticed. Meaner, too. Oh, Earl might not be much on conversatin', but he's got a few other hobbies. Or...well. S'pose just the one. As to what that hobby *is*, well, just go on and take another look at him—at his knuckles, in particular. I guess they tell the story as good as anything, 'cepting maybe his nose. Leastways, what's left of it."

The stranger turned, as asked, looking silently back where Earl stood with the other two. Claude gave him a moment, letting his situation sink in. "Well," he said after a time, "tells a story, don't it?"

"Suppose it does," the stranger said, turning to regard him once more.

"Good," Claude said, falling back into the rhythm of things, feeling for the first time since he'd spoken to the stranger, if not comfortable, at least a damned sight closer than he had. "Now then, since it seems we finally understand each other, are you gonna give me that horse or ain't you?"

"He isn't mine to give."

Earl let out a growl at that, starting forward, and Claude held up a hand, stopping him. "Look, mister," he said, doing his best to keep his patience, "we're gonna have that horse one way or the other, understand? Either you give it to us willingly—or grudgingly, I s'pose it don't matter which—or we'll kill you and take it. You can rest easy that you don't have no choice in the matter."

The stranger stood there for several moments then turned to the horse, giving a single nod. "Go."

The horse seemed to turn to regard him for a moment then it started forward at a slow walk, coming to a stop beside where Claude and the boy stood. "Well, I'll be damned," Claude said. "Trained too." He grinned. "See, that wasn't so hard was it?" he asked. "Now, what else have you got?"

"Nothing you'd thank me for."

Claude frowned. "That a threat?"

"No."

He watched the stranger for a moment then grunted. "Well. And you just reckon I ought to take your word on it?"

"I wish you would."

There was a difference in his tone again, but it didn't sound like a threat to Claude as much as it did a genuine plea. There was something about the way the man said it, something about the whole damned situation that made Claude think maybe he should just listen to the stranger. After all, he had whatever money was in the coin purse—likely not much—and more importantly he had the horse. A good haul, better than he expected when they'd first spotted the man, that much was sure.

He considered it for a moment then grunted. "Well. Maybe you do and maybe you don't. You see, fella, there's plenty of...shall we say, *opinions* regarding people in my profession."

"Bandits, you mean."

"And while *all* of those opinions aren't true," Claude went on as if the man hadn't spoken, "I'm sorry to say that one, at least, is. You see, as a general rule, bandits are believed to be greedy. And I'm afraid that, in my case, at least, that one's all too true. So then I'll be needing to see what you've got in that bundle on your back."

"No."

Claude grunted a humorless laugh, shaking his head. "That's the second time you've told me 'no.' Can't say I much care for it. Never have, truth be told. Now, normally, I'd let Earl make clear our thoughts on such a thing—as he seems just about chompin' at the bit to do. But the sun's shinin' in the sky, the damned birds are chirping in their damned trees, and I've got me a fine new horse, so I'll give you one more chance—the bundle. Now."

"It stays with me. It is my burden and mine alone."

Claude frowned. "Sounds to me like you don't even want whatever's in there, fella. Be a shame to die over something you don't want, don't you think?"

"You have no idea."

"Enough," Claude growled, losing his patience. "Earl, show this bastard what those fists of yours are for."

"With pleasure," the big man growled, starting forward.

The stranger shifted then so that his right side faced Earl and the other two, his left Claude and his nephew. Then he only stood, waiting with apparent calm. Claude frowned at that. He'd robbed plenty of folks in his time, poked a few holes in some of them when they chose not to cooperate. All in all, he was a pretty hard man. But he didn't think even he could stand so calm while that big bastard Earl was stalking toward him, his lips peeled into a wide grin that showed off the gap in his teeth where one had been knocked out during a fight.

Earl, at least, didn't seem to give the man's demeanor a second thought—fact was the big bastard gave very few things a single thought, let alone a second. He moved forward in a rush, like a mountain with legs, charging right at the bastard who just continued to stand there.

Claude found himself tensing, waiting for what would happen when that mountain plowed into the man—the only thing that *could* happen, when a mountain ran into a man—but right before Earl struck him, the stranger moved.

He moved so fast that it was little more than a blur, and even though he'd been watching intently, Claude couldn't have said what exactly happened. All he knew was that, in another instant, Earl was lying flat on his back, wheezing for breath, the stranger standing over him, watching him silently. After a moment, the stranger turned to regard Claude once more.

He couldn't see the man's eyes, but Claude could feel his regard fall on him like a heavy weight. "You sure you want to do this?" the stranger asked calmly, not even sounding out of breath. "There's still time, still a chance. Things go much further..."

He didn't finish but then he didn't really need to. The only person present likely not to understand what he meant was Earl, and the big fucker was too busy gasping like a fish out of water to pay attention to anything.

Claude felt a shiver of fear run through him at the calm in the man's tone, at how quickly he'd dealt with Earl, a man who Claude had personally seen take on bar rooms full of people like it was a game and, if it were, it was one only he ended up enjoying.

He told himself it was fine—after all, he'd been scared before. Any man who had starved, who had *really* starved knew the taste of fear all too well, knew the taste of it even when there was nothing else to taste. Maybe especially then.

And now, like in those times, he took hold of that fear, reining it in, shaping it in his hands, turning it into something he could use. Fear made a man a coward, sent him running, carrying his empty belly and the gnawing sensation of hunger with him. It was useless. Anger, though...anger was a weapon, one that had served him well his entire life.

"*Carl!*" he shouted. "Let's poke a little daylight in this bastard, eh?"

A moment later, something whistled out of the canopy of trees, too fast for the eye to follow. At least, Claude's eyes. The stranger seemed to follow it. In fact, he did a lot more than that. One moment, the arrow was flying at the stranger, then he moved in a blur and the next moment he was holding it in his hand, his hooded face looking up at the trees. He turned back to Claude then, snapping the arrow. "Last chance."

Claude growled in anger. *"Kill the fucker!"* he roared, and then they were all rushing forward.

Brent was there first, eager as he always was when there was killing to be done. He was holding a knife in each hand, and he came on in a flurry of steel that was impossible to dodge. And yet, the stranger did, dodged the rapid blows with an economy of motion that almost made it seem as if he didn't move at all. Then one hand lashed out, too fast to follow, and a moment later Brent was lying next to Earl. He wasn't gasping though, as he was far too busy being unconscious for that.

"Just *wait!*" the stranger shouted, turning to Claude again. "You don't know—" But he never got a chance to finish whatever he'd been about to say for then Dell was on him. Dell might not have had a taste for blood like Brent, and though Claude had no idea whether the man had actually *been* a soldier or not, certainly he had the discipline of one. He came on doggedly, focusing on the task at hand, swinging his sword at the stranger's back even as he spoke.

The stranger seemed to sense it, though only the gods knew how, pivoting at the last moment and striking Dell's wrist with an open hand. Dell cried out in surprise and pain, and his sword went flying. The stranger spun then, planting a kick in his midsection and, in another moment, Dell was flying after his sword.

The abrupt movement caused the cloth bundle strapped to the stranger's back to come free. It hit the ground and rolled, the cloth that had bound it unfurling, revealing a scabbard that let off a metallic chime as the sword it contained slipped out a few inches.

In that same instant, the world seemed to explode in brilliant, bright light, and Claude cried out, squeezing his eyes shut and holding up his hand against the painful glare. After a few seconds, the light began to fade, and Claude blinked, rubbing at his eyes. "What the shit was that?" he rasped.

No one spoke, though, and when he looked up he saw the stranger still standing there, a trembling hand extended at the sword.

"A *sword?*" Claude hissed. "All this for a *sword?*"

"It's too late," the stranger said, seeming almost to be talking to himself. "I tried...but it's too late."

"What the fuck are you talking about?" Claude demanded, not liking the man's voice, for it was not a casual, emotionless tone, not now. A new note was in it, one he had wanted earlier but one that he did not like now—fear.

The stranger slowly turned to him. "You have no idea what you have done. Five years. Five years since the last time, since they were this close, and now..."

"What are you *talking* about?" Claude asked, finding himself being pulled into the man's fear as if by magic, his eyes darting around them as if expecting to see an army appear out of nowhere. But no, that wasn't the truth. He wasn't looking for an army. He was looking for monsters. "It's just a damned sword!"

"It's too late," the stranger said again. He knelt, retrieving the sword, holding the handle in one hand, the scabbard in the other, staring at that small sliver of bared blade as if he could divine the mysteries of the universe within it. "Too late."

"L-listen," Claude said, feeling as if he were losing control of the situation and not liking it, not at all, "you give us all your money, now, and we won't be forced to—" He cut off, his words turning to a shout of surprise as the stranger drew the blade and, in one smooth motion, plunged it into Earl's massive chest.

The big man gave a shudder and then was still. The stranger, though, paid this no attention. He was already moving to Dell, the soldier only now starting to try to struggle to his feet, so intent on the task that he didn't even see the blow that separated his head from his shoulders coming.

Then there was Brent, conscious now, backing away, sliding his ass across the ground, not looking like a killer anymore but a terrified child. "P-please," he muttered, "p-please don't—"

The stranger didn't seem moved by his pleas, though, and Brent just managed the beginning of a scream before the blade darted out like liquid silver, plunging into his heart. "It's better this way," the stranger said, seeming to speak to the corpse. "Better this than what

14

they will do when they come, trust me, for I have seen it. And they *will* come—they always come."

"Bastard!" someone shouted from the canopy of the trees, and another arrow flitted out. The stranger spun, deflecting it with the blade with a sort of disgusted casualness. Then he knelt, retrieving one of Brent's knives, and spun, releasing it to fly into the treetops.

Claude thought that there was no way the throw could be accurate, not when he couldn't even *see* Carl, but he was proven wrong a moment later when the archer fell out of the tree he'd been crouched in to land on the ground below with a *thump.*

Carl turned, staring at the man, lying there unmoving, Brent's dagger sticking out of his eye, in disbelief. "Impossible," he breathed. "It isn't—"

"I told you," a voice said, so close that he thought he could feel the man's breath on his neck, and he spun to see that the stranger was standing right in front of him, his hood still covering his features. "It's too late."

Claude felt a hard impact then, as if someone had punched him in the stomach, and he stared down, confused, to see that he hadn't been hit by a fist after all but by a sword. It had struck him in the chest and driven through it, disappearing nearly to the hilt.

Impossible.

It was his last thought—he did not have another.

***

He missed the bandit leader's heart by inches, and the man did not die as quick as he might have. An inexcusable mistake, one his teacher would have punished him severely for. But then, he was that man, that student, no longer. He was a vagabond, a wanderer upon the face of the earth.

He was the last.

"I am sorry," the wanderer told the dead man, then he pulled his blade free, allowing the corpse to collapse at his feet.

"Wh-who are you?" the remaining man, young, barely out of his teens, stammered.

The wanderer turned to face him, and noted as he did that his hood had fallen away in the brief fight. He raised it again. Not that it mattered, for the blade had been drawn, the damage done. "I am the last," he said in answer to the man's question. "I am the wanderer."

"P-please," the youth said, backing away as he tossed his sword to the ground. "Please don't kill me."

"It would be better," he said to the youth. "Without pain. Worse if they find you, and they *will* find you. They will come—always they come."

"W-w-who?" the youth asked, his voice shaking with his fear.

"Better if I do it," he told the young man. "Quick and easy. A pinch, nothing more. No pain. No suffering...no regrets."

The youth let out a cry at that then turned and bolted in the woods. The wanderer watched him go, considering giving chase only to abandon it a moment later. There was no time.

They were coming. Soon, they would be here.

It almost seemed to him that he could feel their attention, could sense their approach through the sword he held.

"I am sorry," he said to the departed youth. "You have chosen life...and life is pain. More pain than you can imagine." More pain than *anyone* could imagine, in truth. Anyone, at least, save him, for he was the only one who had known it, who had felt their attentions, and lived. "Good luck," he said to the youth who had already disappeared into the tree line, knowing, even as he said it, that it was useless. The man was dead already—he just didn't know it yet.

Better, then, for the youth, had he chased him, better if he had felt the sword's kiss. But his responsibility was not to the youth or to himself, and so...

He turned to gaze at his horse, regarding him with its knowing eyes. "I know," he said. "We have to go."

You spent too long with those bandits, a voice said into his mind. *You should have killed them immediately—you know well what is at stake.* It was a man's voice and one he knew well.

Wrong, a female voice offered. *Prudence was required and prudence shown. The sword is not the only danger—far from it. Six bandits slain on the road, and anyone with eyes to see it would know it the work of a single man. That would bring questions, questions we can ill afford.*

And now? another voice asked, this one a male's as well but different from the first. Older and somehow tired. *Now the sword has seen the sun, and the bandits are dead just the same. Spare the boy, and in his last moments he will not thank him for the mercy, if mercy it could be called.*

It was *mercy,* another female voice said, *mercy to be commended.*

And will that mercy still be commended, the first male spoke, *should they get their hands on the sword, on the power it contains?*

A calculated risk that—

The wanderer reached up and snapped the facing of the amulet closed, shifting the leather thong from which it hung. Not necessary, that, but a nervous habit, one he had picked up over the years. He had picked up many things, for there had been many years.

He paused, considering opening the amulet again, thinking perhaps he had acted in haste, but he quickly dismissed the idea.

They were ghosts, nothing more. His ghosts to bear, it was true, just as the sword was his burden and his alone, but a man could not suffer ghosts always, for they talked incessantly—there was, after all, nothing else that they might do.

Besides, he told himself, now was not the time for listening— now was the time for action. The creatures would be coming. No doubt they were on their way already, answering the blade's call. "Come, Veikr," he said, "it's past time we were gone."

The horse sidled up to him, and he leapt into the saddle. The wanderer knew that they needed to hurry, yet he found himself glancing at the dead men. More to add to the growing list, then. It had been necessary, their killing, a mercy, perhaps, but he felt no better for that. After all, their evil had been of the petty kind, sad and desperate and, in many ways, to be pitied, yet unknowingly their small evil might have called down one far greater, and so he told himself that there had been no choice.

But that made it no easier. Killing, the taking of a man's life, he had learned long ago, was the one thing a man could never get used to.

"We go away, Veikr," he said softly, forcing his gaze away from the corpses. "Only away."

CHAPTER TWO

They rode for three days and nights.

On the sunrise of the fourth day, the wanderer led his horse to the side of the road and reached into his saddlebags for oats only to find that the bags were empty. Veikr turned and regarded him expectantly.

"I know, I know," the wanderer said. "We'll have to stop by the next town, see if we can trade for some food."

It helped, sometimes, to talk to the horse. Pushed the loneliness back. Not all the way, but a little, and sometimes that was enough. It helped even though Veikr didn't talk back—perhaps *because* he didn't talk back. The ghosts, after all, did nothing to assuage his loneliness, and they talked plenty—in fact, they did little else.

Thinking of the amulet, he glanced down at it, considered opening it to consult them. In the end, he decided against it. They would have plenty to say, of course—they always did. The problem wasn't getting them to talk. It was getting them to agree. Or, failing that, to not talk at all.

"Oats," he said, pulling himself out of his thoughts. He got distracted, sometimes, lost in his own thoughts, his own memories. As the years dragged on, years spent largely alone save for Veikr, it had begun to happen more often. Understandable, maybe, but it didn't serve to allow himself to become distracted. It did not serve at all. Distraction caused mistakes and mistakes caused death. That was a lesson he knew better than most, and why not?

There was no better teacher than pain, no greater reminder of one's lessons than grief.

"Come on, boy," he said. "Let's get you fed."

***

It was mid-afternoon when they topped a rise in the trail, and the wanderer caught sight of a pillar of smoke in the distance, stretching up above the trees. That was good, he thought. Smoke meant people—at least most times. And while usually he did his best to avoid them, for people meant trouble—and that, pretty much all the time—Veikr was beginning to cast annoyed glances back at him as they walked. Not that he could blame him. Veikr helped him to flee when fleeing was required, carried the majority of their food and their bedroll and, of course, the wanderer, on his back. The wanderer's part of that deal was to feed him and, right now, he was failing.

As if to remind him of that fact, Veikr snorted, giving his head a toss. "I know, I know," he said, staring off at the distant smoke and feeling more than a little trepidation. He had never been good with people, and the last hundred years spent traveling the face of the world alone had done nothing to change that. Still, there was no help for it. Veikr was hungry, and so was he. He hadn't stopped in the last three days, not even to hunt for food, for stopping meant death. With any luck, the people who lived in the distant house might have some food he could purchase for himself as well.

He grabbed hold of Veikr's reins, but before he started down the path, he turned, glancing behind him, sniffing the air. Three nights and three and a half days had passed since his run-in with the bandits, and still there was no sign. Perhaps there would be none. Perhaps those hunting him had lost the trail, somehow. Even now, after all these years, he knew very little about how they tracked him.

He waited another moment, watching his backtrail, listening to the sounds of the birds in the trees, the squirrels skittering in their branches. Then, satisfied—or at least as satisfied as he was likely to get—he nodded to the horse. "Come on."

He started down the path, Veikr beside him.

After an hour of walking, he became aware of the sound of distant rushing water off to his left, through the trees, and he led the horse in the direction of the sound. A short while later they stood looking at a creek.

Just seeing it, he began to feel parched. His throat was coated in the dust of the trail, and his water had run out over a day ago. Still, when he walked to the creek and knelt, he forced himself to take small sips, scooping the water up in his hands.

A moment later, Veikr ambled up beside him and began drinking as well. "Not too fast," he said. "Easy, boy."

The horse ignored him.

"Fine," he said, "but I don't want to hear any complaining if you end up with a stomach ache."

When he was finished, he sat back while the horse had his fill. Finally, Veikr turned to him, and he nodded. "Alright. Let's go."

The horse gave its head a shake, and he frowned. "What?"

Veikr stepped forward, pushing him with his muzzle, then glancing at the creek.

"What?"

The horse looked at him, and somehow seemed to communicate, in his placid gaze, that he was a fool. Then turned and glanced meaningfully at where the smoke could be seen rising over the trees.

The wanderer grunted. "Okay, so we both need baths."

The horse turned and looked at him again, and he sighed. "Fine...I need a bath. Watch our stuff, huh? Try not to let one of those squirrels make away with it."

Veikr snorted as if to show exactly what he thought of that. The wanderer stripped out of his clothes and stepped into the creek. Winter was coming on, and the water was cool against his skin, but he did not mind.

He waded out into the water, enjoying the feeling of weightlessness, of being buoyed up.

As he stood there, bathing, feeling the cool water and the warm sun, listening to the sounds of the birds and the squirrels, he reflected, as he often had over the years, that many men spent their entire lives looking for peace but that such a quest was a fool's errand. Peace wasn't something a man could find for the looking. Instead, it found him. It found him in brief moments like this, so quick that a man, if he weren't paying attention, might not notice at all, and so rare that he could never be sure that this time wasn't the *last* time.

He took his time, washing the road dust off, running his hands through his brown hair to work the worst of the tangles out, soaking in not just the water but the feeling of being *refreshed,* of somehow being made anew. Finally, though, it was done, and he started back toward where Veikr stood, meaning to retrieve his other change of clothes from the saddlebags.

That was when he noticed the first thing that bothered him. Veikr was not cropping at the grass as he would have expected. Instead, the horse's ears were pulled back, and his nostrils were elongated, sure signs that something was making him anxious. The wanderer froze, looking around him, listening, and that was when he noticed the second thing—the quiet. The birds, which had been chirping and singing when he'd stepped into the creek, had gone deathly silent. The squirrels no longer skittered around the branches of the nearby trees, and even the branches of the trees themselves seemed to have frozen from where they'd swayed in the wind.

The world was silent, so silent that had it not been for Veikr's rapid breathing, the wanderer might have thought he'd gone deaf. He slowly looked around at the trees gathered around the clearing, seeing nothing. But then, that *meant* nothing.

He'd left his sword—*his* sword, not the cursed blade he carried—lying on the shore, only a few feet away now, but it might as well have been a mile, if the silence had been caused by what he thought.

Still, he knew that, without it, he didn't stand a chance, so he sprinted the several steps toward it, diving at the last moment. He hit the ground in a roll, scooping the blade up in his hands and felt a *whoosh* of displaced air as something sawed through the space inches above him.

He finished the movement, coming to his feet and spinning, but whatever it had been was already gone, the only proof it was anything more than his imagination coming in the form of the cracking of twigs somewhere within the trees.

Veikr stamped his foot, giving his head a shake as he snorted in agitation.

"Easy, boy," the wanderer said, his eyes never leaving the nearby copse of trees. "Take it easy." But judging by his tense demeanor, the horse didn't take his words to heart—not that the wanderer could blame him.

Over the years he'd spent on the run, he'd had all manner of men and creatures sent after him and here, now, he faced one of the deadliest.

"Easy," he said again, though this time, had he been asked, he could not have said whether he spoke to the horse or himself.

He waited, tense, his eyes scanning the trees, looking for something that he knew he would not see. Naked and wet as he was, his skin was cold, breaking into gooseflesh but he barely noticed, just as he paid little heed to the sharp pebbles digging into the pads of his feet. Distractions, nothing more, things that could not really hurt him on their own but, should they pull his attention away, even for a moment, might well kill him.

He felt the urge to curse himself for being a fool, for not keeping it in his mind that each moment of peace, like that he'd enjoyed while bathing, was often but a prelude to pain, but he resisted the impulse. It would do him no good. After all, if he survived the next few minutes, then it had all worked out, and if he did not...well. The dead, whatever else might be said of them, at least had no regrets.

He stood, unmoving, his eyes scanning the tree line, searching for the tell-tale shimmer, a sort of warping effect that the Unseen had on their environment. They were difficult to spot but not impossible, yet his efforts were hindered by the fact that he had squandered too much time in the creek. Night was coming on, and as the sun finished its course, setting low on the horizon, shadows began to spring up around him.

He didn't know how long he stood there, naked save for his sword and the amulet which always hung about his neck. It might have been minutes or hours. In time, though, his eyes caught sight of a slight blur in the world, as if he were seeing it through water. Only, the blur was not in the forest as he had expected but less than a dozen feet away.

He called on reactions honed over decades of training and leapt to the side, moving so fast that any mortal would have found it near impossible to track the movement, let alone strike him. But the Unseen were not mortals—perhaps they had been once, but they were not any longer. They were more than mortals, less than mortals, and so he felt the slice of a razor-sharp claw as it dragged across the flesh of his upper arm.

He hissed in pain, swinging his blade in a counter, but the creature was already gone, and the steel sliced through the air and nothing more. He spared a brief moment to glance at the wound and saw three deep, bloody furrows in his arm. Not an immediately fatal wound but one that, if not seen to and soon, would spell the death of him.

Foolish, he told himself, *careless.* But he let his anger go, pushed it aside just as he pushed aside the throbbing pain in his arm, for neither could help him, not now. He scanned the direction he thought the creature must have gone with his gaze and saw several footprints where the sand was damp near the lake, far longer and thinner than a man's.

An idea struck him then. *"Veikr,"* he barked, *"to the water."*

Following his own advice, the wanderer backed slowly into the water, not so far that it might hinder his movements but far enough that he could feel the dampness of the water beneath him. And then, his arm throbbing, blood leaking down his free arm that hung at his side, casting crimson drops into the water, he waited for what would come.

It did not take long. The Unseen were many things, but patient was not one of them. Water suddenly sprayed up in two directions, as if by magic, but some of those droplets did not fall back to the ground. Instead, they clung to the invisible form of the Unseen, a tall, too-thin creature as it charged at him, its long, taloned arms behind it.

He waited, feigning that he did not notice its approach until the last moment, then, as it came at him in a blur, one long arm's talons flashing out, he dropped to one knee, bringing his sword around in a sideways strike.

The force of the creature's incredible speed striking the sword was such that it was nearly ripped from his grip, but he held on and was rewarded with a high-pitched, ear-splitting screech as the blade struck the abomination's midsection and then passed through it. With the force of the creature's momentum behind it, the top half of its body struck the ground and water fountained up in a spray.

The wanderer wasted no time, turning and scanning the shadow-laden woods around the lake, for their lack of patience was not the only truth about the Unseen. There was another, more important truth—they always hunted in pairs.

The wanderer knelt that way for several minutes. He would have waited longer, but the blood was continuing to ooze from his wound, and he knew that if he did not see to it soon, he would be doing the creatures' work for them. Finally, he rose and moved to where the top half of the creature's body lay in the shallows of the lake.

In death, whatever fell magic granted the creatures the ability to be practically invisible to the naked eye dissipated, so that he was left staring at the thing's hideous visage. In some ways, it looked like a man. Or, perhaps, some mad artist's rendition of one. Its torso, at least what was still connected to it, was long and thin, as were its arms, arms which did not terminate in hands but in three cruel claws each as long as a dagger. Its body was covered in a pale, parchment-white skin beneath which he could see black veins running the course of it.

The worst, though, was its face. Thin and narrowed to a jutting chin, its open mouth revealing razor sharp teeth. Its eyes, open in death, were far too large for any mortal and were pitch black. The wanderer stared at it for a moment then plunged his sword into the creature's forehead.

Likely it was unnecessary, but when it came to those creatures that were sent after him, it was always better to be sure. He had made the mistake of taking their deaths for granted before and still had the scars to prove it—he would not make such a mistake again.

He ripped the blade free in a spray of black ichor then shuffled to where he'd tossed his sword's scabbard, wincing at the sickening, throbbing pain in his arm as he knelt to retrieve it before sliding the blade home.

"Come," he said. Veikr hesitated, as if he might argue, before finally stepping out of the water and coming to stand beside him. The horse met his gaze with the eyes that seemed to know so much and gave a snort.

"I know," he said. "There should be another, but it is not here. Perhaps it met some ill-fate on the hunt."

Veikr snorted to show what he thought of that, and the wanderer could not disagree. After all, normal mortals or natural beasts, even the most ferocious or feared, posed little threat to such a being.

"Or perhaps this one came alone," he said defensively. "Either way, there is no other—that much is obvious, and it is enough. There is no knowing where it might have gone."

The horse slowly turned, its eyes going to the distance where, in the failing light, the wanderer could just make out the pillar of smoke that he had first spotted rising above the treetops.

There is only one thing which might keep the Unseen from their task, a man's grizzled voice said. *And that is to feed.*

The wanderer glanced down to see that, at some point during his fight with the beast or, perhaps after it, the amulet hanging from his neck had come open.

He frowned then turned back to regard the distant smoke. The ghost was right, of course. The Unseen were possessed of a shockingly high metabolism. It was for this reason that they were able to move so quickly, but such speed came at a price—the creatures had to eat constantly and even then their lifespans were said to be measured in months, not decades.

He hesitated, uncertain.

Surely you can't be thinking about going there! This was a woman's voice, incredulous.

Whoever has created that fire will die if he does not—you know this. Another woman's voice, older, calmer than the first.

Then they will die, the first voice snapped. *All mortals do, after all.*

"Some more fully than others," the wanderer muttered.

But now, as was often the case with the ghosts, they completely ignored him, and why not? What need had the puppet master, after all, to speak his thoughts to the puppet?

She speaks true, said a gruff man's voice, one that might have sounded like a bear, should a bear discover the talent for speech. *It is a pity, yes, a tragedy, but their deaths will mean little in the scheme of things. You dare not risk it being taken.*

There was no need to ask what "it" the ghost referred to, and the wanderer found his eyes drifting toward Veikr's back, where he'd secured the wrapped sword before his impromptu bath.

A tragedy, he thought. *A pity.* And how many pities, how many *tragedies,* had there been over the years, he wondered. A dozen? A hundred? More? Enough that they all blended together into one, a chain he had built for himself over the years, link by link, one that dragged at him with each step he took, growing heavier and heavier as the years, as the decades, wore on. How long until it became so heavy that he could not move at all beneath the weight of it?

Why do you hesitate, Youngest? Asked a deep, resonant voice that he immediately recognized as Leader.

"Are we sure that it is the right choice?" the wanderer asked. "To leave them to die, I mean?"

Likely, they are dead already, Leader responded, confident as always. *And even if they are not, they will be soon. You will do no good to die alongside them, but you will do much evil. You know this.*

Well? a younger, male voice asked. *Why do you only stand there like some cow waiting to be poleaxed? Have you lost blood or your mind?*

"Both, maybe," he said, then he reached up and snapped the amulet shut before any of the ghosts could respond.

"Really have to get a new clasp for this," he explained to the horse, then moved to the saddlebags to draw out bandaging cloth. They might be out of oats for Veikr and rations for him, but these he had in abundance—he always did. He took a moment, bandaging the wound, closing his eyes as he jerked the bandage tight and a wave of dizziness swept over him, and it was all he could do to keep his feet.

Veikr snorted again, and he glanced at the bandage, already beginning to stain crimson. "I know," he said, "not the best job, but it will have to do. I don't care to be here any longer."

He pulled himself into Veikr's saddle, a far more difficult task than usual given that he only had one functioning arm, then glanced back at the corpse of the Unseen. He knew that he should hide it, for should anyone stumble upon it, they would have questions, questions that would only be answered, in time, with blood. But he felt weak from hunger and blood loss, and it was all he could do to keep his seat in the saddle just then. He knew that, should he try to bury the body, he would likely pass out before the task was done, and that would not serve.

"Come, Veikr," he said. "Away."

The horse turned in the direction of the smoke, and the wanderer let him take several paces before finally shaking his head. "No," he said, his voice a dry croak. "No. They were right on this much, at least—even if the Unseen did go for them, there is nothing we can do. It would kill us both along with them, and you know what would happen then." The horse's eyes seemed to roll backward, as if trying to look at the cloth-wrapped bundle sitting in front of him, then it turned its gaze up to him.

"I'm afraid you will have to wait a bit longer for your meal," he said. "We go."

After all, he told himself, *when the chain of regret and shame you have fashioned for yourself stretches miles behind you, what matters one more link?*

***

They'd been traveling for less than a half an hour, the wanderer swaying in his saddle drunkenly, when he heard a scream. A child's voice, ringing in the early dark, and Veikr paused.

The wanderer turned, blinking away the worst of the dizziness, and stared off in the direction from which the scream had come, the same direction as the smoke. It was beginning then.

Just another link in the chain, he told himself, giving Veikr's sides a soft kick to continue on. Or, at least, meaning to. Instead, he did not move at all, only sat atop the saddle, staring in the distance.

He did not know what it was that caused it. Perhaps it was the sound of that scream, a sound that reminded him of other tragedies, other pities. Perhaps it was the blood loss that made it difficult to think clearly, or maybe it was the thought—no, the *certainty*—that when that chain he had dragged behind him for the last century became too heavy to bear, it would only take a single link to make it so.

Whatever the reason, he found himself snatching up Veikr's reins. But instead of leading the horse down the path before him, he gave them a tug and then they were turning. "*Go, Veikr,*" he barked. "*Ganga.*"

The horse needed no encouragement, setting off at a dangerous gallop through the trees, and despite everything, the wanderer found a smile spreading across his face as the wind rushed past. Likely, he would be too late to save them, likely he would have been too late even had he charged there directly from the lake, but he would try. After all, even the thickest chains might be broken, given time and will enough.

There was another scream as they charged, his mount moving far faster and surer in the forest than any of its normal kin might have, and he heard what sounded like the grunts of a struggle from a clearing up ahead.

The wanderer pulled Veikr to a halt, then eased himself off the saddle onto the ground, nearly falling as he did, and was forced to catch hold of Veikr's side for support.

"Remain," he said quietly.

Then he drew his blade and shuffled through the trees in the direction of the clearing. In time he stood in the trees outside of it, staring in, and indeed he caught sight of a young girl that could have been no more than eight years old. The girl's curly golden ringlets bobbed as she ran through the grass, and a large, lumbering form followed after her.

The wanderer frowned. He knew what he had been expecting, and this was not it. It seemed that the girl was not being attacked by the second of the pair of Unseen after all but by a large mortal man with a thick black beard.

Not a creature sent by those pursuing him, perhaps, but an evil just the same and one far more easily vanquished. The wanderer started into the clearing, flexing the fingers of his good hand, then paused as the girl turned to look back at the man chasing her, and he noticed something strange. The girl didn't look scared—instead, she was laughing, her eyes dancing with mirth.

The wanderer stared at the scene in confusion, continued to stare from his spot in the trees as the man caught the girl and swept her up into his arms, spinning in a circle and bellowing out loud, hearty laughter.

The wanderer stood there watching them, father and daughter, he now realized, and though, outwardly, he was still, inwardly, a storm of emotions swept through him, so tightly bound in their churning that it was impossible to separate them. What did it mean when a man lived so long, saw so much, that he could no longer even distinguish a child's cries of joy from genuine fear? What did such a thing say of the world through which the man traveled? More importantly, what did it say of him?

He was still considering this when he heard a twig snap behind him, and spun, expecting to be set upon by the second of the Unseen. Only it was not some nightmare creature which assailed him but instead an old, gray-haired man holding a walking cane in one hand and a bundle of wood in the other.

The wanderer felt shame then, the shame of a man being caught out doing something perverse, and determining in a moment that the old man was no threat, he slid the sword back into its scabbard, counting on the shadows and his own unnatural swiftness to cover the movement from the old man's view.

"Hello?" a raspy voice asked as the old man narrowed his eyes, peering into the darkness where the wanderer stood. "Someone there?"

Perhaps he should have left then—likely he should have, disappearing into the shadows. But instead he stepped forward. "I am here," he said.

"Ah," the old man said, smiling. "Thought I might have seen someone, though fact is my eyes aren't as good as they used to be."

The wanderer did not know what to say to that, and so he said nothing.

"So," the old man said, coming closer and looking him up and down, "lookin' for a place to stay the night, that it?"

The wanderer blinked, thinking it over quickly. The Unseen had not come yet, but that did not mean that it would not, particularly now that his scent, his *blood*—which had begun to trace its way down his arm and from his fingers in a line of crimson—was here. It was dangerous, perhaps even foolish, but he had made the decision to help, if he could, and so he decided he would see it through. "Yes."

The man nodded. "Had a hard couple of days, I take it?"

"A hard life."

The old man snorted. "Well, ain't that the truth?" He seemed to consider for a moment, then smiled. "Well. I'd shake your hand but..." He glanced down at his arms, one still holding the bundle of firewood, the other his cane. "Well, safe to say it ain't just my eyes don't work as good as they used to. Anyhow, the name's Felden Ruitt."

The old man hesitated then, as if waiting for the wanderer's own name which, of course, he could not give him. Partly because the hearing of it would mark him for death and, more than that, the name to which he had been born was his no longer, for he was that man no longer. He was more than that man...but mostly, he was less. "It's a pleasure to meet you, Felden Ruitt."

The man grinned. "Well. You gonna just stand there, or are you gonna help me with this firewood?"

The wanderer stepped forward, taking the bundle of firewood from the old man. "Thanks," he said, finding himself touched but not really knowing why. Perhaps, he thought, it was because though he had traveled the face of the world for many years, it had been a long time since he had felt as if he were a part of it.

A small thing, maybe, but then the wanderer had lived long enough to know that the world often turned on small things.

"Best bring your horse along too," Felden said. "We'll see if we can't get you both fed."

The wanderer turned, frowning, to find that Veikr had approached when he'd been distracted and now stood behind him. "I thought I told you to stay," he muttered to the horse.

The horse cocked its head, meeting his gaze with a stare that seemed to say that he would follow orders just so long as those orders made sense and not a second longer.

The wanderer sighed, turning back to the old man. "Thank you for your hospitality."

Felden Ruitt grinned. "Oh, don't thank me yet. Knowin' my granddaughter, she'll have pink ribbons tied into your horse's hair before the introductions are through."

The wanderer found himself grinning, found himself wondering, too, how long it had been since last he'd done it. "You know what?" he asked, turning to look at the horse. "I think maybe that'd be alright. What do you say, Veikr?"

The horse snorted contemptuously, and he turned back to the old man who was studying his mount.

"Veikr, is it?" he asked.

"That's right."

"An interestin' name, that is. From the old tongue, ain't it?"

The wanderer blinked. "I'm impressed. There are few left breathing who still recognize the old tongue when they hear it."

Felden shrugged. "An old tongue for an old man, and why not? Anyway, I never knew much of it myself, but...Veikr. That seems to ring a bell. Means 'little,' doesn't it?"

"Weakest."

The old man raised an eyebrow, glancing at the horse which stood approximately twenty-three hands tall and weighed nearly four thousand pounds, its thick muscles visible even in the failing light. "Weakest, is it? Seems somebody's got a sense of humor."

The wanderer glanced back at the horse. "He is the smallest of his line."

"Eternals be praised, but I'd hate to run into the biggest."

The wanderer winced at that. "Yes, well...that would not happen. Veikr is the smallest of his line, and he is also the last."

The horse gave a soft shake of his head at that, and the wanderer unconsciously reached up, giving his muzzle a soft pat.

"I see," the old man said, his voice full of compassion as his gaze traveled between the wanderer and his horse. "A hard thing, being alone in the world."

"Yes."

"Well, come on then," Felden said. "I'll introduce you to my granddaughter and my son-in-law."

He turned then, starting away, and left with no other real option, the wanderer glanced at Veikr and then the two of them followed.

The old man led them out of the darkening treeline into the field, where the large man was currently busy tossing the blonde-ringleted girl into the air and catching her again while the girl shouted with joy and laughter.

The wanderer hesitated, feeling like he was intruding, and some of that thought must have communicated itself to his expression, for the old man gave him a pat on the shoulder, one very similar to the comforting pat he had given Veikr only moments ago. "That's alright now," the old man said. "Dekker's a big man, but he's a good one, so you just relax. You won't find no trouble here."

"Well, I've seen a lot in my day, but a flying princess, now, that's a first!" Felden shouted to the others.

The large man turned at that, setting the girl down, and no sooner did her feet touch the grass than she took off at a sprint. *"Paw-paw!"*

She charged into the old man, nearly knocking him from his feet as she pulled him into a tight embrace, but based on the wide grin spreading on Felden Ruitt's face, he did not mind. "Hi there, sweet one," he said.

"I feel like you were gone *forever*," the girl said.

Felden laughed. "Well, might be I came back with a little more than just firewood, eh?"

The girl turned, seeming to notice the wanderer and his horse for the first time and with a squeal of delight she let go of her grandfather and ran to the horse. But she hesitated at his size, glancing uncertainly back at her grandfather. "Can...can I touch it?"

The old man glanced at the wanderer who gave him a single nod. "Sure, go on and help yourself," he said. The little girl needed no more encouraging than that and began stroking Veikr's muzzle and shoulders. For his part, the horse endured the petting with good grace, even nuzzling her and making her laugh. Then the horse glanced at the wanderer.

He grunted. "Don't get used to it," he muttered to the horse.

"Welcome back, Felden," a voice said, and the wanderer left the horse to his spoiling as he and Felden turned to regard the man who had approached. Up close, he seemed even bigger, of a size to have rivaled some hero out of legend. His face also sported several scars, as did his knuckles, proof that he had been in his fair share of fights over the years. "So," the big man asked, "who's your friend?" He glanced at the wanderer, with an expression not of menace but of a cautious kindness that seemed to say that he was happy to be friendly, but he could also make sure the wanderer had a bad day, if he wanted to. The wanderer might have told him that he needn't bother, for the day hadn't been all that kind so far. But then...they so very rarely were.

"Oh, just a vagabond I picked up, said he was lookin' for a place to rob so I brought him here," Felden said with a grin. "Oh, relax, Dekker, you big ox—I'm just jokin' is all. This here's..." He hesitated, glancing at the wanderer. "Forgive me, friend, but I realize I never did get your name."

"Ungr," the wanderer said.

"Ungr," Felden repeated, watching him closely. "Another old tongue word, ain't it?"

The wanderer inclined his head. "Yes."

"What's that one mean, then?"

"Youngest."

"Anyway," the large man, Dekker, said, "what brings you all the way out here in the wilderness, Ungr?"

It is where I always am, he thought, but then the truth would not serve, not here, just as it had not served for the last hundred years, so he thought quicky. "I was set upon by bandits on the road,"—*true*—"and was forced to leap onto my horse and flee through the forest." *Only partly true.*

"I see," the big man said, eyeing him up and down. "Yeah, I've heard tale the bastards are accostin' folks on the road. Guess that'd go some way to explainin' the bandage on your arm, eh?"

"Yes. One of them wounded me before I fled." *A lie, and no arguing it.* It felt bad, to lie to these people after the old man's kindness, but some truths were better kept secret, for some truths—the worst kind—cut.

Dekker watched him for another moment then finally grunted, giving a nod. "Alright then. You come on in the house, and we'll see what we can do about that arm, but I'll warn you, stranger—you make any move to bring harm to my family, I'll make sure you suffer for it. I'm a farmer now, but I wasn't always. We all have pasts. Understand?"

The wanderer understood that better than anyone, so he nodded. "I understand. And...thanks."

The man grunted, giving him a smile. "Don't thank me yet—you ain't tasted my wife's cookin'. Might be once you have, you'll wish you'd taken your chances with the bandits." He turned to the young girl and the horse. "Come on, Sarah girl, to the house. Your mother'll throw a fit if we're late for dinner."

"Aw, Daddy," the girl said, turning around from petting Veikr, "can't we stay out here for a few more minutes? He's *such* a *good* horse."

The big man shook his head, smiling, and the wanderer, watching him, noting the loving gleam in his eyes, did not have to wonder at what had caused the big man, clearly a fighter once, to leave that life of violence behind him. "Tell you what," the big man said, "you go on in the house like a good girl, and maybe you can help me get that monster of a horse settled in the barn in a bit, how'd that be?" He glanced at the wanderer. "If that's okay with you—seems to me he could do with a bit of rest." He paused, clearing his throat. "You don't mind my sayin', you both could."

The wanderer, well aware of his own exhaustion, not to mention the dirt and blood staining him from his fight with the Unseen, tried a smile of his own. It felt strange on his face, wrong, and he wondered how long it had been since he'd smiled. Wondered, too, how long it had been since he'd had reason to. "That'd be fine."

"As for you," the big man said, turning back to the wanderer, "you come on in the house—the sword stays outside though. Understood?"

"Understood," the wanderer said.

Dekker nodded. "Alright. Well, come on then." He led them toward the house, the old man walking beside the wanderer while the girl skipped around Veikr who seemed to be enjoying the attention.

Then they were at the door, the big man giving the wanderer one final look. "You can tether your horse for now. We'll see to him after dinner—assumin' any of us live through it, that is. You get him tied, just come on in."

The wanderer nodded his thanks and moved to Veikr as the rest went inside. The horse gave a soft whinny, and he smiled. "I know. They're good people, I think." Though the truth was, it was hard for him to tell. He had spent many years away from civilization—it was safer that way, both for him and for civilization—and after so long in the shadows, it was hard to see anything else.

The horse gave another soft whinny. "You like her, don't you?" he asked softly as he set about tying the horse. "Well, we'll see if you still feel that way once she works on you with that ribbon."

Veikr snorted, giving a shake of his head. "I *know* you don't need to be tied," the wanderer said, "but they don't know that. Just relax—it won't be for long. And I'll see about getting you some oats, alright?"

The horse only watched him with a look that said he'd better do just that, and the wanderer finished and moved to the door. He paused, glancing back at Veikr. "One eye open, alright? We don't know where the second Unseen is."

The horse snorted as if he were a fool which probably he was, and the wanderer gave another nod before propping his scabbarded sword on the wall outside of the door and stepping through.

Inside, the small, simple cabin was warm despite the coming winter, the cause of which was a blaze in a stone fireplace in the corner. A woman knelt in front of it, stirring the contents of a large iron pot, and she turned at the sound of the door closing behind. "This'll be your new friend then, Da?" she asked, giving the old man a glance.

"Sure, why not?" Felden Ruitt said, grinning from his spot at the table, "a man never can have too many friends. Well, come on, lad," he went on, waving at an empty chair. "Have a seat."

The wanderer started toward the table then suddenly staggered, nearly falling and only managing to keep his feet by catching hold of the back of a wooden chair with his good hand.

The old man was out of his seat with surprising speed, coming to his side. "You alright, lad?"

"I'm...fine," the wanderer said, though in truth he felt far from fine. His vision was blurry, and his head felt as if it had been stuffed with cotton.

Felden Ruitt grunted. "Sure, and when young women dream of their heroes it's my old wrinkled face they see. It's the wound, isn't it?"

"I...yes," the wanderer said. "Maybe...maybe it is worse than I thought."

"Shit, and here I am thinkin' on dinner," Dekker said, rising. "Come on—we got a washroom in the back, I'll take you. We'll get that wound looked at."

The wanderer felt a surge of panic at that, for as soon as the bandages were removed, it would be obvious that he had lied about the manner of his wounding.

"That's alright, Dekker," Felden said, watching the wanderer's face, "He's my stray—I'll see to him."

The big man frowned. "You sure, Felden? I don't mind."

The old man grunted. "'Course I'm sure. Anyway, we both know I know more of healin' than you." He glanced at the wanderer. "Picked up a bit durin' my time as a soldier. Best way to keep breathin' is to be able to stitch up your wounds yourself. Now, you just lean on me, lad. We'll get your sorted quick enough."

The wanderer was too exhausted and dizzy to do anything else, so he allowed the man to drape one of his arms over his shoulder and lead him in a shuffling walk toward a door at the back of the main room which Dekker threw open for them.

They stepped into the small room and Felden led him toward a chair, grunting with the effort of sitting him down. "Just take it easy, lad," the old man said, though the wanderer noted that the man was panting hard from the effort. "We'll get you sorted alright."

"Da?"

The old man turned to look back at the door where his daughter, Dekker's wife, stood. "Some hot water, Ella," Felden said. "And some needle and twine, if you have it."

"I-I have my darning needle and some thread I was using to patch up one of Sarah's dresses."

"That'll do fine," Felden said, "but the water first, if you please."

The woman nodded, turning and hurrying out of sight. "Now then," the old man said once she was gone, "let's have a look." He lifted the wanderer's arm, sniffing of the wound. "Well. Don't smell infection, so that's somethin' you can be thankful for."

"I'll try."

The old man barked a laugh. "Alright, now let's see what we're workin' with."

He started to unwrap the wound, but paused as the woman, Ella, returned with several rags, her husband behind her with a large bowl of steaming water.

"Just set them down there, please," Felden said, motioning to the table. The two did as asked, and then stood, watching.

The old man glanced at the wanderer then back at the two. "I'll get him sorted. Why don't you all go ahead and have dinner? No use in us all goin' hungry."

The big man, Dekker, frowned. "You'll let us know if you need us?"

"It's a promise," Felden said.

"Alright then," he said, then he turned and walked back out the door.

Ella fidgeted for a moment then smiled. "I'd better go check on Sarah." She turned and disappeared through the door, closing it behind her.

"There now," Felden said, "you can relax, lad."

The wanderer hadn't realized that his body had tensed at the idea of the old man unwrapping the wound in front of the husband and wife, and he winced, relaxing in his chair. "Sorry."

"I know Dekker's a big fella, but you've got to trust me—he's a softy. If he weren't, I wouldn't have let him marry my daughter, would I?"

The wanderer opened his mouth to tell the man that it hadn't been the size of the man that had unnerved him but then closed it again. Better him think that than that he was worried about them seeing his injury.

The old man went about the task of unwrapping the wound then, when the bandage fell away, he hissed. "I've seen some bad wounds in my day, stranger, but this is right up there with the worst. It's a wonder you're still conscious, let alone able to walk all the way here."

"I've had a lot of practice," the wanderer said truthfully. "At walking, I mean."

The old man glanced at him then gave a nod. "I think maybe you have. Anyway, I need to get the worst of the blood away. This might hurt a bit."

Pain was another thing he'd had a lot of practice at, so he only sat while the old man took a rag and soaked it in the steaming water then began to rub at the wound, cleaning the dried blood off to reveal three jagged furrows where the Unseen's claws had struck him.

The old man glanced up at him, raising an eyebrow. "You said a bandit's sword did this?"

The wanderer met his eyes. "I did."

Felden watched him for another moment then finally gave a nod. "Alright." The old man reached over, retrieving the thread and needle that Ella had brought. "Guess I don't need to tell you that this'll hurt too since you seem like the sort of man's probably taken a few wounds in his time and has the scars to prove it."

More than you know, the wanderer thought. "Please, proceed."

The man did, bending to the task, and the wanderer did his best to remain still at each stabbing pain of the needle as it traced its way in and out of his flesh, sealing the wound. By the time it was done he was covered in sweat, and the old man sat back, running an arm across his forehead. "There. Now, I'll be right back—you just sit there, try not to pass out, eh?"

The wanderer gave him a small smile. "I'll do my best."

The old man left then and returned a few minutes later with a small bowl which he stirred with a wooden spoon. "This ought to take the edge off the pain," Felden said as he sat and began applying the poultice to the wound. True to the man's word, the herbal mixture took the worst of the pain away. With that done, the man rewrapped the wound with a fresh bandage, pulling it tight.

"Alright," the old man said. "I'm no healer, but that ought to keep well enough. Though, you want my opinion, you ought to get it looked at by someone, the next town you go to."

The wanderer made it a point to avoid towns, but he nodded. "I will. Thanks."

"Now, you think you could handle some food?"

The wanderer's stomach rumbled in response to the question. "I think I'll chance it."

A few minutes later they were walking back into the main room where father, mother, and daughter all sat, eating and talking.

At the sound of the door opening they looked up. "Everything alright?" Dekker asked.

"As well as can be expected," Felden said. The big man nodded, rising and moving to the wanderer's other side.

"Go on, Felden," he said as he took the wanderer's arm and draped it across his shoulders, "have a seat and get some food—I'll help your friend here."

The old man smiled. "See?" he said to the wanderer. "A softy." But he accepted the offer quickly enough, moving to the table and having a seat.

Dekker guided the wanderer to the table, pulling out a seat and gently lowering him into it.

"Thanks."

"Sure," the big man said. "Go on—have some food."

The wanderer glanced at the bowl of steaming soup in front of him then winced as he thought of Veikr. "I was wondering if, perhaps, I might trouble you for some oats for my horse. I can pay and—"

"Already taken care of," the big man said. "Got your horse situated in the barn—nothin' fancy, understand, but it's dry."

"Thank you," the wanderer said, meaning it. "That...that is very kind."

The big man shrugged, clearly uncomfortable with the praise, "Ain't nothin'. Anybody'd have done the same."

The wanderer had walked the earth a long time, and he had not found such a thing to be true. A quick glance at Felden showed that the old man was smiling sadly, as if he, too, knew that the statement was wrong, no matter how much he might wish otherwise.

"Daddy, can I go see the horsey?" the little girl asked.

"Sure, lass, just let—" Dekker began.

"Dinner first," Ella intoned, raising an eyebrow at her husband who winced.

"You heard your mother, Sarah. Eat, then you can go see the horse. If, that is, it's okay with Ungr here."

"I think that would be fine," the wanderer said.

Then they ate, and despite the big man's words about his wife's cooking, the stew tasted delicious to the wanderer who could not remember the last time he'd had a homecooked meal, having lived the last many years off gamey meat prepared over a campfire or, and this more often, berries and herbs picked as he walked.

He did not know just how hungry he had been until he went to get another spoonful and heard the sound of his spoon striking an empty bowl.

"Would you like seconds?" Ella asked.

"Aw, dear, Felden just now got done fixin' him up. Seems a shame to kill him." This from the big man who grinned widely, narrowly avoiding his wife's playful slap.

"I...if it isn't any trouble," the wanderer said. "It is really quite good."

"See there?" Dekker said, laughing. "I knew the man was a liar!"

The wanderer, who had lied several times to the family since meeting them, struggled to hide a wince at that as Ella took his bowl and walked to the fireplace, spooning out more of the delicious stew.

She returned a moment later, passing the bowl to him. "You'll have to forgive my husband," she said, rolling her eyes, "he's not just the size of a bear but possessed of one's manners as well, I'm afraid." Her husband grinned at that, and she returned the smile, shaking her head before taking her seat once more.

"Thank you," the wanderer said, "for everything."

The woman smiled while Dekker winced, clearing his throat. "Anyway, better eat up. If a man means to take poison, seems to me the best way is fast."

The wandered laughed at that, but he didn't need another invitation, and he began to eat.

"So, Ungr, isn't it?"

"That's right."

"You live around here?"

The wanderer did not have a home, had not for many years, and he shook his head. "Not really, no."

"Ah," Dekker said. "Just visitin' kin, then? Or are you here for work?"

The wanderer considered that. He was the last of his name, had been for some time, and so there was no kin alive who he might visit, neither here nor anywhere else. "I..." He hesitated.

"By the Eternals, Dekker," Ella scolded gently, "what are you, a king's questioner? He's eating, can't you see and, besides, did you ever think that maybe he wants to keep his business *his* business?"

The big man's shoulders hunched. "Sorry, fella," he said. "Didn't mean nothin' by it, was just trying to make conversation is all. You ain't got to say nothin' you don't want to, alright?"

"No, it's me who should apologize," the wanderer said. "It...well, to answer your question, I guess I'd say that I'm here for work." Not the truth, exactly, but as close to it as he wanted to come.

Dekker nodded. "I see, I see. So, what is it you do?"

"*Dekker,*" Ella whispered, but the wanderer held up his hands.

"Please," he said, "it is only right that he should ask questions. After all, I am a stranger inside your home, one who you have been nothing but kind to. As for my profession..." He hesitated then, his mind racing with thoughts. "I, well, I am a sellsword."

Dekker grunted, sitting back in his chair. "That right?"

"What's a sale sword, Daddy?" the young Sarah asked.

"Not a sale sword, lass," the big man said, "a *sell*sword. It means that..." He scratched at his chin, thinking it over, then looked to his wife for help.

"What it means, honey," she said, "is that Mr. Ungr here, well, if someone has been bad, and the guards are having a hard time tracking them down, well, he goes and fetches them."

"You mean...you mean he gets the bad men?" the girl asked.

"That's right," the woman said, smiling apologetically at the wanderer.

Dekker grunted. "So. The bandits—the ones gave you that cut. You didn't just run into them, did you?"

In point of fact, the wanderer *had* just run into them. Certainly, had he known they were there, he would have taken a different path. But he saw where the big man's head was going and decided it would be easiest to go along. "That's right," he said. "A nearby town hired me to try to take care of the bandits but...when I found them..."

"They proved to be a bit more than you thought," the big man finished.

"...something like that, yes."

Dekker nodded. "Used to be I did somethin' pretty similar," he said, glancing at his wife who looked at him with an expression of unadulterated love. "Still got the scars to prove it," he went on, turning back to the wanderer. "And, I hope I ain't steppin' out of line, but you mind if I give you a piece of advice?"

"Not at all."

"See," the big man said, "I learned somethin', back then. Took me a long time—I never been all that smart of a man. But what I learned is that there's one very dangerous thing about a man goin' out looking for violence."

"Oh? What's that?"

"Simple," Dekker said, meeting his gaze. "It's that, if he's very unlucky, sometimes he finds it." He sighed, glancing at his wife and daughter. "I'll tell you, Ungr, fightin' don't ever benefit a man much, but it'll hurt him plenty. Hurt those he loves the most, too. You want my advice, get out of it while you can, find another job, any job. Dig graves, if you want. The Eternals know dirt washes off a damn sight faster'n blood anyway."

If only I could give it up, the wanderer thought, *but there is no one else. All those who might have shared the burden are dead and gone...They are ghosts, no more. Only I remain.* "Thanks," he said to Dekker, "I'll...I'll think on it."

"All I ask," the man said, holding up his hands as if to show he meant no harm.

They finished the rest of their meal in silence, one that the wanderer could tell had been made uncomfortable by his admission that he was a sellsword. He wondered just how much more uncomfortable they would have been if they knew the truth about who he was, *what* he was.

In time they finished, and the girl, Sarah, was up out of her chair the moment the last spoon hit the last bowl. "Can I go now, Daddy? Can I go and see the horse?"

The big man glanced over at his wife who sighed, nodding, before turning back to his daughter and heaving a theatrical sigh. "Oh, I suppose so. Come on then."

The girl ran to him, and he lifted her up, sitting her on his shoulders so that her legs were draped over either one. "Come on," Dekker said to the wanderer. "I'll show you where you can sleep in the barn—ain't much, but like I told you, it's dry."

The wanderer nodded, rising. "Thank you, ma'am," he said to Ella. "For the meal."

"It was our pleasure," she said, smiling and doing a pretty good job of being convincing. Yet for all her efforts, the wanderer could see the suspicion in her eyes at the realization that he was a sellsword, and he could not blame her. He might not be a mercenary, but that suspicion was well-deserved, more than she knew, so he only gave her a nod of thanks and turned back to the big man.

"Ready," he said. He inclined his head to the old man then followed Dekker out onto the porch where he retrieved his sword from where he'd laid it.

The big man watched him. "One day," he said, "maybe you'll put that blade down and choose not to pick it up again."

"Maybe," the wanderer said. "But not today."

The big man heaved a heavy sigh. "No. No, I guess not."

Dekker stepped off the porch, leading him toward the barn, the girl bobbing excitedly on his shoulders.

No sooner were they inside, than the father set his daughter down, and the little girl squealed in delight as she rushed toward the stall where Veikr had been stabled. The horse whinnied, showing his excitement to see her.

"Can I go inside, Da?" she asked.

"Just for a minute," Dekker said. "Then it's time for bed."

"Aw, Daddy, but I'm not even tired!"

"Maybe not, but I am," Dekker said.

The girl gave a pouty face at that then turned and began stroking Veikr's muzzle. "You have family, Ungr? Dekker asked, still watching his daughter.

"I do not."

The big man nodded slowly, turning to him. "Met El, my wife, ten years ago now. I was...well. Let's just say I worked for some bad people, spent my time *around* bad people, and I'd say if I weren't the worst then I wasn't all that far off, neither. I ain't blamin' nobody, you understand. It was my fault—we all walk the path we choose for ourselves, and the one I chose, well, I guess I knew where it'd end, or near enough as to make no difference. You understand?"

We all walk the path we choose. Part of the wanderer rebelled at that, so long had he carried his burden alone, yet he knew that it was true. Many years ago, decades, he had chosen his path, and it had led him here, to this place. But what if he was no longer the same man he had been? Did it make any difference? He supposed not. "I'm...trying to," he said.

Dekker nodded. "Anyhow, my path ended up in a back alley, me with a few extra holes poked in me, bleedin' out. Even now, I don't know the name of the man who done it, and I wouldn't care if I did. Woulda been someone else, if it wasn't him. Anyhow, I managed to drag myself to the healer's. El, she was the old man's apprentice, opened the door, and I guess I just about passed out in her lap. Woke up, and she was there, offerin' me water. In time, she offered me more than that. A new life, a new way to be, to live. I've done a lot of things I'm ashamed of, Ungr, very few of which I'm proud, but takin' it, that way she offered? I guess I'd say that's the proudest moment of my life." He glanced back at the girl, playing with the horse. "Folks always talk about how it's a man's job to take care of his woman, his kids. Truth is, though, they take care of me a damn sight more'n I do them." He shrugged. "Anyway, that's all I'll say on it. Sleep well, Ungr."

"Same to you," the wanderer said softly.

The big man nodded. "Oh, don't look so glum, friend," he said, clapping him on the shoulder and giving him a wide grin. "There's still time to make a change." He winked. "Until there's not."

Before the wanderer could give any sort of answer—which was just as well, for he had none—Dekker turned away. "Alright, Sarah. It's time for bed, lass."

"Aw, Daddy, just a few more minutes?"

"Best not, love," Dekker said.

The girl risked one more quick pet of Veikr's muzzle, then she turned and hurried to her father who scooped her up in his arms.

"Good luck, Ungr," he said. "And hey—some people make it out of the path you're on, right? After all, I did." Then he turned and left.

The wanderer watched him go. He was right, of course. Some people made it off the path of blood, but what he had not said, what he had not *needed* to say, was another truth—most of them didn't.

The wanderer sighed and turned to the stall where Veikr stood looking after the girl. "Seems you've got a fan."

The horse, unsurprisingly, said nothing. Instead, he turned away and lay down. The wanderer understood that well enough, for he felt like being alone as well, perhaps lying down and waiting for sleep that, likelier than not, would never come. But he could not sleep, could not even try, for the other Unseen was out there somewhere, and so he secured his scabbarded sword across his back then walked toward the barn's entrance.

As he stepped outside, he caught sight of Dekker and Sarah's shadows silhouetted against the darkness and the warm light spilling out from the house. Only a moment, and then they were through the door and gone. The wanderer wondered, for a moment, if he would see them again, but he did not wonder for long. In the morning, he would leave, and that would be the end of it.

He would be alone again.

There was a chair outside the barn, so he removed the scabbard from his back, then sat and propped the undrawn blade on his knees. And then, as he had done for what sometimes felt his entire life, the wanderer watched the darkness.

He was not sure how much time passed, perhaps five minutes, perhaps as much as an hour, when he heard a creaking sound and turned to see the door to the house opening. The old man, Felden Ruitt, stepped out onto the porch, and the wanderer was not surprised, for he had expected the visit.

The old man was carrying something, and as he drew closer the wanderer saw that it was a large tub filled with water. "For washin' the worst of the road dust away," he said by way of explanation. "My daughter, Ella, meant to bring it to you."

"And yet, you came instead."

"Yeah, suppose I did," Felden said.

"I thank you for it," the wanderer said, "if you would like to leave it—"

"Ah, best to use it now, while it's hot."

The wanderer met the man's eyes for a moment then nodded. He glanced once more out at the darkness of the surrounding forest. He saw nothing, but that gave him little comfort. Evil, after all, only announced itself in plays. In the real world, it came upon a man unaware. "Very well," he said, taking the bowl and moving inside.

He sat the bowl on a stool near Veikr's stable and stripped his shirt, hanging it from a nearby peg. That done, he began to use the rag inside the tub to scrub his face, then his chest and back.

When he was finished, he returned the rag to the bowl and redonned his shirt, turning to the old man who had said nothing.

"Got some pretty nasty scars," Felden observed.

"Yes."

"Particularly that big one, on your chest there. I couldn't help but notice that it's got a twin on your back. As if you were impaled, maybe."

The wanderer watched the old man for a moment. "You have something you want to say."

"Oh, nothin' untoward," the old man said, smiling. "Just makin' conversation, is all. Still, might sound crazy, but I've heard about another had that same sort of scar."

"Oh?"

The old man nodded. "That's right. It was a story my da used to tell me, a long, long time ago. About a man who, with his companions, fought against the world's greatest evil only to betray them and be killed before they achieved a great victory. Seem to recall there was a song about it too, though I'm afraid I can't remember the words."

"I imagine other people have such scars."

"Maybe," Felden agreed. "Only, seems unlikely to me that they also go by the name of the 'Youngest' and have a horse that looks like it'd have no problem eatin' any normal one. A horse that seems a mite smarter than he ought."

"You know more of the old tongue than you let on."

The old man gave him a small smile. "All men are fools, but the one looks least foolish is the one doesn't let on all he thinks he knows."

The wanderer said nothing, for there was nothing to say, and after a moment, the old man nodded, going on.

"Anyway, you can't be that man, Youngest, I mean. Why, the man my father told me of, his woundin', why it happened more'n a hundred years ago, I reckon. If somehow he *did* survive—and by all accounts he did not—then why, by now, he would have died of old age...wouldn't he?"

"What do you want?"

"Me?" the old man asked, seemingly genuinely surprised. "Well, *Ungr,* I don't want a whole lot. Not riches, that's for sure. I've had 'em a few times, and you ask me, a man is rarely better off with 'em than he is without 'em. Mostly, he's worse. I guess all I really want is to spend what's left of my days with my daughter and granddaughter, and I suppose my son-in-law, too. To spend them out here, in the quiet, in peace, for I have seen enough of the world, more than enough, truth be told."

"I see."

"What I *want,*" the old man said, his smile fading as he met the wanderer's eyes, "is to keep them safe, in any way I can. What I *want,* Ungr, is to know why you're really here. You didn't stumble onto this place by accident, did you?"

The wanderer could have lied, but he saw no point. "No."

"And I don't suppose you came to sample my daughter's cooking."

"Not quite."

"Well, then I guess my question, Ungr, *Youngest,* is why are you here?"

"I...don't know."

The old man frowned. "I don't mean to be a nag, Ungr, but considerin' that my daughter and her family are asleep less than a hundred feet from where we stand, I'm wonderin' if maybe you can't do a little better than that."

The wanderer had never been good with words—there had been others of his comrades far better suited to such a task. But they were dead, ghosts, gone or, at least, nearly so, and there was no one else. He hesitated, thinking. How to tell the man that with his simple invitation, he had made the wanderer feel like something he had not felt in a very long time—a person. Not just a traveler moving across the face of the world, but a part of it, one who *belonged.*

"I...I came because I thought that you all may be in danger."

"I see," the old man said. "And just what sort of danger?"

"Better if you didn't know."

The old man cocked his head, seeming to consider. "Well, I believe that much at least. But tell me one more thing, Ungr. This danger you're talkin' about. Why did it come here?"

The wanderer took a slow, deep breath. He did not want to meet the man's eyes, and so he did. "Because I brought it."

"You brought it," the old man repeated.

"Yes."

"And...did you do it intentionally?"

"No, but does it really matter?"

"I suppose not," Felden Ruitt said. "So what do you aim to do, then? Guard us from...whatever this danger is?"

"If I can."

"And if you can't?"

"Then, once I am dead, that should be the end of it."

"And if it isn't?"

The wanderer did not answer that, for the only answer he could give would offer the man no comfort. For that last had been a lie. If he died, if he was taken, and that which he carried taken as well, then his death would not be the end—it would only be the beginning. "It is late, Felden. I am grateful for all that you and your family have done but...perhaps it would be best if you got some sleep."

"And you? Will you sleep?"

"No."

"What will you do then?"

What I have always done. "I'll watch."

The old man nodded slowly. "I heard plenty of stories about you when I was a kid. You and the others. They say you were a traitor, an evil man of the worst kind."

"Yes."

"Well," the old man said, shrugging. "Screw 'em. I'm too old for stories anyway. I hope you have a quiet night, Youngest."

Youngest. How long had it been since anyone had called him that? Anyone, at least, save the ghosts and never mind that he was far older now than any of them had been before they'd died. It was strange, hearing it from another person's mouth. It cast him back to a time long ago, a time when he had been a different man. Not the wanderer, not then, but a man who wanted to make a difference, full of hope and, admittedly, himself. Young enough to think that the world could be changed and arrogant enough to think that he was the one to change it.

When he finally pulled himself back to the present, the old man was gone. And he was alone. Again.

He glanced at Veikr, saw the horse watching him. "Rest," he told him. "I will keep watch."

The horse gave a soft neigh at that, as much argument as he was likely to give, for he knew that he was exhausted. "Relax, old friend," he said. "I will rest too. In time."

Veikr gave a soft snort, as if to say what he thought of that, but in another moment he lay down. The wanderer watched him for a moment. A fine beast, it was true, one that, as the bandit had said, would have fetched quite a bit of coin at market. And why not? He was the last of his kind, all those horses now walking the earth only a pale comparison. A fine beast—the finest—but more than that, a fine friend. His only friend.

"Sleep well, my friend," the wanderer said softly. "I will see you soon..." He turned to the door, shifting the shoulder of his wounded arm as he took up his scabbarded sword and regarded the barn door. "Or I will not."

He moved back to the chair outside the barn, sitting once more and laying his scabbarded sword across his legs so that it would be in easy reach if—*when*—he had to draw it.

The night was still, quiet, and seeming quieter still for having so recently hosted the sounds of the little girl's laughter, the father's loving words.

There was a slight breeze in the air, cool against skin which felt slightly feverish from his wound, but he did not mind. He had been cold before. The only sound was that of the gentle swaying of the tree branches in the wind, no voices now, for he was alone, but he told himself that he did not mind this, either. After all, he had been alone before. In fact, he could hardly remember a time, in truth, when he had been anything else.

And he told himself now, as he had so many times over the years, that it was okay. A man could only walk the path placed before him, and if he were meant to walk it alone, then the bravest thing he could do, the *only* thing, was to walk it.

But unlike those other times, this time, no matter how hard he tried, he could not make himself believe it. The sound of the little girl's laughter was too fresh in his mind, the sight of her mother and father smiling as she shoveled her dinner into her mouth in order to see Veikr sooner too clear.

Although there was no one there to see it—perhaps *because* there was no one there—the wanderer's mouth turned up into a small smile in the darkness.

Later, in the weeks, in the months to come, he would wonder what happened, would wonder *why* it happened. Maybe it was that for the first time in a very long time, he felt as if he was exactly where he wanted to be. Or perhaps it was that he had spent the last three days and nights without sleep, forcing his weary body on to put as much distance between himself and place where he had fought the bandits, where the cursed blade had broken free of its scabbard. Perhaps it was that there were no gods after all or, if there were, then they were cruel. Possibly it was due to his wound, or to the small chair upon which he sat, more comfortable than it had any right to be. Maybe it was the cool wind caressing him, the night, full in its stillness.

Whatever the reason, less than half an hour passed before the wanderer committed one of the gravest mistakes, one of the gravest crimes, of his life.

He fell asleep.

***

As the wanderer slept, something stirred in the darkness, but he did not know it, for as he slept, he dreamed.

He dreamed of kneeling in a great hall, bloodied from several wounds he'd taken in one duel after another. Those who he had fought, who he had bested, stood lining the wall on either side. At least those who could stand. It had been a long day and not all those who had walked into the great hall that morning would walk out of it again.

Before him, on a raised dais, sat the twelve. The Eternals. Men and women out of legend, men and women who were said to be closer to gods than mortals. "Rise," a deep voice intoned. "Rise, Youngest, and kneel no longer, for your seat awaits you. Your journey begins."

And so he did. He rose, casting off his old life, his old name, as if it were a cloak that might be stripped and thrown away. Gods help him, he rose.

And he walked to her. Standing there by the tree, their tree, the one in which their initials had been carved, carved the way the young and in love so often did. Convinced that their love, that they, were eternal, that neither they nor it would ever die or fade.

She turned to him, as beautiful in memory as she had ever been, and though she offered him a smile, he knew her, knew her better than he knew himself, and he could see that she'd been crying.

"So..." she said softly. "It's time."

"Yes," he said.

"You must leave...but...you will come back?"

He walked to her, holding her hands in his, and then he leaned in and kissed her. "Of course," he said. "I will come back."

But that had been a lie, for while those two young fools might have believed their love eternal, they, like so many who had come before and who would come after, were wrong. He left...but he never came back.

He turned, walking away from her, from his old life, and stepped into...

The past week had been one heavy snowfall after the other. At first, it had seemed magical to the boy of nine who now stood by the window of his room in their small cabin, staring out at the woods surrounding their home. At least, that was, what he could see of it.

It was the first snow of his life, and there had been something about the white fluffs falling from the sky that seemed magical. It spoke to some part of him, that magic, seemed to transport him into the worlds his mother told him of in her stories, the ones that always made his father shake his head and sigh with disapproval.

The snow, though, had not slowed, had only began to fall heavier, then heavier still. It was still piling up, thicker and thicker on the ground, and he did not think it felt magical now. Or, at least, if it did, then it was an evil magic, for despite the fact that it had been snowing for days, it did not seem to be letting up at all. It seemed to him that the world would end, that it would never stop falling. An end that did not come with some great battle or with roars of outrage and fear but, with the world smothered as it was by the thick blanket of snow, an end that came with only silence. He said as much to his mother.

"Shh, it's not the end, only an *end, child," she told him, pulling him close. "It is snow, that's all."*

It took another three days but despite his childish fears, the snows did abate. As it turned out, his mother had been right. But in the years to come, years that would make of him not a timid child any longer but a young warrior eager to prove his worth he would find that he, also, had been right. For the world had not ended during that blizzard, but when it did end, it did so in silence. So quietly that among those still living he was the only one who was even aware that it had ended at all. The rest of the world and its people stumbled on like a chicken with its head cut off. Finished, destroyed, but not able to see it, not yet, at least.

Another image, then, of a man—him—snatching a blood-stained sword off the ground.

Run, they had told him, and he had. Gods help him, he had.

The wanderer woke to the sound of a little girl's screaming. He knew it for what it was, this time. Some people, waking in the darkness to such a sound, might have been confused and, their thoughts muddied by sleep, might have hesitated. The wanderer, though, did not hesitate, for he had learned long ago that to do so was to invite pain. The scar on his chest, where he had been impaled, served as a daily reminder of that.

Instead, he drew his sword from his lap, tossing the scabbard aside, and leapt to his feet.

Then he was running.

He heard Sarah scream again, and as he ran he thought that surely he was a fool to have mistaken her sounds of girlish joy for screaming, for the two could be no further apart, the screams seeming to cut into him, to claw at him.

The wanderer rushed for the front door. He did not pause to try to open it, sure that it would be locked. Instead, he continued forward, charging his shoulder into the door, and the wood snapped as he struck it, the door swinging open.

He was in the main room then, and he swept it with his gaze. Part of his training had been to use his senses quicker and better than others, picking up details another man would miss and in only a fraction of the time, so he needed only a moment to understand the situation.

Ella stood in one corner of the room, her back pressed against it, Sarah behind her legs, squished into the corner save her face which poked out from behind her mother's skirts, pale and terrified.

Dekker, the kitchen table, and several chairs lay in a heap where they'd clearly been knocked over, the big man even now extricating himself from the pile.

The wanderer has just begun to wonder what had happened to Felden Ruitt, the old man, when he turned to the other side of the room to see him lying on the ground, writhing and moaning, his shirt, where it covered his chest and stomach, a bloody ruin. Behind him, there was a massive hole in the wall, taller than a man, where the Unseen had not bothered with the door but had instead made use of its unnatural strength and speed to break through it.

Felden screamed as a bloody furrow suddenly appeared in his arm as if by magic, and the old man seemed to levitate upward. There was a shimmer of displaced air above him as if the wind itself was attacking him. Only when some of that blood splashed up, it stuck, revealing some small bit of the Unseen's form.

"*Leave him alone,*" the wanderer growled, the words coming out with harsh fury that surprised even him. It had been a long time since he had felt anything more than the weak ghost of anger, not anger itself but only its memory. Just as it had been a long time since he had felt happiness—as he had when watching the girl with Veikr—or anything at all, for that matter, save a deep, hollowing, abiding fear.

The old man's form paused there, hanging limply in the air like some puppet whose master had tired of it, but he did not fall.

"Go on," the wanderer said angrily, bringing his sword before him with his good hand. "It's me you're after. So come—let us finish this."

The old man pawed weakly at the creature, ineffectually, as if trying to break free of its grip. In the end, though, his efforts made no difference save to mar the creature's form with the blood which had stained his fingers so that, as the creature dropped the old man and turned to face him, the wanderer could see much of its form, outlined in crimson.

His eyes moved to the old man who was gasping in pain but who met his eyes. The man's efforts to break free had failed, but then, noting the gleam in the old man's eyes, the wanderer realized that breaking free had never been his intention. He had marked the creature and for a creature who relied on its enemies' inability to see it, that was no small thing.

The only real question was: would it be enough? The wanderer was aware of the girl and her mother cowering in the corner, crying. He was aware, also, of Dekker, the big man still trying to make his way to his feet, blood running down his face from a wound on his head. The wanderer might have helped him, just as he might have tried to comfort the girl and her mother, but he knew that to do either would mean not just his death but theirs as well.

Instead, he focused on the creature, standing above the old man's writhing form, blocking out everything else, blocking out the big man, stumbling as he struggled drunkenly to his feet, blocking out, also, the little girl and her mother crying in the corner, and the old man lying on the ground in a spreading pool of his own blood. There was nothing but him and the creature, could *be* nothing but him and the creature, if he wanted any chance of saving them.

The creature, based on the way it began to slowly circle the room, away from the old man, seemed unaware that he could see it. The wanderer let it continue to think as much, not looking at it directly but instead tracking it out of the corner of his eye, making a show of looking around the room, as if searching for it.

The creature worked its way behind him, and the wanderer let it, tracking it with quick glances out of the corner of his eye. Then, he *felt* more than saw it move, rushing at him and meaning to finish it quickly.

At the last moment, the wanderer spun, calling on speed and strength, on reflexes honed over years of training, and the steel of his blade struck the creature's outreaching, taloned arm, severing it near the shoulder. The Unseen let out an unearthly wail that continued until the wanderer's back stroke took it at its throat, tearing its head from its neck in a spray of ichor.

Only then, when it was done, did the wanderer become aware of the girl's terrified cries once more and the way the big man, responding to her cry, was stumbling toward them. He took a slow breath as the world, which had slowed to a standstill for him during the fight, sped up once more.

Then he moved to the old man, kneeling before him.

"Did you...get it?" Felden Ruitt asked in a wheezing croak, bloody spittle foaming around his mouth as he did.

"Yes," the wanderer said.

The man heaved a shaky sigh. *"Well,"* he managed. *"That...that's good then. So...how bad is it?"*

The wanderer glanced down at the man's torso, his guts visible from where the creature's claws had torn into him, then back up at the man's face. "Bad," he said softly.

The old man gave what might have been a soft laugh, then broke into a coughing fit, more blood, so dark it was almost black, leaking from his mouth. *"Thought...so,"* he wheezed. *"And that...that thing, it was what you were looking for?"*

"Yes."

"And my family...they're...they're safe?"

For now. "Yes."

The old man gave a nod, his eyes seeming to close of their own volition. *"Well, that's...that's alright then."*

The wanderer was not good with people—he never had been, even before his century long exile from civilization, and those years spent traveling the world alone had done nothing to change that. Still, he found himself taking one of the old man's bloody hands in his. "I'm sorry, Felden" he said, surprised by how difficult it was to get the words out past the lump in his throat.

"For what?" the old man asked, slowly opening his eyes and meeting the wanderer's gaze.

"For..." The wanderer hesitated. "For all of it. I...I did this. I brought this here."

The old man coughed, shaking his head. *"A man can't hold himself responsible for all the evil...in the world, Ungr. Not even you. Just as easy to say it's...our fault, for livin' here. Might as well say it's anybody's fault...for livin'...at all."*

The man's breath was quickening, and the wanderer knew it would not be long now. "But...Felden...I...this happened...because of me."

"Funny," the old man said, *"didn't remember seein' you be the one that clawed me all up. 'Course..."* He paused, letting out a wheezing laugh. *"Didn't much see that bastard either. Anyway...I'm...an old man, Ungr. I was goin' to die, sooner or later. It's what...well, it's what people do, isn't it?"*

"People...yes. It is what they do."

The old man gave a small, bloody smile. *"Speakin' as if you ain't one. Look...I don't know...what all you've been through, but I imagine it's safe to say...it's more...than most. True?"*

"True."

The old man heaved a heavy breath. *"Well. You just remember, lad, whatever happens...you're a person too, you're part of this world. A man...spends too much time...alone, sometimes, he forgets that. But you are. And people, Ungr...people need people. Alright?"*

"Alright."

Felden gave a slow, weak nod. *"That's settled then. Now...you just keep on doin'...whatever it is that needs doin'. For this world...for your world. Understand?"*

The wanderer was opening his mouth to speak, perhaps to ask the man what he thought that *was.* And in that moment, had the man told him to give up his quest, he thought that likely he would have done so. But before he could say anything, there was the sound of footsteps, and he turned to see Dekker shuffling forward, a bloody rag pressed against his head.

"Oh gods, Felden," the big man said, dropping to his knees beside him. "H-how are you?"

The old man gave a weak snort. *"I'm dyin', you big bastard, that's how I am,"* he said, offering the man a small smile to take the edge off his words. *"You...take care of my daughter and my granddaughter, alright?"*

Dekker turned to the wanderer as if searching for help, but the wanderer had no help to offer, and after a moment the big man turned back to his father-in-law. "I will," he said, his voice thick with emotion. "But listen, Felden, we can get you to town and—"

"I'll...be gone, long before that," the old man said, glancing at the wanderer who gave a grim nod. *"You just...bury me, alright? See that*

I'm laid to rest next to...Hilda. Been...missin' her...an awful lot...these last years." Suddenly, he reached out, grasping the big man's wrist. *"And don't...don't let the little one see...alright?"*

"O-okay," Dekker managed in a quiet, weak voice, then the old man's eyes slowly closed, his hand fell away, and he was still.

They remained there for a moment, still, unspeaking, then finally the big man sniffed, running an arm across his face and turning to the wanderer. "Hilda was his wife. Died ten years ago, taken by the fever."

The wanderer didn't know what to say to that, so he said nothing, only giving a nod.

"Dekker, what—" the woman began from the other side of the room, but the big man thrust out a hand toward her.

"Stay there, Ella, keep Sarah, tell her...tell her to close her eyes." He turned, glancing at the corpse of the Unseen lying on the ground then paled before turning back to the wanderer, his expression grim, angry. "I ain't never seen nothin' like that, that *thing*, but from the way you acted, I'm thinkin' maybe you have, that right?"

"Yes," the wanderer said.

Dekker watched him for several seconds, his eyes narrowed. "And that monster...it was after you. That also true?"

"Yes."

The big man frowned, seeming to consider, and the wanderer thought that the man looked just then like he wanted nothing more than to kill him. And the wanderer, feeling grief at the old man's death, the truest, most painful grief that he had felt in a very long time, thought that, should he try, he would let him.

In the end, though, Dekker only gave a heavy sigh, seeming to deflate, the menace going out of him as he glanced back at the old man's corpse. "Take what you can carry—oats and food for the road. Then you get out of here. Tonight, you understand?"

"I understand."

Dekker tensed then gave a single nod, still eyeing the old man. "I'm a changed man, Ungr, a better man. But...I'm thinkin' it's probably best I don't see you again."

"Okay." He turned to leave, stopping when a big hand grabbed his arm. He thought, perhaps, that Dekker had decided on violence after all, but when he turned, the man was watching him, not with an angry expression but a fearful one.

"There...that is, are there more of these things?"

"Yes," he said, and the big man deflated. "But not here," he finished.

Dekker frowned. "And you, what? You fight them?"

"When I have to."

The man turned to look at the corpse of the Unseen again, an unmistakable look of disgust on his face. He seemed to consider something else for a moment, then finally shook his head. "I ain't that man anymore, Ungr. Like I told you. Leastways, not mostly. And I got a family to think about. I wish you luck but...well. That's all I can do, understand?"

The wanderer knew well what the man meant, for he had carried the burden of the blade, of the *truth*, alone for so long, and if given a choice, he would not have done so any longer. How, then, could he blame the man for not wishing to risk that which he loved most? "I understand. Do you mind if I take the body?"

The big man tensed at that until he followed the wanderer's gaze to the creature lying dead in the floor and realized he hadn't meant the old man's. "Feel free," he said disgustedly.

The wanderer nodded. "Thanks."

"Safe travels, Ungr."

"You'll be okay?" he asked.

The big man nodded. "There's the city of Celes only a few days away. I'll find a place to leave Sarah and El until I can get all this sorted."

The wanderer nodded, glancing at the woman and the child still standing in the corner, the young girl with her face buried in her mother's skirts, the mother with her arms wrapped protectively around her, gazing at him as if he were a monster himself.

And aren't you? He glanced down at the amulet on his neck, thinking perhaps that it had come open during the fighting, but he saw that it had not and after a moment he realized that the voice he'd heard had not been from the ghosts, not this time. It had been his own.

He wished there was something he could say to make it better, but he knew that there was not. Sometimes, words failed, and even if there were words he might say, words that might give them comfort, they were ones he did not know, so he only turned and walked out of the door, moving to the barn to wake Veikr.

CHAPTER THREE

He traveled through the night, leaving the family, or at least what remained of it, behind him. Veikr turned from time to time, glancing back, no doubt thinking of the little girl who had sewn the pink ribbon into his hair—ribbons the wanderer had not had the heart to remove.

The wanderer said nothing during these times, too preoccupied with his own thoughts, ones of guilt and shame, mostly. He had known better, known that he should not go to them. Yet he had and, because of it, because of his weakness, Felden had died, an old man who had wanted nothing more than to live out his remaining years with those he cared for the most.

The wanderer pushed Veikr through the next morning, not stopping to break his fast but chewing on some dry, tasteless bread as he rode. From time to time, he would glance angrily at the Unseen's body thrown over his saddle bow, and the sack, containing its head, that hung from Veikr's saddlebags.

By the time evening began to cast shadows over the world on the second day, another feeling had begun to work its way past the shame and the guilt—loneliness. Loneliness that felt like an ache in his chest, as if some vital part of him had been torn away when he left the family. He knew that was not true, for that part, whatever it had been, had withered decades ago, yet meeting the family, eating with them, he had been reminded, for the first time in a very long time, of just what he had lost, just what he had given up.

The corpse on his saddle had begun to stink some few hours ago, but he paid it little mind as his eyes traveled both sides of the path, looking for a landmark that might signal that he was near his destination. The problem was that it had been years since he'd traveled this part of the world. Much had changed since then, some things dying while others grew, and even had it not, likely he still would not have remembered, for he had traveled many other roads since last he'd been here, so many that they all felt like little more than a blur.

He gave Veikr's reins a pull, and they came to a stop as he glanced around. "Any ideas?" he asked the horse.

Veikr snorted as if to say that his time was far better spent on more important endeavors, and the wanderer sighed. "I didn't think so." Either the horse did not remember or he did not care—perhaps he was still sore about them leaving the little girl. It didn't matter which, for the wanderer did not remember the way either. The ghosts would, he knew, for they remembered everything—after all, there was little else for them to do.

Still, he hesitated. He did not like speaking to them—or, more accurately, *listening* to them—for they never showed any indication that they cared about his opinion on the matters they discussed, instead directing him this way and that like a puppet linked to them by invisible strings. Which, in many ways, he was.

Yet as exhausting as the ghosts were, he thought that perhaps they might be better than the silence, a deafening, living silence which had seemed to grow with each step he'd taken away from the family and their home. A silence that seemed to press in all around him, threatening to crush him and leaving him to decide whether or not he wanted it to.

He opened the locket.

Immediately, twelve voices began speaking at once, a riot of tones ranging from annoyed to furious. The wanderer sat and waited, weathering the barrage of sound much the way a man might weather a rainstorm it was impossible to avoid.

He waited for it to stop only, it did not, and after a time, he sighed. "I cannot understand you when you speak all at once."

That was ill done, Youngest, a voice said, a young woman's voice, one that said "Youngest" with a certain amount of scorn.

Oh, what do you know of it? This a man's voice, near the same age as the woman. *He did what he had to do, that's all!*

Yes, the first voice said, *and because of it that old man is dead.*

And likely had he not gone he would now be dead, and they would have the sword! Are you truly so foolish?

Foolish? the woman demanded. *I will not sit here and—*

Enough, a voice growled, loud, Leader's voice. And even now, after all this time, the ghosts responded to it much as they had in life, going silent immediately. *Whether his choice was correct or not makes no difference,* Leader said into the silence. *It has been made already, and there is no changing it, and since he lives yet, since the sword remains out of their hands, I think that the choice can only have been the right one.*

Of course, the male ghost responded, an obvious note of pleasure in his voice.

As you say, the woman responded, an equally obvious note of frustration in her own.

Still, Youngest, that was wise, taking the body, though had you but allowed us to speak the fate of the old man might yet have been avoided. In future, you would be wise to remember that.

Had I allowed you to speak, the wanderer thought, *I would have still been standing and listening when the Unseen came.* But he did not say as much, for there was no point. The ghosts were what they were and no amount of speaking to them would change that—the dead, after all, never changed.

The leader must have taken his silence as acquiescence, for he left it, moving on. *Now, you seek the cave, do you not? The one you stayed in once before?*

"Yes," the wanderer said. "Ten years or so ago."

Twelve years, seven months, and eleven days, to be exact, an old man's voice said.

Very well, Leader said. *Open yourself—Scholar will perform a Sojourn.*

The wanderer winced. "It isn't necessary, if you could just tell me, then—"

I'm afraid it is, Youngest, a wizened voice said, one belonging to the scholar. *You did well, bringing the creature, but you remain some distance from the shelter you seek, and if the body is left untended much longer, it will rot without us learning anything from it.*

As far as the wanderer was concerned it was useless, for they had done this before, examining the bodies of those sent against him, and though they had learned some of their anatomy and how they were fashioned, they had not so far learned anything of any significance. But he sighed, giving way to the inevitable. "Very well," he said, closing his eyes.

He cleared his mind, pushing away his grief and shame at the old man's death, pushing away, also, his own weariness, a weariness that pervaded his mind and body, his soul. Then, when that was done—or as close to it as he was likely to get—he imagined a room. He stood within that room, and at its end was a door. The room was but a backdrop, seen through the corner of his eyes. What he focused on, though, was the door. He pictured each nick in the wood, the rust on the brass handle, the way it sat slightly askew in its frame.

No sooner had the image come to him then there was a knock on the door and slowly, he reached out, not with his hand but with his mind, grasping the handle and pulling it open.

A hunched, ancient-looking man stood on the other side of the portal, a great white beard running down his chest, his hair frazzled and unkempt. Scholar looked the same now as he had in life as he should, for his representation here was not physical but instead a manifestation of his own image of himself. *Hello, Youngest,* the man said, smiling.

Hello, Sc—He did not manage to get the words about before the man seemed to surge forward, and despite the door, despite that he was invited, when the man stepped into his mind, now, like every other time, the wanderer felt as if he were being invaded. It was as if someone had overtaken his mind, sweeping his own thoughts, his own *being,* away.

Relax, the old man's voice said, *this will not take long.*

The wanderer thought it was easy for the ghost to say as much, for he had never had his body taken over by another, had never become little more than a passenger in his own mind and despite the ghost's attempt at comfort, the wanderer thought he could hear an almost eager giddiness in his tone. And why not? If the dead wanted anything, it was to live again, and while taking over the wanderer's body was not exactly that, it was as close as any of them would ever get.

Why does he *get to do it*—the young woman's voice began.

Quiet, Leader's voice intoned. *Scholar—begin.*

The wanderer watched, helpless, from within his own mind as Scholar gave Veikr's sides a kick. The horse, likely sensing something strange, did not move at first, instead turning and regarding him.

"Come, come," Scholar said impatiently, sounding like little more than an excited child now. *"We must be off."*

He gave the horse another kick in the flank and, this time, Veikr gave a snort before turning and starting down the path. Fifteen minutes later, Scholar led them off the road and into the trees, following a seemingly random path, until they eventually crested a small rise.

Scholar, still in control of the wanderer's body, dismounted, walking to a large pile of tangled brush. He drew his blade and set about hacking at it until, finally, enough was pared away to reveal the opening to the cave.

The wanderer was left stunned by the man's impeccable memory as he had been in the past. The ghosts were annoying, it was true, frustrating, but it could not be denied that, on occasion, they were also useful.

Scholar sheathed the sword, missing on his first two attempts and finally managing it on the third. The ancient man had been renowned, in his time—and in fact, was renowned still—for his knowledge, but he had never been known for his skill in battle.

He walked back to where Veikr stood, eyeing him and sniffing at the air, then with a grunt of effort, pulled the body from the saddlebow. He tried to heft it gently but tripped and nearly fell, resulting in the unceremonious dumping of the corpse onto the ground.

There, Scholar said panting, *now for the head.*

He moved to the bag hanging from Veikr's flank and, in another moment, head and body were laid out side by side. Then the scholar drew the knife the wanderer always kept at his side and began to cut away pieces of the creature's lifeless, gray flesh.

Scholar did not speak as he went about his grisly work, and the wanderer found himself casting his mind about for anything to distract him. Perhaps unsurprisingly, his thoughts went back to the house, two days' ride away, and to the family which, according to Dekker, would no longer be there.

The family, he realized, had come to represent something to him, something more than a husband and wife and their child. Instead, they had come to represent the life he might have had, had he but made different choices. A life full of love, filled with small pleasures and small inconveniences, his biggest worry putting food on the table or of bandits on the road. Worries that might keep him up some nights, but ones which were far more manageable than the constant fear that dogged the wanderer's steps, that haunted his dreams. The worry, the *knowledge,* that should he fail, the world failed with him.

But then, he told himself, a man had to look at all sides of it, didn't he? If he *had* made a different choice, would there have been anybody left, when the others had been killed, to steal the enemy king's cursed sword and spirit it away? For that was the only thing keeping the enemy from having total dominion over the world. Perhaps another would have taken the wanderer's place, but even still there was no knowing if they would have managed to escape with the magic blade.

He thought that should make him feel better about the choices he'd made. A hundred years ago, when first he'd started out, it certainly would have. Fifty years ago, it *probably* would have. But he was old now, the oldest living man in the world, he was certain, and he was so very, very tired.

Perhaps, if he could find another, one who might—

Done.

He was pulled away from his thoughts by Scholar's voice and his gaze alighted on the bloody, disgusting remains of the man's probings.

"Good," the wanderer said. "Then can I have my body back?"

Of course, of course, the ghost said, *only...perhaps I had better examine it more closely.*

The ghosts were always reluctant to give back his body once they had overtaken it, but that didn't keep him from feeling a slight panic, for if there was a fate worse than his own, it would surely be being trapped in his body watching, helpless, while it was controlled by another.

"Now, Scholar," he said, doing his best to sound authoritative, powerful, instead of frightened.

Very well, as you say, the ghost said with obvious reluctance.

The wanderer imagined the door again, imagined himself standing at it, opening it and waving the old man through. Scholar hesitated for a moment then, with a heavy sigh, stepped through the door. As soon as he was through, the wanderer slammed the door closed, imagining a lock which he promptly fastened.

Now then, Leader said once it was done, *what have you learned, Scholar?*

It is as we thought, the old man answered. *The creatures, the Unseen, as the Youngest names them—though I must say it is a bit on the nose and not quite accurate for all—*

Scholar, Leader said in an admonishing tone.

Very well, the old man said. *Well, it is as I thought. The creatures' metabolisms have been sped up to an incredibly drastic degree, and it is no doubt this that we can thank for their speed.*

"Didn't plan on thanking anybody for it," the wanderer muttered.

In fact, Scholar went on as if he hadn't spoken, *had it not been slain, the creature would have died in a matter of weeks. Already, its internal organs, put under such great strain, were beginning to fail.*

How long then, do you estimate, the creatures might survive from the moment they are created?

A few weeks, the Scholar said, *perhaps a month, not much more than that.*

Well, Leader said, *that's something at least.*

As far as the wanderer was concerned, it wasn't much of anything. After all, when the creatures moved as fast as they did, they could cause quite a bit of havoc in a month and knowing that the beast would soon die would be of little comfort if it killed him. Besides, it wasn't as if the enemy didn't have plenty of other creations to send at him, for the Unseen were just one of the many weapons within their seemingly limitless arsenal.

What of you, Oracle? Leader asked. *Might you divine anything from the creature's remains?*

No, a woman's voice said, *not now. Too long has the life been gone from its body. The body has forgotten itself, and there is no way to make it remember any longer.*

A shame, Leader said. *Still, there is nothing to be done for it. Now,* he went on, *I think it best that we come up with a plan. Youngest, you must—*

The voice cut off as the wanderer snapped the amulet closed, his body feeling, as if often did after one of the ghosts' invasions, strange, as if it weren't his at all, and he knew from experience that it would take several days for the feeling to completely wear off.

Veikr snorted, and the wanderer turned to him. "What?" he asked. "I have a plan—sleep." Sleep that might help to heal the wound in his arm, the one that still throbbed, sleep that might, more importantly, serve to put some distance between him and his own dark thoughts, thoughts which centered around the family he had very nearly killed.

He walked to the cave entrance and glanced back at Veikr. "Coming?"

The horse met his eyes then turned, looking back in the direction of the distant cabin.

The wanderer felt a spike of anger at that, but he resisted the urge to lash out. After all, what had transpired was not Veikr's fault—it was his and his alone, so he gave a weary sigh. "Suit yourself."

CHAPTER FOUR

The wanderer spent the next two weeks in the cave, ostensibly to give his wounded arm an opportunity to heal. He ventured out only at night so that there was less chance of being seen, for that would invite questions, and in his experience, questions invited death.

Even then, he only went out when he was forced to collect more herbs to poultice his arm or, alternatively, when hunger or thirst drove him out to hunt or to venture two hours' deeper into the wood to refill his waterskin. He told himself he was doing the right thing, the smart thing. After all, he didn't like his chances if he should find himself going up against another of the enemy's creations with a wounded arm—he had only succeeded the last time because Felden Ruitt, while dying, had been clever enough to mark the Unseen.

The truth, though, a truth that became harder and harder to ignore as the days stretched into weeks, particularly in those quiet times as he lay in the darkness of the cave, was that giving his wound a chance to mend was only an excuse.

The real reason that he remained in the cave was simple—he was hiding. Not hiding from the enemy, really, for experience had taught him that when it came to avoiding them, staying on the move was always better. Instead, he was hiding from the world, from the pain, from guilt and shame brought on by the knowledge of what his actions had caused, getting Felden killed and risking an entire family.

But on the morning of the fourteenth day of hiding, he removed the poultice from his arm and found that the wound did not hurt any longer, at least no more than small twinge when he flexed the arm experimentally. Nor was there the putrid stink that might warn of infection. The wound was closed, the flesh mended back together, and in its place was a long, jagged scar, one that blended with the dozens of others covering him, scars picked up in one desperate battle or another over the years.

Part of who he was, *what* he was, meant that he healed from wounds quicker than a normal man might. At least, the physical ones. Now, as always, the emotional wounds lingered, and Felden's death was as fresh now as the day it had happened, the two past weeks having done nothing to blunt the edge of it.

He found himself thinking of the old man's words, thinking of him telling him that he was a part of the world, a part of its people, and that people needed people. Suddenly, he did not want to be in the cave any longer, alone with his misery and his shame.

Pulling on his boots in the gloom of the cave, he packed up his belongings and stepped out into the daylight, wincing as eyes that had grown accustomed to the darkness protested at the bright, morning sun.

Veikr cut off from where he'd been cropping at grass to look up at him, a question in the horse's eyes, as clear—after nearly a century of having traveled with the beast—as if he had spoken the words aloud.

"We're leaving," the wanderer said in answer. "That okay with you?"

The horse raised up, stomping the ground with his two front hooves, and giving a loud neigh. The wanderer allowed himself a small smile. "I thought so." He secured his belongings in Veikr's saddlebags. It did not take long. He had been largely idle in the last two weeks and the provisions Dekker and his family had given him had long since ran out. The cursed blade, he secured across the bow of Veikr's saddle, leaving his own sword scabbarded behind his back.

That done, he glanced around the small clearing and at the cave which had been his shelter for the last two weeks. He decided that he would not miss it. Perhaps Felden had been right, perhaps people needed people. Or perhaps it was simply boredom that drove him. Whatever the reason, he could remain idle no longer.

He climbed into Veikr's saddle, grabbed his reins, and turned him back to the road. The horse glanced back at him as if to ask where they were going.

"Follow the road," the wanderer said. "And we will see what we will see."

The horse's gaze traveled down to the amulet hanging from the leather thong at his neck. Two weeks had passed, but still the wanderer remembered well the feeling of being cast aside, of being no more than a passenger in his own mind while Scholar performed his examination of the Unseen's corpse. He shook his head. "Not now."

The horse gave his head a shake as if to say it made no difference to him, then turned back to the road and began to walk.

Away from the damp cave, and the small, somehow sad clearing in front of it, the wanderer began to feel better. It was peaceful in the woods, the sun shining through the green canopy of the trees and splashing onto the dirt path in golden puddles. The birds sang in the trees, and squirrels scurried along the branches, storing nuts in preparation for the coming winter which was likely no more than a few weeks away. Veikr, too, seemed to enjoy it, moving with his head high instead of hanging low as it had in the two weeks following their departure from the family's homestead.

As he rode, the wanderer stretched his left arm, flexing it this way and that to limber it up in case he had need of it. After all, in his experience, peace was, more often than not, no more than a prelude to violence; this time, should violence come, he would not be caught unaware.

But despite the fact that he expected something to attack him and that he spent the majority of his time scanning the trees on either side of the road, the day wore on with no sign of any danger.

In time, the sun began to sink low on the horizon, signaling night's approach. They crested a rise in the trail and in the distant valley, the wanderer caught sight of a small town. He hesitated then, thinking. For years he had shunned civilization, at least as much as he was able, thinking that it was safest for him and everyone else if he carried his burden alone.

He was just about to order Veikr to go around when Felden Ruitt's words came back to him, so strongly that the old man might have been sitting right beside him. *You're a part of this world, and its people. And people, Ungr, need people.*

Veikr glanced back at him as if to ask what the hold up was, and the wanderer sighed. "How bad could it be, right?"

Veikr snorted, and the wanderer nodded. "Right. Let's go find out."

***

An hour's riding later, they arrived at the entrance to the town, though in truth it was barely more than a village with a single dirt trail running through the center of it, flanked by buildings on either side. There was a wall surrounding it all, at least of sorts, one fashioned from wooden logs that stood four feet high. And in the opening in the wall, what the wanderer supposed served as a gate, stood two men, obviously meant to be guardsmen, though they, if it was possible, seemed even less equal to their task than the gate they guarded was to its own.

Their clothes were filthy, their shirts untucked, and their idea of "guarding" apparently meant to sit at a small, collapsible wooden table drinking ale and playing cards.

The wanderer pulled Veikr to a stop a dozen feet away from the two men, waiting for them to notice him. When neither did, he cleared his throat. "Hello, the gate!" he called.

The two men started, one of them nearly falling out of his chair.

"—*the fuck,*" one hissed.

"Shit," the other said, wiping at his pants where he had spilled his ale while leaping to his feet.

Both of their hands were on the swords belted at their sides without even so much as a sheath covering the rusty blades. "What do you want?" one demanded.

The wanderer frowned. "I suspect the same thing that most want who arrive at this...gate."

The man, who had a piggy, chubby face to match his piggy, chubby body, scowled, his eyes narrowing, nearly completely hidden in rolls of fat. "You bein' a smart ass, mister?" he demanded.

"Come lookin' for trouble, that it?" the other said, glancing nervously at his friend.

The wanderer winced. He had really been away from people for too long, and he had forgotten how easy it was to give offense. He held up his empty hands. "I want no trouble, only entrance into your town..." He paused, glancing up at the wooden sign hanging crookedly from a post. "Fulwell."

The two frowned at him for several seconds, then the fat man—the thinker of the group, it appeared, at least so much as they *had* one—slowly grinned. "Well, that's alright then. We folks of Fulwell, well, the way we see it, the more the merrier, ain't that right, Paul?"

The man in question, Paul, glanced between his companion and the wanderer, licking his lips as he thought it through. Finally, he grinned. "Oh, sure. The more the merrier, that's exactly right."

The wanderer was beginning to think that it had been a mistake, coming here, but he was here now, so he nodded. "Thanks," he said. He gave Veikr's reins a small snap, and then they started forward.

"There's just the tax to take care of, o'course," the fat man said when he'd drawn even with them.

The wanderer sighed, unsurprised, then turned in his saddle to regard the man. "Tax?" he asked, playing his part.

"Aye, sure. What, you don't think all this—" the man paused, gesturing expansively at the small town with its run-down looking buildings and unpaved street—"is done by elves, do ye?"

The second man laughed at that. "Elves. That's a good one, John."

"How much?" the wanderer asked.

"Question is how much you got?" the man asked, grinning. "See, it's a percentage is all."

"I see," the wanderer said. "And if I choose to go around your town, to avoid it altogether?"

The man laughed. "Well, now, that'd be the Goin' Around tax, wouldn't it?"

"The 'Going Around' tax."

"Sure," the man said, nodding. "You go trompsin' through with that mighty beast of yours, why, you're liable to dig muddy ruts all in the ground, ain't ye? Ground the good folks of Fulwell like to walk when they get a minute to themselves, want to see the countryside. Don't seem right you'd go messin' up the ground like that just for someone else to have to pay to fix it, does it?"

"How much to enter the town?" the wanderer said, finding himself growing tired of the game.

"As I said, see, that's a percentage and—"

"*How much?*" the wanderer growled, losing his patience.

The fat man tensed at that. "Now, look here—"

"*Now, just what's all this about?*"

The two guards made faces like children caught acting out. They spun, and the wanderer followed their gazes to two men riding up on horses.

The first, who rode in the lead, was a heavy-set man, wearing a uniform with a badge emblazoned on the front of it. There was a sword sheathed at his side, but by his look, the wanderer suspected it had been a long time since the man had drawn it.

The second, though, who rode slightly behind him, was a different matter. The man wore all black, and he was thin—not emaciated or unhealthy, but instead possessed of the wiry muscularity often seen in skilled duelists. The way he rode, too, gracefully swaying in the saddle, also reinforced the idea.

It was the first, though, who had drawn the two men's attention. "H-howdy, Constable," pig man said, licking his lips. "J-just welcomin' a new visitor to town, is all."

"A visitor," the constable repeated as he pulled his horse to a stop a few feet away. "Why ain't that a treat!"

"Y-y, uh, that is, y-yes sir," the second guardsman said.

The constable turned in his saddle, and though the man was grossly overweight, there was a keenness, a sort of lupine cleverness in his eyes. "Just take it easy there, boy. Why, you look as if you done seen a ghost."

"Y-yes, sir," the man managed.

The constable watched him for another moment, a smile on his face that never reached his eyes, then he turned to the wanderer. "So," he said, "you mean to visit our fine town of Fulwell, that it?"

"Yes."

"I see. Well, what's all the hold up then?"

"W-we was tryin' to get him to pay the tax is all," the fat man said in a whining voice like a child trying to convince his parents it hadn't been him who'd started the argument. "He's bein' difficult."

The constable frowned. "Difficult?" he asked, turning back to the wanderer. "That right?"

"If difficult means asking how much the tax was, Constable."

The constable snorted. "Please, call me Walter. That'll do fine." He glanced back at his companion. "You hear that, Gene?" he asked. "Clever one, ain't he?"

"Clever," the black-garbed man repeated, his narrowed eyes watching the wanderer.

The constable sighed, turning back. "You'll have to forgive Gene, here. He ain't much for conversatin', truth be told, though he's a fine hand with that blade he carries. Finest I ever saw and that's the truth. Anyhow, the tax is—" He paused, glancing the wanderer up and down. "Well, it'll just be one eternal."

The wanderer blinked. "An eternal?" he asked. "To enter your town?"

"That's right," the constable said, smiling widely.

The wanderer grunted. "Seems like you probably don't get many visitors."

"Some," the constable said. "Anyhow, I know it's a lot, but hey, if it helps, all that money is used to keep the town up—believe me, it ain't fillin' my pockets." He grinned at that, but once again, the expression did not touch his eyes.

The wanderer frowned, reaching for his coin purse. He opened it, peering inside. Two eternals, and a few dozen copper, that was all. Not much to be getting on with, that was sure. Not much at all.

"Anyhow," the constable said, a note of eagerness in his voice he didn't completely manage to hide, "if you ain't got the coin, I understand. Might be we could work somethin' out. Why, how about this? How about I buy that horse you got from you? Why, I'd say you'll even walk away with quite a bit of coin in your pocket off the deal."

"But not tax coins, of course."

The constable grinned, "Just right. So, how about you lettin' me get that hor—"

"No."

"Well, now, don't be hasty fella," the heavy-set man said, frowning. "I'll offer you a fair pri—"

"My horse isn't for sale."

The man frowned, clearly annoyed, and like a dog reading his master's anger, the black-garbed man went for his sword. "Easy, Gene," the constable said, raising his hand, "just take it easy." He glanced at the wanderer. "As I said, you'll have to forgive Gene. A man has a talent—and believe me, with that blade of his, he's got talent to spare—then, my experience, he's always lookin' for a reason to show it off. Anyway, you're sure? About the horse, I mean?"

He watched the wanderer carefully, and the wanderer nodded. "I'm sure."

The constable sighed, shaking his head. "As you will, though I gotta say it's a shame. Beast like that, why, you'd make a fortune off him. Biggest damn horse I ever saw, what about you, Gene?"

"Big."

The constable sighed again. "Anyhow, I'll be takin' that eternal now."

The wanderer reached into his coin purse, retrieving the shining gold coin, and handed it over.

The fat man took it, smiling pleasantly, then bit into it, nodding. "No offense, friend, but you can't be too careful, can you? Why, we get all sorts here and some, I hate to say, are less honest than others."

"No," the wanderer agreed, "you can't be too careful."

"Alright then," the constable said, easing his horse to the side and holding out a hand in invitation. "Welcome to Fulwell, Mister— I'm sorry, I'm afraid I didn't get your name."

"I didn't give it," the wanderer said, then he gave Veikr's reins a snap, and they walked through the opening between constable and duelist, the black-garbed man eyeing him as if he wanted nothing more than to draw his sword and go to work. For the wanderer's part, he was annoyed, the feeling of peace he'd had while riding completely gone now, and he almost wished the man would go for his weapon.

At least it would provide a distraction from the returning grief. Anyway, the man carried himself like an expert duelist, one who had spent years in training. Perhaps he was good, maybe even great, maybe even good enough to win, to kill the wanderer. And would that be so bad, really?

In the end, though, the black-garbed man did nothing, only watched him, and the wanderer rode past, feeling more than a little disappointed.

"We'll talk again," the constable called after him. "About the horse, I mean—you'll find that I'm a stubborn man, once I see somethin' I want."

The wanderer didn't see a need to argue with that—in fact, he didn't see a need to say anything at all, so he did not. Instead, he rode on down the street, aware of several faces peering around corners and out of windows as if they had been watching the spectacle but had also been too scared to venture out into the street.

The wanderer wasn't surprised, for the constable, whatever else he was, was clearly a man accustomed to getting his way, and one that, from what he'd seen, didn't mind trying to bully his way into it. Still, the wanderer didn't concern himself with it. After all, he had seen this sort of petty rule of a town before, many times in the hundred years since he and his companions had lost the final battle, since the legendary talents of the Eternals had failed. The constable, in his greedy, selfish rule, only mirrored that of the world's current rulers.

For now, for the last hundred years since the final battle, those whom he and his companions had fought wore their visages, their identities like masks, masquerading as the legendary Eternals when, in fact, those famous men and women were dead.

Or, at least, nearly so.

He found his hand drifting toward the locket hanging from his neck, the locket which contained within it the essences of each of the Twelve. Legendary heroes, each great in their own right, but each not strong or clever enough to have withstood the enemy in the final battle. Save him, the Youngest, who had not stood but had instead stolen the enemy king's sword and fled with it, thereby not saving the world, but at least delaying its destruction.

Left with none to stand against them, the creatures assumed the mantles of their defeated foes and tricked the entire world into believing that the Eternals had been victorious. With that done, they painted the wanderer as a traitor, claiming that he had attacked the Eternals during the battle, meaning to steal their sword and give it to the enemy. For his crimes, the creatures claimed that he was cursed to walk the world for eternity until some righteous chosen finally took his life.

A lie, of course, but one that had caused him no end of trouble over the years as men and women sought to claim the significant reward that went along with being a "righteous chosen." It was the main reason why he had begun to shun civilization in the first place. At least, that was, until he had spoken with Felden.

He caught sight of eyes watching him from the windows of the shops and buildings he passed, nervous, frightened eyes, but he paid them no attention, pressing on deeper into the town, leading Veikr at a slow walk.

In time, they came to a building with a sign hanging from the front that simply read, "Inn and Tavern." The wanderer supposed that, when you were the only such establishment in town, there was really no need to get creative with the name.

He secured Veikr at a hitching post at the tavern's front—one that he couldn't help but note was empty of any other mounts. "Back in a minute, boy," he told the horse. "I'll go see about getting you some oats and a place to stay for the night, how'd that be?"

The horse gave him a long-suffering look that seemed to say that that was the very least he could do, and the wanderer smiled before walking through the door of the tavern.

The common room of the inn was much as he had imagined it would be, with wooden tables and chairs that had been built with an eye to practicality instead of beauty as one might have seen in a bigger city. Why bother spending money to fancy the place up, he supposed, when a potential customer would have to travel several hours to the nearest town to find any competition?

A dozen or so people sat scattered about the tables, surprisingly subdued, and they eyed the wanderer warily as he stepped inside. He did his best to ignore the suspicious stares, just as he tried to ignore the feeling—increasingly strong—that it had been a mistake to come. Instead, he made his way to the bar where a thin man that was nearing the point of emaciation was wiping down a glass with a rag.

The man glanced at him, raising an eyebrow. "New to Fulwell, are ya?" he asked as the wanderer took a seat on one of the stools.

"Just passing through," the wanderer said.

The barkeep grunted. "Sure. So how can I help you?"

"I was looking for a room for the night, and a stall for my horse."

"Horse?" the man asked, surprise in his voice.

The wanderer frowned. "That's right. Why is that surprising?"

The man glanced at the door then back, shaking his head. "No reason. Anyhow, probably I can figure out a room. As for your horse, well, there's an old stable out back. Hasn't been used in a while, but I imagine it'll serve. Anything else?"

"Dinner," the wanderer said, "and some oats for my horse."

The man nodded. "It'll be three coppers for the room, another one for the dinner—it's beef stew. My Matty makes it, and it's about the best you've ever had."

"Sounds good," the wanderer said. "And how much for the stall and oats?"

The man waved a dismissive hand. "The stall you can have for free—the Eternals know it ain't like anybody else'll use it anytime soon. As for the oats...well, I'll have to see what I can scrounge up. Been a while since we had anyone come through with a horse needin' fed. Still, I reckon I'll find somethin'."

"Huh," the wanderer said. "I'd have thought just about everybody would own a horse in a town like this."

The barkeep's eyes cut to the door again before coming back to him. "Aye, well, you'd think that, wouldn't you?" he muttered. Then he glanced around the room nervously. "Anyway, I'll go see what we can do. Want an ale while you wait to wash some of the road dust off? It ain't nothin' special, but it's wet anyway."

"Just one," the wanderer said. The man nodded, pouring the drink and, in another moment, it was sitting on the counter before the wanderer.

"Thanks."

"No problem," the barkeep said, "now, you sit tight, and I'll go see about the rest."

"Alright."

The man turned, disappearing into a doorway behind the counter, and the wanderer sat, taking his time with the ale. He did not often drink because drinking led to a loss of control and, with the burden that he carried, any loss of control could prove catastrophic.

As he sat waiting on the barkeep to return, he was surprised by how quiet, how subdued those in the common room were. There was no laughing or joking, no fighting either, all of which were typical in such places—or at least had been the last time he'd had cause to visit them. Instead, those seated at the tables leaned

76

forward, talking in hushed whispers, constantly glancing over their shoulders at the door, much like the barkeep had, as if expecting a madman to come charging through, blade in hand, at any moment.

The wanderer had not survived as long as he had by ignoring such things, so he grabbed his ale, rising, and made his way to the end of the bar. He sat in a stool at the end so that his back was to the wall, and he could keep an eye on the doorway.

He'd been sitting there for no more than a few minutes when a raised voice came from a table near the center of the common room. "It's true, I tell you!"

The speaker looked to be young, in his mid-twenties, perhaps, and he was shaking his fist furiously. "The Eternals aren't benevolent rulers, nor are they gods! They are just *men,* that's all, greedy, selfish men who care nothing for their people anymore—if they ever did! And Soldier, why he's the worst of the lot!"

Soldier. Of course. The wanderer was well aware that, following the battle, the one in which the Eternals lost, those who had taken their place had split up the kingdom in to twelve parts, one for each of the impostors. But he had been too distracted by recent events to realize that, by traveling south, he had wound up in Soldier's territory. Not that it much mattered really as all twelve would have been more than happy to see him dead.

"He's our rightful ruler," one of the men said, his eyes shifting left and right, "and he ain't done nothin' but right by us."

"Yeah, just let off, why don't you, Scofield?" another said. "We've heard all these speeches before, haven't we? Anyway, what do I care if the Eternals sit with their feet propped up, pretty women poppin' grapes into their mouths? Ain't none of my concern. That's their business, ain't it?"

"Is it?" the young man, Scofield, demanded. "Is it? And what of the bandits roaming the forest? Or the monsters that are sometimes said to be seen in the countryside, killing the unwary? Is *that* your business, Shem?"

The man named Shem snorted. "Monsters. It's just *stories,* Scofield, that's all. Stories told by old drunks too lazy to work, only tryin' to figure out the next thing they can say when they're in their cups."

"Stories," the young man sneered. "And the livestock? The ones found butchered, slaughtered the way no wild animal would do? Are those stories too, Shem? What about you, Davie?" he asked, turning on another man on the table. "You yourself lost some sheep, didn't you? Nearly torn in half from what I heard! Are those just *stories?*" he demanded, his face red with passion.

The man, Davie, fidgeted uncomfortably. "I don't want no trouble, Scofield, alright? Not with the Eternals and that's a fact. Sometimes, animals, well sometimes they get killed is all. Ain't no tellin' what done it. Might be it was a wolf or—"

"A wolf with six-inch claws?" the young man asked, then shook his head. "I can't tell whether you all were born blind or you chose it, for you'd have to be one or the other not to see what's going on around you. Children who wander too far into the woods come up missin', animals are slaughtered *inside* their pens, and our *ruler,* the very man who's supposed to help us with such things, does nothing!"

"And just what do you mean for us to do about it, you long-winded bastard?" someone else demanded, a big man from another table. "Have an election?" He snorted. "The Eternals are *eternal,* in case you hadn't realized. They been rulin' for more'n a hundred years, and they'll still be rulin' long after you and I ain't naught but dust. So why don't you shut your damned trap before you cause trouble. Sit, have a drink. Unless, that is, you mean to deal with those bandits and those *monsters,* yourself? And maybe Soldier too, while you're at it, that it? I heard he's a real treat with a blade. How about you, Scofield? Got any trainin'?"

"You know I don't," the young man admitted, his face pale. Then he seemed to rally, his chest puffing out. "And maybe I can't do anything about the bandits or the monsters *or* our corrupt ruler. But there are those who can. The Perishables—"

"Oh, Eternals be good, not this again," the man named Shem said. "Enough about these damn Perishable fools, Scofield. Like we told you before, ain't nobody here interested in signin' up to be the next one whose blood decorates the headsman's block."

"Perishables," Davie said, shaking his head, a grin on his face. "What a name. Sound like food you don't want to carry on a long journey."

"Or perishable like your sister's virtue, maybe, Davie," the big man from the other table said, and everyone laughed at that, even

Davie. Everyone, that was, except the young man, his face flushed with frustration.

"This isn't a joke, damnit!" Scofield said, clearly angry now. "You all just sit back and let it happen, but if you helped, if enough people *helped,* we could talk to Soldier, make him understand. And if he won't listen, then...then maybe it's time we *did* have an election!"

There was silence for a moment, and the young man slowly began to smile, likely thinking that he had finally reached them. "I elect to check on the virtue of Davie's sister, that's what I elect to do," Shem said, and everyone burst out laughing again.

There was the sound of a door opening, and the wanderer glanced to the side to see that the barkeep had returned holding a bag. "Be a minute on the stew," he said, "but I got your horse's oats here and—" He cut off, glancing into the common room, at the young man standing there. "Ah, the poor fool's at it again. As if we don't all have enough trouble as it is without somebody comin' through and stirrin' up more."

"The Perishables sent me here," the young man was saying. "Sent me here to find brave men for the cause, and—"

"All the fruit was busy, I expect," Davie said to another round of laughter.

"On account of it perished," offered another man, and the room devolved into laughter again.

The young man waited for it to pass then spoke on, "But it seems that there aren't any brave men in Fulwell, not anymore. Maybe there never were!" The men in the room at least had the good grace to look ashamed at that, pointedly avoiding meeting the young man's gaze. Scofield, though, wasn't finished. "Don't know why I expected any different. What with you all too scared even to do anything about a corrupt constable who keeps raisin' your taxes until you can't hardly afford to eat, rigged it so that you finish a hard day of work more broke than when you started."

Still they said nothing, and finally the young man, apparently exhausted, collapsed into his chair, a resigned expression on his face.

"Well," the barkeep said quietly to the wanderer, "coulda been worse. Thank the Eternals that's over at least before anything else ha—" He cut off as the door opened to reveal three men. The first was dressed in the sort of foppish finery that was normally worn by the gentry of large cities. He wore a light blue silk shirt with long sleeves, ruffled at the end, and tight-fitting trousers. An ostentatious scabbard that looked more like a piece of art than anything that might hold an actual weapon was belted to his side.

The man didn't walk so much as saunter into the common room, running a hand through his slick, black hair. Behind him came two others, broad at the shoulders with mashed, scarred faces that marked them as street toughs. These two said nothing, only walked slightly behind and on either side of the first, eyeing the patrons of the common room as if they would like nothing more than to pick a fight with any of them—or all of them. A fight, the wanderer suspected, that they would inevitably win.

Just before the door closed, he caught sight of three horses picketed beside Veikr. These men, at least, didn't seem to be suffering from the mount shortage that the barkeep had alluded to. All conversation in the common room cut off as the door swung closed.

"Shit," the barkeep hissed from beside him.

"What?" the wanderer asked quietly. "Who is he?"

"Trouble on two feet, that's who," the barkeep said.

"I say," the foppish visitor said, smiling across the common room, his hands on his hips, a king in his domain. "Who owns that fine stallion picketed out front?"

The barkeep turned then, apparently remembering something of the utmost importance that he needed to do in the kitchen as he vanished through the doorway.

"He's my horse," the wanderer said. "But I don't claim to own him."

The man turned, smiling wider. "Why, if it isn't a visitor! And here I was beginning to think that our little town of Fulwell had been forgotten about altogether. Tell me, stranger," he went on, "what brings you to Fulwell?"

"I'm just passing through."

"Of course," the man said with a sigh. "Why else would anyone bother stopping in such a shithole as this? I have tried to civilize it, of course, but..." He paused, glancing meaningfully at the common room's patrons who all avoided his gaze before turning back to the wanderer. "Well, no amount of coin, however benevolently spent, can turn a hillbilly into a nobleman, now can it?"

The wanderer frowned. "You're assuming that would be an improvement."

The man flashed him another smile, but there was an edge to it this time. "Ah, a clever one, that is very nice. It is so *droll,* spending my time among these, these *savages.* It does my heart good to speak with another thinking man."

"I'm thinking, right now, that I'm going to go to my room," the wanderer said, rising and pocketing the key the barkeep had left on the counter before his hasty departure. "But first, I need to go see to my horse."

"Leaving so soon?" the young man asked, grinning to display his teeth. "Ah, but that's a shame, isn't it! But first, please, pray tell me how much you want for that enormous beast of yours—that is a fine bit of horseflesh and one that..." He paused, glancing up and down at the wanderer's form, cloaked in dust from the road. One that I fear might be wasted on you."

"He's not for sale."

One of the big men let out a low-throated growl and started forward, pausing like a dog come up short on its leash when the fop raised a hand. "Oh, come now," he said. "*Everything* has a price."

"Not my horse."

The man frowned then, the look of a child accustomed to getting his way and discovering, for the first time, that the world might not revolve around him after all. "You are being quite rude, you know. I will offer you a fair sum, for I would make of it a gift to my uncle. He does *so* love a fine horse."

"I'm not rude," the wanderer said, hefting the bag of oats in his left hand, keeping his right free in case he had to draw his blade. "I'm just leaving."

He started toward the door, and one of the big men stepped to the side, blocking his path. The wanderer only stood, watching him, waiting for what would come.

In the end, the young fop gave a laugh. "Oh, do get out of his way, Henry. You heard him—the man wants to leave."

The big man eyed him for another moment then stepped to the side, just enough to allow the wanderer to walk past.

The wanderer did so, moving toward the door.

"My, but is that young Scofield, I see there?" he heard the finely-dressed man—who, the wanderer would have guessed, was of an age as the other—ask from behind him. "And here I thought I told you I didn't want you sullying our fine town with your presence any longer."

The wanderer glanced back at the table where the young man who had been trying to recruit for the group known as the Perishables sat. The others who shared the table had begun to rise, vacating it and moving to sit at other tables at the far end of the room, leaving the youth alone. His face was pale, but he cleared his throat. "I-I'm free to go wh-wherever I like," he managed.

"Oh, Scofield," the finely-dressed man said, shaking his head, "you do have some funny notions. Come, Henry, let us have a little conversation with—" The man paused as he turned, looking at the wanderer. "You're still here? I thought that you had to see to your horse."

The wanderer glanced at the youth, sitting alone. He was scared, that much was sure, as well he should be as he was likely in for a beating. But then, in the wanderer's experience, the lessons a man learned the best were those learned through pain and, besides, the last thing he wanted to do was advertise his presence by getting in a fight in the middle of town. "I do," he said, then he turned and walked out the door, leaving the young man to what was coming.

It didn't feel good, leaving him, but then, save for meeting Felden Ruitt and his family, very few things in the last hundred years had and he had no reason to expect that to change anytime soon.

He moved to Veikr, tying the feedbag around him, and the horse obligingly began to eat. "Quickly now," the wanderer said. "The sooner we get you to your stall and me to my room the better." The fact was he was beginning to grow more and more sure that his visit to town had been a mistake after all. He would have saddled up Veikr and left then, but they were both tired and, more than that, he needed to stop and get supplies first. It was the reason, after all, that he'd come here in the first place—that and the voice of Felden Ruitt, the voice he couldn't seem to shake no matter how much he tried.

Still, he thought he would be okay. As long as he avoided the young fop, whoever he was, and the constable, at least. And that ought to be easy enough. When Veikr was done, he would put him in his stall, and then he would go to his room. He would rise early in the morning, get his supplies, and be gone before anyone was the wiser. It seemed simple enough—but then, most things were.

Right up until they weren't.

No sooner had he had the thought then the door to the tavern suddenly burst open and the young man, Scofield, came flying through it. The man hit the ground hard, rolling and coming to a stop about a dozen feet from where the wanderer stood with Veikr.

The wanderer glanced at the man and saw that his face, where it wasn't covered in dust, was bloody. The man himself was clearly in bad shape, wheezing for breath, still doing so as the young man with the slick black hair walked out of the tavern, followed by his two bruisers who were flexing their bloody knuckled hands.

"Ah," the fop said, smiling widely as he noticed the wanderer. "Still here, then? Well, it seems that you're going to get a free show." He winked. "Careful I don't charge you for it."

The wanderer ignored him, turning back to Veikr, as the man and his two hired toughs moved to where the other young man lay in the dirt, gasping for breath.

"Now, Scofield," the man said, his tone amused, "where were we?"

"Listen, L-Lee," the young man said, trying to scoot away, "please, I-I didn't, that is, I don't want any trouble, please—" He cut off, crying out in pain as one of the toughs lifted him to his feet by his shirt collar, his feet dangling in the air.

"Oh, Scofield," the young man, Lee, said, shaking his head. "Imagine thinking that what *you* want makes any difference at all. Didn't I tell you, the last time, that if I caught you here, in Fulwell, spouting your revolutionary nonsense again, that I would make you suffer for it?"

"Y-yes, but—" Scofield never got to finish as the young, slick-haired man chose that moment to bury his fist in the defenseless man's stomach.

Veikr neighed softly, and the wanderer ran his hand along his muzzle. "I know," he said softly, "but it isn't our fight. We can't risk it—you know that. He'll get a beating, that's all. Likely, he'll be better for it."

The horse met his gaze with its own, and the wanderer was forced to look away from the accusation he saw there. "Are you finished?" he said, not waiting for a response as he began to remove the feedbag.

He glanced over to see that one of the toughs was now holding the young Scofield's arms twisted behind him at what was no doubt a painful angle. As the wanderer turned to look, the young man, Lee, struck him again, this time in the face. Scofield cried out, and blood sprayed as his head was slammed to the side by the force of the blow.

"You filthy *swine*," Lee hissed, looking down at his light blue shirt, now stained crimson at the sleeve. "Do you have any *idea* how much this shirt cost?" Scofield never got a chance to answer—not that he likely would have—for the man struck him again, this time in the stomach.

Scofield doubled over and would have fallen had the tough holding him not been there to keep him upright. Lee brought back his hand, clearly preparing for another strike, but just then Scofield somehow managed to wriggle one arm free, and the fop let out a cry of surprise as it was *he* who was struck in the face.

Lee stumbled away, nearly falling, then stared back at Scofield, his eyes wide, his face crimson with fury, a small line of blood trickling out of one corner of his mouth. "You *dare*," he screeched, his voice breaking in a high pitch. "You, you, *worm*, dare to strike *me?*"

The fop, shaking with fury, went to draw his blade but fumbled the first attempt, hissing a curse as he was forced to use both hands to extricate his sword from its uselessly ornate scabbard. "I'll kill you for that, you filthy swine."

He started forward, and the wanderer watched him, knowing he shouldn't get involved. The best thing, the *smart* thing, would be to pretend he hadn't seen anything at all, to turn and take Veikr away before the thing was done and the fop went looking for someone else to vent his anger on. But then, it seemed to him that he had rarely done the smart thing—leave that to Scholar.

Before he knew it, he was moving forward, catching the slick-haired man's wrist before he could bring his blade down.

"Enough," the wanderer said. "Whatever lesson you meant to teach him—I'd say he's learned it," he finished, glancing at the young Scofield who dangled limply in the tough's grip, barely still conscious.

"This is no concern of yours, stranger," Lee hissed, trying to jerk his arm away but unable to wrest it free of the wanderer's grip.

"I'm making it my concern," the wanderer said. "Now, you've given him his beating—it's done. Why don't you just leave it? Go have a drink, maybe?"

"If I say yes, will you let my arm go?" the man said, clearly putting in an effort to keep his voice steady.

"Sure," the wanderer said casually, releasing his arm.

As soon as his hand was free, the nobleman took a step back, behind his two toughs, then grinned. "I didn't *say* yes, you understand. Your mistake, I'm afraid."

"Is it?" the wanderer asked softly, glancing between the two toughs.

The young man rolled his eyes. "I tire of this—Henry, Eli, show this visitor a welcome to Fulwell he won't soon forget."

"You got it, boss," one growled.

"My pleasure," the other agreed.

Then they moved forward, coming at him with their fists raised, taking their time.

The wanderer, though, didn't like the idea of wasting anymore time out here than he had to, for the longer the thing dragged on, the more people would see and the better chances that those hunting him would hear of it.

So instead of waiting, he rushed toward the one on his left. Whatever the big man had been expecting, it certainly wasn't that. He let out a surprised grunt, swinging a meaty fist at the wanderer, one that, had he stood there to take it, likely would have knocked him unconscious. Only, he didn't. Instead, he ducked under the blow, stepping to the man's side as he did and planting one precise strike in his attacker's underarm, targeting the pressure point there.

He didn't have to wonder whether or not his aim had been true, for the man bellowed in agony, his arm going suddenly limp as he stumbled, which made it easier for the wanderer to pivot and plant his fist in his face.

The big man collapsed, unconscious before he hit the ground, and dust rose around him at the impact.

"*Bastard!*" The second—Henry or Eli, the wanderer wasn't sure which, and he didn't much care—didn't waste any time, barreling toward him the way an angry child might, counting on his greater size and greater strength to decide the matter.

Which, likely, they would have done, had the wanderer chosen to meet the man on those two fronts. But, of course, he did not. The man was so intent on charging at him, so intent on bowling him over, that it was an easy enough thing to step to the side, sweeping out one of his legs. Then the man was charging no longer but falling, his face smashing hard into the dirt. He hacked and spat out dust, beginning to rise, but abruptly gave it up when the wander struck him once in the soft place where his head connected to his neck.

Not hard enough to kill, but enough to know that the man would be far too busy being unconscious for the next several minutes to give him anymore problems.

There was a shout from behind him, and the wanderer rose, turning in time to see the young man, Lee, rushing toward him. The man brandished his sword in both hands, high over his head, as if he thought the wanderer was a log and the blade he held an axe.

Still, the wanderer found himself surprised—he wouldn't have thought the youth would have had it in him. In truth, he'd expected him to run.

But while the grimace on the young man's face as he approached showed fear as well as anger, anger, it seemed, had won out. As it often did, in truth, and, more often than not, to the grief of everyone involved.

This time, though, the wanderer decided that the grief would go to the young man and him alone. His first instinct was to draw his own sword, still scabbarded at his back, but he resisted it with a will. Drawing a sword, Soldier had told him—the *real* Soldier, long ago—was like asking a question, a question with only one answer: blood. And violence, blood, they never made things simpler—only more complicated.

So instead, he waited until the man reached him, bringing the sword down with a shout—he supposed to let him know it was coming in case he'd somehow missed the unsubtle telegraphing. *Anger is a weapon, it's true, but one that very few men know how to wield.* Another of Soldier's sayings—there had been a lot of them over the years—but the youth had clearly never learned this one.

He roared in what he must have supposed was a furious, intimidating cry, was still roaring as the wanderer side-stepped the blow, and the fine sword buried its fine tip in the ground. The wanderer stepped up, and in one smooth motion, brought the ridge of his hand into the youth's throat. Not hard enough to crush the windpipe there, but hard enough to make it take a temporary break from its job.

That cut the roar off quickly enough. The youth dropped his sword, stumbling backward, wheezing and hacking, both his hands cupping his throat as if he meant to strangle the life out of himself. The wanderer walked with him until the man, Lee, took his third step and fell sprawling on his back. Then the wanderer crouched above him.

As the man continued to paw at his throat, his previously slicked-back hair now in wild disarray, the wanderer drew the knife from his belt, and the man watched it with wide, terrified eyes.

"*P-pl—*" the man tried, croaking but breaking off into a coughing fit.

"Don't talk," the wanderer said quietly. "The time for talking's done. It's time to listen now, understand?"

The man nodded so hard the wanderer suspected he'd be dealing with a sore neck in the morning. Well. A sorer neck, at any rate.

"Good. Now, I'm going to let you and your...friends go."

The man nodded more, tears of relief gathering in his eyes.

"Sure, you're grateful now," the wanderer said. "But listen—later, hours from now, maybe days, that gratefulness, that relief at still being alive, is going to fade. What's going to be left is a wounded throat and, worse than that, a wounded pride. That's about the time you're going to start thinking some things. Thinking that you could have taken me, that you *still* could, if given another chance."

The man hissed, retrieving a knife from his boot. The wanderer caught his wrist and punched him in the face, hard, breaking his nose. Lee cried out, gasping and whimpering at the same time. The wanderer sighed, tossing the knife away. "You'll convince yourself, in the hours, the days to come that I just got lucky, that you stumbled, or that there was dust in your eye or some other fool thing. And then you'll start thinking about coming after me again. You'll think that you have to do it, that your wounded pride will allow nothing else. But let me tell you something, kid. In all my life, I've never met a single man who made it to old age because of his pride. I've met plenty, though, who didn't. Nod if you understand what I'm telling you."

The man gave another vigorous, shaky nod.

"And just so we're both clear," the wanderer said, "because I'd hate for there to be any confusion. If you come for me again—I'll kill you. Now, get up and get out of here. And take your dogs with you."

Lee didn't need a second invitation. He scrambled across the dusty road. The wanderer rose, sheathing the knife, and watched as the man shook his friends, rousing them, and in another few minutes they were all stumbling down the road, casting frightened glances behind them.

The wanderer waited until they turned a corner on the street. When they were gone from sight, he turned and walked over to the man, Scofield, who had managed to drag himself halfway to his feet and was currently sitting with his back propped against one of the tavern's hitching posts.

"You okay?" the wanderer asked.

The man stared at him. "I-I've never seen anything like that," he said. "You...you just took them apart as if, as if it was nothing."

The wanderer thought it best to leave that for the time being. "Can you stand?"

"I-I don't know."

"Well," the wanderer said. "You won't—until you try."

The man did, and after several grunts and hisses of pain, he managed to drag himself to his feet.

"T-thanks," he croaked.

The wanderer glanced around, all too aware of the fact that they were being watched from nearby shop windows. "Come on," he said. "We'll get you an ale. It won't make the pain go away, but it might make you forget about it a little, and sometimes that's the best you can hope for."

He draped the man's arm over his shoulders and led him in a shuffling walk back into the common room. As the door opened, the tavern's patrons—who'd been crowded around the windows—hurried back to their seats.

The wanderer winced inwardly at that. The last thing he needed was to draw attention to himself. Still, what was done was done, and there was no changing it. That sounded more like something Leader would have said, but either way, it was true.

He led the bloody man to a chair and sat him down in it before taking one opposite. The barkeep showed up a minute later with a bottle of whiskey and a rag. "Here," he said, handing both to Scofield who took them, a confused expression on his face.

"For cleanin' your wounds, lad," the barkeep explained. "And, when the pain of that gets too much, the whiskey's for drinkin'."

"Th-thank you," the young man said.

The barkeep waved it away, turning to the wanderer. "That was some kind of show you put on there."

The wanderer winced. "Think anybody saw?"

"I'd say just about everybody in town, and those who didn't will be hearing about it before the night's out. A small town like Fulwell, news travels fast, and bad news, well, that's fastest of all. My mother told me that, a long time ago, and I've always found it to be true."

"So have I," the wanderer said with a sigh.

"Now then," the barkeep went on. "How'd you do it?"

"Do what?"

"You know exactly what I mean—I watched you break those two big bastards down, fold 'em up like they was chairs. And that prick, Lee, well, I imagine he'll think twice before drawin' that sword of his."

"Probably he won't."

The barkeep gave a sigh. "Aye, probably he won't. Still, it was a damn fine show. So you gonna tell me how you did it? It'd be nice to have the truth before the town gossips get their hand at it. By tomorrow evenin', you'll be a demon or an angel, maybe both."

"I'm neither of those things," the wanderer said. "I'm just...well. Lucky, I guess."

The barkeep snorted. "Don't know if I'd say lucky."

The wanderer frowned at that. "What do you mean?"

"Well," the thin man said, "you know Lee, there? The fella with hair looks like it's slathered in bacon grease? The one you beat like a blacksmith poundin' iron into shape?"

The wanderer met the man's eyes. "I remember—that a problem?"

The barkeep grunted. "Not for me it ain't. But you see, Lee, while he's an almighty prick, also has the dubious honor of bein' our fine constable's nephew."

The wanderer sighed. "Well, he would be, wouldn't he?"

The barkeep gave him an apologetic smile. "S'pose he would." He glanced around the room, and the wanderer did the same, noting that all the patrons quickly looked away, doing a poor job of hiding their eavesdropping. "Look," the barkeep said, leaning in and talking in a whisper, "I don't give a shit about Lee. I wouldn't piss on that prick bastard if he was on fire and holdin' a bag of money. I'd say about the same for his uncle, but I'd say it quiet, you understand?"

The wanderer watched him. "I'm starting to."

"Oh, Lee's a little shit, spoiled on account of his uncle's the constable. Dangerous the same way a child might be dangerous if given a blade. His uncle, though...well, the constable's a different matter. A mean one, make no mistake, but clever, too, and a damned sight more dangerous than that fool nephew of his."

"I see," the wanderer said, thinking it over. "And he and the nephew...they're close?"

The barkeep snorted. "No, I don't guess I'd say the constable's close with anybody, save maybe that sullen bastard that's always followin' him around like a mongrel looking to be thrown some scraps. Nah, I don't reckon he gives any more thought to that nephew of his than a man gives to a shit, once he's had it. Only..."

"Only it's *his* shit."

"Exactly," the barkeep said.

The wanderer was about to say something more when there was a clatter, followed by a hissed curse, and he and the barkeep turned back to the table to see that Scofield had spilled the whiskey, and it was pouring onto the table.

"Damnit, lad," the barkeep said, "I know it ain't the finest whiskey, but that ain't no cause to go pourin' it out like its poison." He took the bottle and glanced at the wanderer. "Which it is, o'course. Only, the good kind." He sighed again, shaking his head and pulling up a chair beside the young man, taking the rag. "Just sit there and try not to whimper too much, eh? I'll get you cleaned up, and then we'll see what needs doin'."

The wanderer rose, and the young man looked at him. "Y-you leavin'?" he asked, sounding more than a little like a child scared that their parents would abandon them in the darkness alone.

"Just checking on my horse. I'll get him in the stall and then stay the night." He paused, turning to the barkeep. "Assuming I still have a room?"

The barkeep considered that, seeing the out, then finally he sighed. "Shit, why not? Probably I shouldn't even charge you—I won't lie to you, it did my heart good to see that bastard Lee get what was comin' to him. Though, be honest, I'm surprised, given what you now know, that you ain't leapin' on that giant horse of yours and gettin' out of town just as fast as he'll carry you."

The wanderer shook his head. "Better if I don't. As you say, it's a small town, and somehow I doubt Lee decided to go home and sleep it off. I'd say it's likely he's gone to tell that uncle of his, if he hasn't told him already."

"Maybe I'm missin' something," the barkeep said, "but it seems to me that'd be all the more reason for you to get out of town now while the gettin's good."

The wanderer shook his head. "By now, he's already told the constable everything. Either he's decided to do something about it or he hasn't. If he hasn't, then there's no harm done. If he has...well, if it were me, I'd station men at either end of town. There don't seem to be a lot of ways to sneak out of here."

The barkeep snorted. "That much is true. Why, if there were, I reckon I'd have taken 'em a long time ago. Still...you sure? There's a good chance that bastard Walter'll be sendin' some of his men to find you, likely he'll come himself."

"If they do, then I'd rather *see* them coming," the wanderer said. "Better that then stumbling over them out there in the dark. And listen...if they do come...I don't want to cause you any trouble."

"Oh, you won't," the barkeep said. "I wish you all the luck, stranger, I surely do, but I live here in Fulwell, and, my experience, life is hard enough without goin' lookin' for ways to make it harder. The key you got's the only one to your room, but I imagine an axe'd do the trick quick enough, and I for one ain't plannin' on getting in its way, understand?"

"I do."

The barkeep turned from where he was ministering to the young man's wounds and glanced at the wanderer. He watched him for a moment then nodded. "Alright, then. Well, Scofield, you're about as good as you're gonna get."

"Don't *feel* good," the youth muttered.

"Well, maybe that'll be some incentive," the barkeep said, "you know, to keep from gettin' the shit kicked out of you in the future.

Anyway, at least you're alive to feel anythin' at all—if the stranger here hadn't showed up, you wouldn't be. I like you, Scofield, but not enough to get my own self killed just so you'll have company." He sighed. "I think maybe I've got somethin' in the back, might help. Wait here." He rose, glancing between the two of them. "And hey, while I'm gone, do me a favor and try not to get into anymore scraps, eh?"

"Reckon I'm about all scrapped out," Scofield mumbled, then turned and glanced at the barkeep, offering him a wide, if slightly pained smile, one that seemed to transform his already young face into that of a kid. "Thanks, Ellum, really."

The barkeep shifted, clearly uncomfortable. "It's nothin'. Just try not to give me any more work tonight, eh? It's late, and I'd just as soon get some sleep."

The young man grinned again. "I'll do my best."

Ellum grunted, rising from the chair, and without another word he moved toward the back room. The wanderer stared after him, was still staring when the young man spoke.

"So...where did you learn to fight?"

The wanderer glanced at the young man. "Does it matter?"

Shofield gave a soft laugh at that. "I'd say that, so far as Lee and those two dogs of his are concerned, it matters quite a bit." When the wanderer only continued to watch him, he winced. "Right, no, you're right. It's your business and none of mine. Still, however you learned, I'm thankful for it."

The wanderer gave a single nod, accepting the thanks. "What do you plan to do now?"

"What do you mean?"

"I heard you before," the wanderer said, "talking about the Perishables."

The young man nodded eagerly. "That's right, that's exactly right. Hey, now that you mention it, would you be—"

"No."

Shofield winced again, giving a self-deprecating laugh. "Sorry. You save my life and here I am pestering you about joining."

The wanderer watched him for a minute, and he decided he could understand why Ellum, the barkeep, and the others in the inn seemed to like the young man. He was one of those people who seemed impossible not to like, his expressions and his words open and innocent, childlike in some way that was hard to define.

"So?" the wanderer asked.

"What?" the young man said. "Oh, you mean about what I mean to do."

"Yes."

The young man seemed to consider that, scratching at the beard—if one might be generous and call it that—stubbling his jawline.

"Will you leave Fulwell?" the wanderer prompted.

The young man winced. "I've considered it. Anyway, when Lee and his thugs were beatin' the shit out of me I guess I was thinkin' little else except, if they'd let me, I'd leave Fulwell that instant."

"So you mean to?"

Shofield frowned, then slowly shook his head. "I don't think so."

It was the wanderer's turn to frown then. "You know them better than I do, but this Lee doesn't seem like the sort of person who lets things go. Seems much more like the kind that finds a grudge and nurses it."

Another laugh, another charismatic smile. "Oh, you're right there. Lee isn't the forgiving type, that's for sure, the bastard."

"So?" the wanderer asked. "Aren't you afraid that they might come back and find you here again?"

"Terrified," the young man admitted with that childlike innocence the wanderer had noted earlier. "But then...well, being scared, that doesn't give us an excuse to do nothing, does it? I mean, I know you said you heard some of what I was telling the others—don't worry, I'm not trying to recruit you. All I meant was that, well, there's a lot wrong in this world, with the Eternals, with that damned Lee and that damned uncle of his. Most of it I can't change. But I was sent here to recruit and recruit is what I mean to do. I can do that much, at least." He looked at the wanderer, an almost defiant expression on his face as if he was expecting an argument and was more than ready to put it down.

The wanderer didn't argue, though, he only nodded. "You mean to stay, then."

"At least for a while," the young man said, then, apparently aware of the note of contrition in his own voice, cleared his throat and squared his shoulders. "The work I'm doing—it's important work, work that *needs* doing. And my pa, he always told me that what makes a man a man is always doing the thing needs doing."

"Where is your pa now?"

"Dead," the young man said, his jaw working.

The wanderer gave a single nod. "I can't make you leave, and I wouldn't, even if I could. A man has to make his own decisions—good or bad. If you mean to stay, to continue what you're doing, then I wish you luck. But only, remember this," he said, rising. "A man has to make his own decisions—that's true. But he also has to live with the consequences. Good luck, Scofield."

The young man grinned widely, the grin of a young man who was convinced that, despite what had nearly happened, he was immortal, convinced the way so many his age were. "And to you as well."

The wanderer opened his mouth, meaning to say something else, but in the end he let it go unsaid, heading upstairs to his room. He unlocked the door, stepping through and swinging it shut behind him as he glanced around his room.

A small bed sat in the corner, small but clean looking. A table stood beside it, and a wardrobe had been placed along the opposite wall. The wanderer moved to the table and took a seat, wishing he'd brought his ale with him instead of leaving it downstairs in the common room.

He wasn't much of a drinker, and it had been more than a hundred years since he'd been drunk, but he thought he would have liked to have been drunk now. The young man, Scofield, had gotten to him—or, more particularly, his words had.

Being scared doesn't give us an excuse to do nothing. That had felt like a punch in the stomach, had stolen the wanderer's breath. Then, as now, he wasn't even sure *why* the words had had such an effect on him, only that they had.

He wondered if, perhaps, the words—and the young man's plight—mattered so much to him because of the fact that, long ago, he had been much like him. Fired up and passionate about his cause, eager to go out into the world and fix all its problems. That had been a long time ago indeed, before he realized that the world didn't *want* its problems fixed, and it would punish, most severely anyone who took it upon themselves to do so.

He had seen it before, plenty of times, but how, he wondered as he moved across the room to sit at the table, could you make a young man, so full of passion and the inherent, inarguable belief that he would live forever, see the truth of it? Some lessons might be learned at the hand of an engaged teacher, but others...others could only be learned by pain, could only be remembered by the scars they left.

He thought of her, waiting there in the glen, standing by the tree they had carved their initials into, wondering, as he had so many times in the years since, how long she had waited. He thought of standing before the Twelve, waiting to be judged, and of the hundred years since their final battle, since their failure. He had not been able to let his own burden go, no matter how much he might have wished it, for while he might once have been full of passion too, that passion had faded over the years. Died a little each time he heard about one of those whom he had known in his own life passing from the world, and he unable even to attend their funerals, including that of his father. To do so would be to give the enemy a chance to find him, a chance to finish what they had begun and destroy the world in truth.

His secret—the secret he did his best to hide, even from himself—was that he wished that he had never gone to the Eternals. He wished that, instead, he had stayed with that woman, *his* woman, in the woods. They would have most likely led a small life, a quiet one, but a fine one, too. It was too late for him to change anything, for she was dead and gone, along with all but the memory of his old life. But for the youth, Scofield, there was still some time yet. Probably the youth wouldn't listen, but then that didn't mean that the wanderer shouldn't try.

After all, as Scofield's father had told him, what made a man a man was doing the thing that needed doing. Even if he suspected, even if he *knew*, that doing it would make no difference.

With a sigh, the wanderer rose and moved to his door, unlocking it. Then he was stepping out on the landing, heading down the stairs toward the common room again. He started toward the table where he and Scofield had sat, pausing when he realized that the young man was gone, the table empty. The barkeep, Ellum, looked up from where he'd been wiping at the blood stains the young man had left on the table to meet the wanderer's gaze. "Lookin' for the lad?"

"I thought I might...speak to him."

"Well, I'm sorry to say he left, shortly after you, in fact."

The wanderer nodded. "Left the city?"

The barkeep sighed, shrugging. "I don't know, but the gods know I hope so. The lad's...passionate, I'll grant you, can be annoyin', but then sometimes I think that maybe the world could do with more folks with that kind of passion, folks that aren't content to get drunk and bitch about the things they don't like about the world but who instead set out to fix it." He paused, considering, then gave a grunt. "Most times I think as much, really."

The wanderer nodded again, for he found that, despite the fact that his own passion had led to a solitary life, wandering the world for a hundred years, his only ambition to keep the magic sword out of the enemy's hands, he found that he agreed.

He stood there, thinking about the young man, Scofield, about the man he himself had once been, and didn't realize how much time had passed until the barkeep spoke again.

"Everything okay, stranger?"

"Fine," the wanderer said. "Thanks." Instead of heading back to his room, he walked toward the common room door and out of it, into the street, looking first one way then the other in the vain hope that perhaps he might see the young man.

He didn't, though. Wherever Scofield had meant to go, he was well on his way now. The wanderer could only hope that he had left. Fulwell would not be safe for him for some time—perhaps ever. He could have looked for him, maybe, but he knew that such a search would be folly. After all, it was dark, and he was in a town he did not know. He had far better chances of being found by the constable's nephew or the constable himself than he did of finding Scofield. Besides, he told himself that it was none of his concern, or at least, it shouldn't be. His duty was the sword, that and that only. His duty was to save the world, not one young man, assuming he even needed saving, which likely he did not. Likely, the man had already left and was well on his way out of town.

The wanderer looked around one more time, then sighing, walked back into the tavern. He made his way back up to his room and closed the door, locking it behind him. He glanced around the room then moved to the chair to drag it toward the door where he propped it so that its back was beneath the latch. Should someone try to break into his room, the chair would make the task more difficult. Not a particularly sturdy chair—it would only buy a few more seconds before a determined intruder was able to break it. But then, the wanderer had lived long enough and had been in enough life-or-death situations to know that when it came to such things, a few seconds often made all the difference.

He shuffled to the bed, shifting his left arm that ached where his exertions had pulled at the recently healed wound. He removed the scabbarded sword from his back and placed it beside the bed so that it lay less than a foot from the cursed blade, still wrapped in its bundle where he had put it under the bed before going downstairs. Then he removed his boots, placing them beside the bed, and lay down.

The bed was more comfortable than he would have first guessed, far more comfortable than he was used to, though considering that he spent the majority of his days sleeping on the forest floor or in abandoned barns he supposed that didn't count for all that much.

Yet as comfortable as the bed was, he found that, no matter how much he searched for it, sleep eluded him. Thanks to the change that had been worked in him so long ago, the wanderer did not sleep as much as normal people. At first he had thought this a great boon, one that allowed him far more time to do the things that needed to be done.

Now, though, a hundred years into his exile, he felt differently. Sleep, after all, was a cure for all the problems and pains of the waking world. It was an escape, a means of forgetting, at least for a little while, the many worries, the many regrets that a man accumulated over his life, that hung from his neck like some great, ever-growing chain of iron.

He wanted to sleep, *needed* to sleep, if for no other reason than to forget about the young man, Scofield, and his plight, to forget about his own. And yet...sleep eluded him.

His emotions were too unsettled, memories of his past pushing at him, like a building wave threatening to sweep him away. It was strange to him that, no matter how much a man traveled, he could never leave his past behind him. He felt the memories of his life coming on and, in sudden desperation, he clawed the locket at his neck open.

Immediately, a deluge of voices swept over him, most of them scolding, angry at the fact that he had risked himself to save the youth from being killed. Some might have thought their comments cold, and they would be right to do so, for the ghosts *were* cold. Warmth, after all, was only for the living. The ghosts thought of no one, of nothing except the mission, saving the world. They had no time or concern for the individuals which made it up.

They were, to the wanderer, like guards who stood in defense of a castle, fending off the battering ram, rallying against the catapults, and yet unaware of the danger presented by a lone man who walked up and began, slowly, to chip away at the great edifice stone by stone. And they would, if left to their own devices, remain ignorant of the man's efforts until the entire castle came crashing down around them.

The wanderer did not respond to their scoldings and soon they were no longer speaking to him at all but to each other, arguing really. The wanderer lay there, letting their bickering voices wash over him, for they at least served to distract his mind and his thoughts from memories of his past, driving back the wave that had threatened to overcome him.

And then listening to the voices of the ghosts like the susurration of the tides, the wanderer finally found the escape he had been looking for, and he slept.

***

The wanderer slept light. He always had, even before becoming the Youngest, and the last hundred years had only heightened that tendency, so that he could wake at the sound of a pin dropping on carpet. Only what woke him now was not a sound at all. Instead, it was a smell. Specifically, the smell of something burning.

He was up in an instant, his gaze moving first to the door to his room only to see that the chair he'd placed there had not been disturbed. He frowned, then, as a thought occurred to him. It had been pitch black when he'd lain down, and he should not have been able to see the chair at all from the bed. Yet he could, for it, like the rest of the room, was bathed in sporadic, flickering orange light.

A fire then, but not in the tavern itself, for no smoke roiled underneath the doorframe, and anyway the smell was not strong enough for that. The wanderer rose, taking a moment to pull on his boots and to secure his scabbard over his back, the bundle of the magic sword there as well, then he moved to the window and looked out, scanning the street for the source of the flames.

He found it immediately and, as he did, a shock of fear ran through him. The fire was not coming from the inn—about that much, at least, he had been right. Instead, it was coming from somewhere far worse. The stables. The same stables where he had penned Veikr only hours ago.

He rushed to the door, throwing the chair aside and slinging it open. Then he was running, sprinting across the landing to the stairs which he took two at a time.

"What is it?" a man asked in the common room, raising his head drunkenly to glance at the wanderer.

The wanderer ignored him, shouldering into the door and out into the night. He sprinted around the tavern's side toward the burning building. There was no crowd yet, which meant that the stables had not been burning for long, yet their sides were wreathed with flames, great tendrils of fire flicking this way and that as if hungrily searching for something else they might devour.

The wide front doors of the stables were thrown open, and the wanderer did not hesitate, rushing inside. "*Veikr!*" he shouted, holding an arm in front of his face to protect his exposed skin from the worst of the heat as he scanned this way and that, struggling to pierce the smoke with his gaze. "*Weakest!*" he shouted.

The horse did not answer. Instead, the wanderer heard a loud *crack* from above and leapt back in time to narrowly avoid being crushed by a burning wooden beam which fell from the rafters to land in a shower of sparks where he had stood. "*Veikr!*" he roared.

The horse did not answer, and the wanderer told himself to relax. The horse was not here—could *not* be here. He would not stand still and burn, after all, and the barn had not been built, the stall constructed that could hold the giant horse if he did not want to be held.

He heard a cough and spun, his hand going to the handle of his sword peeking over one shoulder. But no attacker rushed toward him out of the smoke. Instead, a figure lay a short distance away on the ground. Frowning, the wanderer rushed over, dropping to his knees and seeing that his fear was confirmed—the man lying there was Scofield.

"Come on," he said, "we need to get you out of here."

"Too...late," the young man said, giving him a bloody, pained smile.

The wanderer glanced down at the youth's form and saw that indeed, he was right. There was a spreading pool of blood beneath the man, and with the sword wound in his stomach it didn't take a genius to figure out where it had come from, just as it didn't take one to see by the fresh scrapes and cuts on the young man's face that he had been beaten before he was stabbed.

"I-I'm sorry," the young man said, breaking into a coughing fit.

"Sorry?" the wanderer asked, genuinely confused. "Why?"

The youth grimaced, giving his head a weak shake. "Should have...listened to you. Should have...left. Only, I thought...I thought maybe I could go and talk to Lee, you know, make things righ—" He cut off then, crying out in pain.

"Shh," the wanderer said, putting his hand on the youth's shoulder. "Don't talk."

"C-can you d-do me a...a favor?" the young man asked, coughing again so that a line of blood leaked from the corner of his mouth. He gave another weak grin at that. "I mean...another one?"

"Name it."

With a visible effort, the youth reached into his tunic and withdrew a rolled parchment which he offered to the wanderer with a trembling hand.

The wanderer took it, frowning. "What's this?"

"A-a message," the youth said. "R-report, really, for...for the leader of the...Perishables. C-can you see that...that he gets it? H-he's in the city of Celes, a few days ride s-south of—"

"I know where it is," the wanderer said. In fact, there were very few, if any, cities on the face of the world that he had not been to during his hundred-year journey.

The young man coughed again, giving a weak nod. "T-there's a b-bar called *The Spilled Tankard*. Y-you can find him th..." The youth trailed off then, taking a breath, his eyes closing.

The wanderer waited for the man to finish but he never did, and by the sudden stillness of his chest, he never would. Gritting his teeth, the wanderer rose, sliding the rolled parchment into his tunic. He had thought that his long life had inured him to the sharpest of grief's stabs. He had been wrong. The grief was back, stronger than it had been in a century, and there was something else, too.

Rage.

He did not look for Veikr any longer, for he knew that the horse was not here. Which meant that he was somewhere else, and it didn't take much work to consider where that could be.

The wanderer walked toward the door of the barn, the flames all around him nothing compared to the flame of fury raging inside his chest, making his hands knot into tight fists at his sides. He stepped out of the burning barn and into the night.

They were waiting for him there, as he'd known they would be. Seven in all, sitting atop their horses and arranged in a semi-circle in front of the barn.

The constable was at the front. His nephew, Lee, sat beside him, a cruel, satisfied grin on his face. At the constable's other side was the man in all black, Gene, who held Veikr's reins. Spread out to either side were four men the wanderer did not know but all of whom, he saw, had swords sheathed at their sides.

"Constable," the wanderer said, turning to the fat man.

The man shook his head, a small humoring smile on his face like that a father might use when speaking to a willful child. "I thought I told you to call me Walter. Seems you really do have a problem listenin'."

The wanderer said nothing, aware of his fists clenching and unclenching at his sides, aware, too, of his jaw, squeezed so tightly shut that it hurt.

"Damn shame about the stables," the constable said, shaking his head with feigned regret. "And is that poor Scofield I see in there?" He winced. "Must have succumbed to the flame."

"That's the story?"

The constable considered then shrugged, grinning like a man caught out at an innocent prank. "Well, it will be. After all, I'm constable in Fulwell, aren't I?"

The wanderer said nothing, and the constable sighed. "You really aren't much of a talker. Still, I told you we'd speak again about this horse of yours." He paused, glancing over at Veikr who stood watching the wanderer.

"A damn fine bit of horseflesh that is," the constable said. "And I want to tell you again, I'd be interested in buyin' him." He held up his hand as if to forestall any comment. "I know, I know, he ain't for sale. Only, the thing is, if it hadn't been for me and my men here happenin' upon him, why, this beautiful horse would have burned up along with poor Scofield. Seems to me that, if you can't protect what's yours no better'n that, probably it'd be best if I took him off your hands. And, considerin' that I *did* save him, it only seems right that I get him at a bit of a discount."

"A discount."

"Sure," the constable said, grinning wider, "free, I was thinkin'. Yeah, that'd do me fine."

"Listen," the wanderer said, deciding he should give it one more try even though he didn't want to. "I don't want any trouble." A lie, though. In truth, he wanted all the trouble these men could stand and then some.

"No?" the constable asked, then shrugged. "Well, I'll tell ya somethin', stranger. I don't want my sister comin' to me bitchin' about how a visitor comes into town and beats her boy so bad he looks like a doll belongin' to a child with a mean streak. And I *damn* sure don't want to have to tell that sister that, seein' her boy like that, I didn't do nothin' about it. That wouldn't be right at all. Would it, Gene?"

"Not right," the black-garbed man said.

"So you see," the constable went on, "somethin's got to be done. At least, that's my thoughts on the matter." He turned to look over at Lee, his nephew, the young man sitting his horse with an expression somewhere between a sneer and a smile on his face. "But then, what about it, Lee? You prepared to drop it, let it go? All of us go on about our lives?"

"No," the young man sneered. "You should have left town when you could," he said to the wanderer. "Now I'll do to you what I did to Scofi—"

The man never got a chance to finish, though, for before he did the wanderer moved in one smooth motion, drawing the knife he kept sheathed at his waist, pivoting, and extending his arm in the man's direction. The knife flew true, burying itself in Lee's throat, and the man's eyes went wide in shocked terror. He wavered in his saddle then fell off, collapsing to the ground, dead.

The wanderer turned to look at the constable who, along with the rest of his men, was staring in wide-eyed horror at the corpse. "I told him that if he came for me again, he'd find his death," the wanderer said. "I meant it."

"You *son of a bitch*," the constable hissed, all traces of his feigned good humor gone now. "*Kill this fucker!*" he roared.

The four men sitting their horses behind the constable and the black-garbed man dismounted, drawing their blades. As he waited for them to slowly approach, the wanderer drew his as well. Then, with a roar, the first charged in, wielding his sword in a two-handed grip, raising it above his head as if he meant to cleave the wanderer in half. Before he even began to bring the blade down, though, the wanderer lunged forward and his questing steel struck the man in the throat and then went through it.

The man stumbled to a stop, a confused look on his face as if he were trying to solve a particularly difficult puzzle, then the wanderer ripped the blade free in a spray of blood, and the dead man collapsed in a heap at his feet.

The others hesitated at that, beginning to circle him warily. As they did, the wanderer knelt, retrieving the dead man's blade. A heavier one than he liked, but it would serve. He rose, holding the new sword in his left hand, his own in his right.

"Last chance," he said to the three men. "You won't have another."

Unsurprisingly, the men liked their odds, and after a moment the wanderer nodded, relieved that they would remain, that he would have their bodies upon which to vent his unflagging rage. "Very well," he said. Then he rushed the nearest.

The man brought up his sword, parrying the first blow that had been aimed at his neck—or at least meaning to. The blade never struck home, for it had been a feint, and the wanderer immediately spun backward, dropping to one knee and bringing the other sword around where it struck the man in the back of his knees, lopping his legs off.

The man screamed as he fell to the ground, now legless, but the wanderer paid him no mind as he rose, spinning in time to catch the descending blade of the third man crossways between his two swords. Then he forced the sword up and before the man could recover, brought his own blades across his opponent's torso in an X, tearing two great gashes into his stomach.

As the man fell screaming to the ground, his hands covering the ruin of his stomach, the wanderer turned to the last who watched him with eyes the size of dinner platters in the moonlight.

"N-no," the man said, as if he were not staring at a man at all but some avenging avatar of destruction. "No." Then he turned, dropping his sword, and ran.

The wanderer watched him for a moment before heaving the sword after him. The man screamed as the blade pierced his back, and he fell to the ground.

The wanderer walked up to him, writhing on the ground, pawing desperately at his back as he tried and failed to remove the sword that was just beyond his reach. "Too late," the wanderer said, then he brought his blade down, severing the man's head from his body.

That done, he turned back to the constable and the man in black. The constable was staring at the dead men as if trying to understand what had happened. Meanwhile, the man named Gene was smiling a sharp smile. "You're good," he said.

"Thanks."

"Not good enough, though," he said.

"What are you *talking* about?" the constable demanded. "H-he just killed four me—"

"*Shut your fucking mouth, you fat pig,*" the man in black hissed, and the constable recoiled in shock.

"G-Gene?" he asked, as if the man had somehow been possessed by someone else.

The man in black said nothing, though, only dismounting from his horse and letting Veikr's reins drop to the ground. He came forward with a measured pace, removing his sword from its scabbard as he did, then stopped ten feet in front of the wanderer.

"Doesn't seem fair," the man said. "You bein' tired and all after fighting the others."

"What is?" the wanderer asked.

The black-garbed man inclined his head as if to acknowledge a point. "Now, before we get started, will you tell me your name? It seems only right that I should know it for when people come asking after what happened to you."

"They won't."

The man shrugged. "Very well."

Then the talking was done. The black-clothed man rushed forward, and the wanderer did the same. Their swords flashed out, twin bolts of silver in the darkness, and they froze, their faces inches from each other.

The black-garbed man was still smiling, but as the wanderer stared at him, he saw a line of blood begin to leak from the man's mouth. "A...trade it is then," the man hissed. "I'll...take it."

"Not a trade," the wanderer said, looking down. The other man followed his gaze to see that, indeed, the wanderer's blade had impaled him through the stomach but his own blade had missed by a hair's breadth.

"Im...impossible," the man said. "No...no one's that fast."

The wanderer stepped back, ripping his blade free, and the man stumbled, falling to his knees. "Will...will you not now tell me who you are? *What* you are?"

The wanderer considered, watching the man for a moment, and in the end, he decided it made no difference. He leaned forward, so that his mouth was inches from the man's ear. "*Youngest, they call me. I am the last. The last Eternal.*"

The man raised his gaze to look at him as the wanderer leaned back, and the swordsman's face seemed to have been bleached of all color. "Y-you're him," he said.

The wanderer did not answer, at least not with words. His sword licked out, too fast to follow, and a moment later the swordsman's body fell to the ground, his head rolling for a few feet before coming to a stop.

"*Yaaah!*"

The wanderer looked up at the sound of the shout to see that the constable had turned his horse and was kicking its flanks hard, sending it in the direction of the street.

"No," the wanderer said, as he had to the dying man, "it's far too late for that. Come, Veikr."

The horse did as requested, moving up to stand beside him, and the wanderer leapt into the saddle. "Go."

The constable was urging the horse on, and his mount seemed eager, but for all their efforts the two had made it no further than the front of the tavern when Veikr's powerful strides caught them up.

The wanderer rode up beside them, pulling himself over to ride side-saddle, then grabbing hold of the saddle-horn, he lifted himself up and gave the constable a kick. The man screamed as he went tumbling out of his saddle. As the constable's horse ran off into the night, the wanderer urged Veikr to a stop, then turned him around. He dismounted then, leading Veikr back to where the constable lay on the ground, almost in the exact same spot, the wanderer noted, where Scofield had lain after Lee and his men had beaten him.

The constable didn't look in much better shape. Falling from a horse was never fun, but when that fall was unexpected and was taken by a man who was at least a hundred-and-fifty pounds overweight, injury wasn't just likely—it was pretty much assured.

Plenty of scrapes and scratches where he'd rolled across the ground, his body covered in the dust of the road, but what had him hissing with pain was neither of those but instead the fact that one of his arms, judging by the angle at which it lay, had been broken in the fall.

The constable saw him coming and mewled desperately as he backed away, sliding across the ground. The wanderer walked after him, aware of the people, drawn by the commotion, beginning to gather on either side of the street.

Still, he paid them no attention—in that moment, they might as well not have existed. There was only him and the constable and the blade in his hands. Nothing else.

"J-just hold on a damned minute," the constable hissed as the wanderer caught up to him. "Y-you just hold on, damnit," he said. "Listen, I-I can give you gold, more than you can—"

"I don't want your money," the wanderer interrupted.

"Fine, *fine!*" the constable said, a panicked desperation in his voice now. "Horse then, one for every day of the—"

"I already have a horse."

"Damnit, then what do you *want?*" the man screeched. "Just tell me, and I'll give it to you!"

"I want you to die," the wanderer said simply.

The constable let out a sound somewhere between a sob and a growl. "You can't *kill* me," he hissed. "I'm the *constable* of this town, and you, you're *nobo*—" His words turned into a scream as the wanderer casually stuck his blade into the man's shoulder.

The constable backed up again, and the wanderer followed. "L-listen to me, you *bastard*, you won't get away with this, understand?"

"Maybe, maybe not," the wanderer said. "That's not going to make any difference to you, though."

"Look here, you, I'm the constable and..." He looked around, apparently just becoming aware of the people now lining the street, dozens in all and, the wanderer suspected, the better part of the town's population. *"What are you all doing?"* the constable screamed. *"Can't you see this man means to murder me?"*

The wanderer glanced around, saw that no one moved forward. "They're waiting," he explained.

"Waiting for *what?*" the constable hissed.

"This."

The blade went in smoothly, taking the man in the heart. The wanderer would have liked to have believed that he took no joy in it. That what he did was only a service, the same, in its way, as a man putting down a dog that's gone mad. But it wasn't true. The fact was, his mind was on the young man lying, dead in the barn, and he *did* enjoy it.

He pulled the blade free, wiping it on the dead man's shirt, then sheathing it at his back once more. He became aware of the sound of footsteps and spun, thinking that someone in the crowd had decided to attack him after all. Only the man wasn't attacking but walking up, his hands held before him as if to show he meant no harm and the wanderer realized that it was Ellum, the innkeeper.

"He dead?" the man asked quietly.

"As they come."

The barkeep nodded. "Listen," he said, "about your room—"

"I'll leave town tonight," the wanderer said.

The man sighed, visibly relieved at that. "It's no offense, understand, only, well, what with all that's happened..."

"You don't have to explain anything," the wanderer said. He started toward his horse, pausing as the man spoke again.

"What about the lad, Scofield?" he asked. "Did you ever find him?"

The wanderer's first instinct was to tell the man that no, he had not. After all, the fire in the barn would burn all the evidence that the young man had ever been there, and should he lie, the man might go on for the rest of his life thinking that Scofield was still alive, only that he had gone somewhere, traveling perhaps. But after spending a hundred years with the entire world believing that their rulers were the actual Eternals instead of impostors who had taken over their positions when they were dead, the wanderer had learned something.

The truth was always better. Sometimes it hurt—most times, in facts. And the truth, laid bare, often caused far more pain than pleasantness, far more grief than relief. And yet...the truth was better.

"Dead," the wanderer said.

The barkeep's eyes went wide at that. "No, it can't be. Can it? I mean...are you sure?"

"Yes."

The man swallowed hard, running a hand across his mouth. "Then...this bastard was responsible?"

"Yes."

The barkeep turned to look at the constable's corpse, his eyes dancing with anger. "I wish you would have made him suffer more before you killed 'em."

"So do I," the wanderer said honestly. Then he turned and walked to Veikr, swinging up in the saddle.

They did not boo or shout curses at him as he rode away through the street, but neither did they cheer. They only stood, silently regarding him, until he disappeared into the night...like a ghost.

CHAPTER FIVE

The wanderer left the town of Fulwell behind, traveling south for two days. On the third day, he'd only been traveling for an hour after waking when he turned a corner in the trail and saw, in the distance, the great city of Celes, known around the world as the Jewel of the South.

For his part, looking at it, now, as with the other times he had been to the city, the wanderer could not deny that it lived up to its name. Great walls of white marble surrounded a city which had been around for a thousand years in some fashion or another, making it one of the oldest cities in the world.

Yet despite their age, the walls were immaculate, for they were regularly maintained by crews of hundreds of workers given the constant task of their upkeep. As clean as they were, they seemed to shine in the early morning sun, like the jewel after which the city was named.

But as beautiful as the distant city was, as magical as the effect of its shining was, the wanderer, staring at it, felt only disquiet. After all, as fine as the city was, it was also massive, housing hundreds of thousands of people, so big some people lived their entire lives within its walls without ever setting foot outside of them.

That many people meant far too many chances of being discovered, of being marked out for one reason or another. It had been a hundred years since he and the other Eternals had waged the final battle, a hundred years since he had been marked as a traitor, but his name, instead of fading into history, had become a by-word for evil men, his likeness commonly used by authors to represent traitors. The city was full of danger, yet he would go anyway. He would go because he had told Scofield that he would. He was not sure why he would keep this promise when he had broken so many others over the years, but he would just the same.

Since leaving Fulwell, the wanderer had not consulted the ghosts for their opinion on the matter, for he knew already what those opinions would be. They would all call him a fool who risked everything for nothing—the only time they agreed was when they were discussing how foolish he was—and in some ways they might even be right. After all, objectively speaking, the lives of millions of people would undoubtedly be of greater value than the dying wish of one man. Brutal arithmetic, perhaps, but no less true for all that.

Only, life was not objective—it was as far from that as anything could be, in fact. A responsible man might indeed look to logic for answers, but that same man must be willing to follow his feelings, his morality. Priest, another of the ghosts, had taught him as much, many, many years ago, had claimed that while knowledge and logic might *inform* a man's decisions, they could not make them for him. Indeed, he had to make them on his own, calling on what sense of morality he possessed to do so.

True, it might not make objective sense to risk so many lives to fulfill a promise to a dead man, but how many such decisions might a man make, how many such logic-based courses of action, before he was a man no longer but some unthinking, unfeeling, un*caring* automaton?

You are part of this world. Felden Ruitt's voice in his head, and this time, at least, the voice was not a source of shame or regret but comfort.

At least, mostly.

The worst part about the city of Celes was not the fact that it was brimming with hundreds of thousands of people, not the fact that those beautiful marble walls looked to the wanderer like some giant cage. Instead, it was that Celes was the capital of the southern kingdom of Aldea and, as such, was the home of Soldier. And while the wanderer had once looked at the real Soldier as a mentor and a friend, the enemy had taken his identity, his face. And now, the wanderer meant to venture into to the heart of that enemy's power, an enemy who, along with his eleven companions, had been hunting the wanderer for a hundred years.

And yet, he would go, had known it from the moment the young man, Scofield, had asked it of him. He would go because, as Felden Ruitt had told him, he was a part of the world, and it a part of him.

"Ready?" he asked, turning to look at his horse.

Veikr gave a soft snort as if to say that he was far less likely to have an issue with the city than the wanderer and, since that was no more than the truth, the wanderer said nothing, only started forward.

It took him another hour to reach the city. Or, more exactly, to reach the great line of people awaiting entrance into the northern gate. It was early in the morning, but even at this hour, hundreds of people were lined up, men and women from the outlying areas come to sell their goods at the daily market mostly.

The wanderer stood with Veikr in the line, aware of the attention of those nearest him as they took in the enormity of his mount like spiders crawling over his skin. Still, he told himself that it was alright. It had been a hundred years, after all, and even the story the enemy had planted about him being a traitor was—in most places, at least—forgotten.

It was unlikely anyone would recognize him and, if things went the way he intended, they would have little time to do so anyway. He would find the leader of the Perishables, deliver the letter, and leave the city as quickly as he could.

He could not save Scofield, but that much, at least, he could do, and so he would. Despite the dangers, despite the fact that he knew the ghosts, if given chance to speak, would call him a fool. He would do it. After all, he was a part of the world.

So he waited in line, doing his best to ignore the stares of those around him and slowly, as the morning waned on, he drew closer and closer to the gate.

Finally, he was third behind an obviously wealthy merchant sitting atop his ostentatious, gold-gilded carriage, with four men, just as obviously hired guards, positioned around it. Ahead of him, was a far different sort. A small wagon filled with vegetables being pulled by a pair of exhausted-looking mules. Sitting atop the wagon was a large man who appeared to be in his thirties and, going by his dirt-stained, simple linen clothes, was a farmer. The man's wife sat beside him.

The two rode up to the gate and the four waiting guardsmen there, the man pulling the mules to a stop. One of the guards glanced at the others, not bothering to hide his grin before moving forward. "Well, look at this here, now," the guard said. "Ever hear of a bath?"

The farmer said nothing, only kept his head down, avoiding the guard's eyes. A big man, the farmer, nearly half again as large as the guard, yet he crouched timidly in his wagon as the guardsman strutted up, glancing it over.

"Turnips and carrots, is it?" the guardsman sneered. "Wouldn't happen to have any fine wine hiding under all that, would you?"

"No, sir," the farmer said.

"No?" the guard asked, glancing back at his fellows, making a game of the farmer's discomfort. "You sure? No contraband, nothin' of that sort?"

"No, sir," the farmer said again. "Only these turnips and carrots. I mean to sell them at market."

The guard snorted. "As if anyone would be interested in your dirty vegetables. Still, best I check—folks been tryin' to sneak a lot of stuff into the city, you know? And what with those Perishable pricks all about, why, you can't be too careful."

The man made a show of strutting to the back of the wagon, grabbing several turnips and carrots and throwing them out onto the dirty road.

"Hey," the farmer began, starting to get out of the wagon and stopping as his wife grabbed him by the arm.

"Don't, Finn," she said quickly.

The guard glanced up from tossing another vegetable onto the roadside, then made his way back to the front of the wagon, taking pains to step on several of the vegetables as he did. "What's that?" he asked. "You got something you want to say to me?"

Veikr snorted softly beside the wanderer, and he patted the horse's muzzle. "Easy, boy," he said quietly, his eyes never leaving the guardsman. "Easy."

"No, sir," the farmer said for the third time, but this time there was a strangled sort of quality to his deep voice that made it clear he was struggling to contain his anger.

"I didn't think so," the guardsman said, smiling smugly. "Anyhow, I guess you're clean. Go on, pick this shit up—can't be litterin' the road with your filth."

The wanderer saw the farmer's jaws flexing, but he glanced at his wife, gave a weary sigh and nodded before stepping off the wagon. The entire line was forced to wait as he set about the task of picking up the vegetables the guard had tossed in the road, putting them back in the wagon one handful at a time.

The guard stood watching with a smile on his face. When the farmer was done, he started back toward the wagon, but had to stop as the guard stepped in front of him. "Just one more thing," the guard said, grinning a grin that the wanderer had seen before, one that a cruel child might wear as he threw rocks at a mongrel dog in the street.

"I thought we were good," the farmer said, apparently also aware of the guard's expression and what it meant.

"Oh, we are, we are," the guard said. "Only, well, there's the tax, of course."

The farmer frowned. "Tax?"

The wanderer sighed. Whatever else the cruel men of the world were, they were rarely original.

"Just so," the guard said, nodding.

"I was just here two weeks ago," the farmer said, a note of defensiveness in his tone now, "there wasn't a tax to enter the city then."

"What can I say?" the guard said. "Times change. You see, with all the trouble those bastard Perishables have been kicking up, well, our wise leader, Soldier, has deemed it necessary to increase taxes to fix the damages in the city that they've caused."

"I see," the farmer said, his jaw working again. "How much?"

"Only an eternal," the guard said, then grinned. "An eternal for the Eternal."

"An eternal?" the farmer said, his voice aghast. "But that's more than I'll make on this entire wagon and—"

"Well," the guard said, "if you don't have the coin..." He paused, glancing meaningfully at the farmer's wife, still sitting in the wagon and watching the scene with a worried expression on her face. "Perhaps we can come to some other...arrangement."

The farmer's hands were flexing at his sides now. "No," he said, his voice a rough growl. "We'll leave—we can sell our goods at Bevaton."

"As you wish," the guard said, shrugging.

The farmer moved past him, starting to climb in the wagon then pausing as the guardsman spoke again.

"Only, before you go, we had best settle up."

The farmer glanced back. "Settle up?"

"Of course," the guard said. "What, do you think that you can just waste so much of the city's time, as you have, and not pay for it?"

The farmer's jaw was working again, so hard that the wanderer thought it was a wonder the man had any teeth left. "How much?" he asked, his voice a harsh growl.

"Oh, it ain't you I'm interested in takin' payment from," he said, glancing over at the farmer's wife. "Your whore, there, though—"

He never got the chance to finish, for the farmer's fist lashed out. Powered as it was by a body that had spent the better part of its life at manual labor, the punch did a thorough job of rearranging the guardsman's face in a splatter of blood before he struck the ground, hard.

Any satisfaction the farmer might have felt though, no doubt vanished a moment later as the other three guards gave a shout and came forward, their swords drawn. In short order, the farmer was manacled and led away to the dungeons by one guardsman while his wife looked on helplessly.

"Get that damn wagon out of here," one of the remaining guardsmen said while the other tried to revive his fallen companion who, it seemed, had gone from asshole to unconscious with remarked quickness.

The woman hesitated, clearly nervous and unsure of what to do. "B-but my husband—"

"You can see him when he's brought before the magistrate tomorrow morning. Until then, get this wagon out of here."

"But I don't know where to—"

"*Now!*" he roared, and the woman grabbed the reins, urging the team of donkeys away.

The wanderer watched her go, thinking that he should do something, but knowing that the thought was a foolish one. He could help no one. After all, he had tried to help the man, Scofield, and what good had it done? None for Scofield, who breathed his last in a burning barn that smelled of dried old horse shit, and not for himself, for if the enemy had not learned of his presence in the town of Fulwell following the incident, it was only a matter of time before they would.

So, he only stood, watching as the woman, crying now, rode the wagon away. The guard waved the wealthy merchant forward as if nothing had happened. This time, though, he did not so much as check the wagon, only shook the merchant's hand—a handshake in which some coins were not-so-subtly passed from one man to the other—and then waved him through. The merchant went, smiling, no doubt pleased at how easily his wealth paved his way through the world, creating for him roads where for others there were none.

And it was true, the wanderer couldn't argue it, but he might have told the merchant, had he asked, that roads paved with money often fell through without warning, and that friends who were bought were easily lost.

It was his turn, then, and he walked up to the guard.

The man looked him and Veikr up and down, his eyes widening slightly as he took in the size of his horse. "Fine horse."

"Yes."

The guard glanced at him. "What's your business in Celes?"

"Visiting a friend."

"Friend?" the guard asked, glancing him up and down with a doubtful expression that seemed to say that he couldn't imagine the wanderer had friends. Which, of course, he did not.

"Yes."

"I see," the guardsman said. "Well, there's the tax you'll be needin' to pay, of course."

"So I heard." The wanderer withdrew his coin purse, reaching into it and removing his last eternal, leaving only some few measly coppers to jingle around. It bothered him, being extorted, but not so much as it would if the enemy should find him, so he handed the coin over.

The guard took it, smiling. "Alright then. Go on through—and is that a couple of swords you got there?" he asked, nodding at the wanderer's back where the two blades were secured.

"Yes."

The man nodded, frowning. "Make sure they stay there, understand? I won't have any trouble in my city."

"I'm not looking for any," the wanderer said, which, of course, was the truth. But then, he thought as he led Veikr past, what a man looked for and what he found were rarely the same thing.

CHAPTER SIX

A common saying in the world—one that had even been common a hundred years ago when the wanderer had first begun his endless journey—was that when meeting someone for the first time, a man should always put his best foot forward. And the city of Celes was proof that its engineers, at least, had taken that saying to heart.

The street beyond the gate was fashioned from cobbled marble, the same, he suspected, as that which had been used to shape its massive walls. And while the marble was inevitably cracked in places, what was there was so clean that it shone in the sun, making it difficult to look at.

The shops that flanked either side of the lane were also fine, expensive-looking affairs. No rundown buildings or decrepit inns here—here, a traveler visiting to the city for the first time could only be impressed by the majesty of everything around him. Which, of course, was the builders' intent.

The wanderer had been to Celes before, but that had been many, many years ago, when he and other young men and women had begun their training under Soldier, long before he and the other Eternals had fought the enemy in the final conflict. Long before they had failed.

On the surface, the city looked, now, much as it had then, yet the wanderer did not think he imagined the undercurrent of fear that seemed to thrum within the city, that seemed to hide behind the doll-like smiles of the merchants as he passed. Neither did he think it was only his imagination that made it seem like the people in the street weren't walking from place to place so much as scurrying like rats. As they hurried this way or that, he saw them casting anxious glances at the guards patrolling here and there, as if the men weren't given the task of protecting them but were instead members of some invading army.

Veikr, too, seemed to notice the oddness, whinnying softly. "Easy, boy," the wanderer said, patting the horse on the muzzle. "We're just going to deliver the letter, that's all. Then we're out of here."

He made his way past fine shops with expensive and fragile glass windows, though ones not as fragile as the smiles on the faces of those he passed. Once, he had called the city of Celes home, had lived and resided and trained within it for over two years, yet he felt as if he walked in a completely different city. Celes, once, had been home to artists and bards, actor troupes and all manner of creatives trying to make their way in the world. It might have seemed strange to some that the home city of an Eternal who was lauded for his physical prowess such as Soldier might be so, but then people, like the city itself, were always more complicated than they first appeared, and Soldier had been a lover of the arts.

Now, though, the wanderer saw no performing troupes or street bards, only men and women who cast worried glances over their shoulders as they hurried about their day. Celes no longer seemed like a thriving city full of innovation and experimentation—instead, it seemed like a city under siege.

A thought that was reinforced as he walked past a tailor's shop and saw that the door had been broken in, and all the man's wares thrown out into the street. A man, likely the owner, was on his hands and knees doing his best to scoop the fine garments off the dirty ground. Two guards stood around him, their arms folded. Someone passing by might have thought that the men had come to investigate a crime, but something about the way they only stood while the tailor struggled to save his livelihood, mixed with the frightened glances the tailor shot at the guards, made the wanderer think that such was not the case. In fact, he thought it far more likely that the guards were the cause of the damages.

The people who passed ignored the scene, not daring to so much as even glance in the direction of the pitiful tailor who, the wanderer noted, had a bloody nose. The wanderer thought that out of all the talents people had, complacency and the ability to ignore the pain of another was probably their greatest—and their worst. Yet he also did not stop, only moved past. After all, the tailor's suffering was only a small tragedy in a world full of them, and should a man think to stand against all the world's evils, even the petty ones, he could only be crushed, for those evils, taken together, were a great mountain, one that could not be stood against.

Besides, he told himself that it was not his problem. Part of the world he may be, but the burden of the blade was enough, more than enough for one man to bear without adding more to it.

He walked on, leaving the tailor and his problems behind him as he had so many others over the years. But then, that was the thing about trouble—no matter how much of it a man left behind him, there was always plenty more ahead. Trying to avoid it was like going for a swim and trying to avoid getting wet.

He walked on until he saw a tavern sign. Not the one he was searching for, but his throat was dry from his travels, and it had been many years since he'd been in Celes, the city having grown and changed much since then. He walked up to the tavern, hitching Veikr to the post. Then he took out the horse's feed bag, filled it with oats and strapped it to him. "Just stopping for a drink and directions, old friend," he said. "I won't be long."

The horse didn't respond except to begin enjoying his oats, and the wanderer patted him softly before turning and moving into the tavern. The common room of the tavern was filled with people, perhaps unsurprising considering that it was only a little over an hour from the city gate. And, if the wanderer's long and tedious experience there was anything to go by, those who entered the city would be looking for a chance to sit down and relax, perhaps have a drink.

Unsurprising, perhaps, but discomforting for all that and as several sets of eyes swiveled to him, the wanderer was tempted to turn and leave. He told himself, though, that such a choice would be foolish. Celes, after all, was a very big city, and he could easily wander around it for days without ever finding the tavern he was looking for. Days in which he would be risking discovery by Soldier or one of those in his employ. No, it was better to stop, to ask for directions.

He made his way to the bar and sat.

"What'll it be, stranger?" the barkeep asked.

"An ale," the wanderer said. "And a question—have you heard of a tavern in the city, one called the Spilled Tankard?"

The bartender seemed to consider that, scratching at his chin. "The Spilled Tankard. Sure, I think maybe I have. It's on Fetter Lane, as I recollect."

"Fetter Lane?" the wanderer asked, not recalling the name of the street.

"Aye," the man said, "in the poor district."

The wanderer nodded. It made sense, of course, that the Perishables would hide their operation and their leader in the poor district of the city. After all, the people of a city's poor district were often well-versed in hiding and, more importantly, keeping quiet. "Thanks," he said.

"No problem," the barkeep said. "I'll get you that drink."

The man stepped away, and the wanderer became aware of the rolled parchment Scofield had given him pressing into his chest inside his tunic. He realized, now, that he hadn't even read it. He had been far too busy being angry with himself for allowing the young man to die than to even think about the message he had asked him to carry.

He shook his head. Foolishness of the highest order, and something the ghosts, if allowed to speak, would have quite a bit to say about. Not that he was likely to give them that chance anytime soon. The ghosts had never seemed satisfied no matter what he did, but he had no interest in hearing their thoughts on him bringing the sword that was his to safeguard into the very heart of the enemy's power.

He removed the document and unrolled it, glancing over the text. *"Fools,"* he hissed quietly as he read, for the paper detailed what appeared to be a planned outing by none other than Soldier, the ruler of Celes and its outlying areas. And it didn't take much work to figure out why a revolutionary group might want to acquire information regarding the movements of the leader they had formed to protest. Perhaps they meant to kill him, perhaps to only kidnap him or perform some other aggressive act. Whatever it was, though, the result would be the same.

The bartender returned with his ale, and the wanderer nodded his thanks, too distracted by the parchment to even so much as turn away from it. He read the parchment again, taking a long pull of the ale as he did. He was distracted by thoughts of what would happen should the Perishables attempt their mission, frustrated that they could be so stupid, and so he did not notice the faintly odd taste to the ale until he had already swallowed it.

Shit, he thought. He was on his feet in another moment. His legs felt watery, uncertain beneath him, and he was forced to catch himself with one hand on the bar as he spun to regard the barkeep who flashed him a smile.

"Hey there, fella," the barkeep said, his voice full of mock-concern, "you feelin' alright?"

The wanderer opened his mouth to answer but didn't manage any words before the drug, whatever it had been, took hold, and the darkness which had crowded the corner of his vision rushed forward, sweeping over him.

***

Youngest, you must wake—
Get up, damn you, before—
I knew he should not have come to the city. It was a foolish choice, and one that...
—allowed yourself to become distracted and now, here, is the consequence.
...not too late. But you must awaken, Youngest.

The voices washed over him, as they had for so many years as he lay in a pool of shadow, rocked back and forth by a lulling tide of darkness. Again and again they spoke, but their words were like moths, flittering briefly against his skin before fading away again, leaving him alone in the dark.

Mostly, he thought that that would be better. To forget about the voices, to forget about the world and just float here, to float on the waters until he could float no longer and then, when that time came, to sink. To sink further and further until the world forgot about him too. Until, in time, perhaps he might even be able to forget about himself.

You are part of this world.

Felden Ruitt's voice. Strange, perhaps, that he might be haunted by the voice of a man he had known for less than a day, strange, too, that it might affect him so. After all, he had been haunted by the voices of the Twelve for a hundred years and more. Yet, the voice *did* affect him.

What makes a man a man is doing the thing that needs doing.

Scofield's voice this time, repeating the words of his father.

The wanderer still did not want to go, but what difference had his own wants ever made?

He opened his eyes.

"Ah, you're awake. Thought that was you I heard mumbling."

The wanderer blinked in an effort to clear the worst of the blurriness from his sight. As he did, he saw that, sitting in a chair in front of him, holding a knife in one hand, was the barkeep he had spoken with what felt like moments ago. The man sat regarding him calmly, and why not?

Taking stock, the wanderer realized that his hands had been tied behind his back against the chair in which he had been sat. He felt a terrible moment of panic and swept his gaze frantically around the room until he caught sight of the wrapped sword propped against the wall, still, thankfully, within its sheath.

Continuing looking around him, he saw that the room he had been brought to was small, and that there was a second man standing near a simple fireplace, tending to the fire there.

"Might be you're wonderin' where you are," the barkeep said, drawing his attention back to him, and the man gave him a big smile. "Well, we'll get to that. But first, tell me, how'd you like the ale?"

The wanderer met the man's eyes. "A bit more of a kick than I was expecting."

The barkeep howled with laughter at that, turning to regard the other man. "Hear that, Jack?" the barkeep asked. "Looks like we got us a funny one here."

"Funny indeed, Walter," the second man said, raising the fire poker he held out of the fireplace and looking at its glowing red end. "For now, anyway."

"Yeah, for now," the man, Walter, agreed. Then he turned back to the wanderer. "As for the ale, well, might be I put a little somethin' extra in there for ya—free of charge, as it were."

He sat back in his chair, crossing one leg over the other, slowly tapping at the knee of his trousers with the bared blade. "My, but I can't help but wonder what's goin' through your mind. I guess you're just about scared shitless right now, ain't you?"

The wanderer said nothing to that, and the man frowned for a moment before slowly grinning again. "Go on, look as hard as you want, if it helps. Some do." He nodded his head down at the floor at the wanderer's feet, and the wanderer followed his gesture, looking down at the dusty wood boards of the floor, stained liberally with crimson.

"The man that did all that bleedin' there," the barkeep said, "he did a lot of hard talkin'. Leastways, 'til the screamin' started."

"Did a lot of that, too," the second man, Jack, said, grinning and sticking the fire poker back into the fireplace.

"Sure, 'course, I like to think we parted on good terms," the barkeep, Walter, said. "Why, that's his hat there," he went on, nodding his head at his companion's head and the brown hat he wore. "Made Jack a sort of, well, I guess you'd say he made him a gift of it, and that no small thing—by all accounts, the man loved his hat."

"Sure," Jack agreed, grinning. "After all, he won't be needin' it anymore, will he?"

The wanderer had to fought back the urge to sigh. It wasn't that his life wasn't in danger. It was just that his life had been in danger by a lot more dangerous people—or creatures—than those in front of him, and all the talk was boring him. "So what, then?" he asked, deciding to try to get them back on track. "You just randomly drug people who come to your bar asking for a drink and then torture them?"

The barkeep clapped a hand to his chest, his eyes opening in mock surprise. "Why, I'm *offended* that you would even say such a thing," he said, then grinned. "Of course it's not *random.* In fact, it ain't even my bar. Not that the owner's likely to complain."

"Not anymore than the fella gave me this hat."

"Anyway," Walter went on, "you see, it ain't a matter of doin' the thing at random. What it is, you see, you said the magic word."

The wanderer frowned. "The magic word?"

"Why, sure," Walter said, nodding companionably. "Only, I don't mean please—you did not say that, and don't think I didn't notice, young man." He grinned, waggling his finger at the wanderer. "No, you see, you said 'The Spilled Tankard.' That's the magic word." He paused, frowning. "Well. Three words. Anyway, you understand what I mean."

"I'm afraid I don't."

The man sighed, shaking his head as if with regret. "Seems like we've got another difficult one on our hands, Jack."

"Seems like it, Walter."

"Well, he won't be the first one."

"Nor the last."

"No, nor the last." Walter turned back to the wanderer. "See, friend, me and my companion here, we was given a very particular job. Not just us, understand, but I like to think we're the best of the bunch. Anyhow, that job is to...let's say, ask some questions of folks we hear come through the city lookin' for The Spilled Tankard. Most of the others, well, they go on throughout the city, that sort of thing. Me and Jack here, though, well, we don't like to move as much as that on account of—"

"I got a bad knee," the man, Jack, said from the fireplace.

"Sure, a bad knee," Walter agreed. "And me? Well...guess I'm just lazy. Anyhow, we took to noticin' that folks tended to come in this here bar quite a bit, askin' about the same place you just asked about. Funny, I thought, as I've seen the Tankard, and it ain't nothin' but a shithole. Funny that so many folks'd all of a sudden find an interest in it. Only, turns out, it weren't the tavern those folks was interested in."

"No," Jack agreed. "It's the Perishables."

"The who?"

Walter laughed. "That's funny. I appreciate the effort, I really do. Only, we know, just as much as we know that you're sittin' here now, that you come lookin' for the Perishables. You like every other sad son of a bitch that has found himself sittin' in that chair that you're in now. Lot of 'em, when we first ask, also try to deny it, but in time, they all admit to it. By then, though..." He sighed heavily. "Well. Just say the damage is already done, if you catch my meanin'. So, why don't you just tell us everythin' you know about the

Perishables and their plans, their members all that, and then we can all get on with our day, no muss no fuss."

"Am I to understand that you're telling me that if I told you what you wanted to know, you'd let me go?"

"Why, sure," Walter said, clearly doing his best attempt at an innocent grin, "we ain't monsters, are we?"

"Not monsters," Jack agreed.

"No, just honest men—" he paused, and the two shared a grin as if it was a scene in a play, one they'd rehearsed a thousand times— "well, *men,* anyway, tryin' to do their job. I take pride in that, doin' my job well. You understand?"

"Sure."

The man nodded. "Good, maybe we can save ourselves some time and trouble after all, eh? Anyhow, the folks we work for— important folks, *powerful* folks, understand—well, they know all about you Perishables and, thanks to me and Jack here, all about your shitty little tavern in the poor district. Shit, they've known for weeks now. I reckon they could have dealt with you all easily enough anytime they wanted to. But they're patient, these here, and they figured, I guess, that the spider that kills a single caught fly eats for a day. But that same spider, when he waits, lets the fly invite all his little fly friends, well, he can eat well indeed."

The wanderer blinked. "Not very particular on the intelligence of the people they hire, your employers, are they? I've no idea what you just said."

The barkeep sighed, shaking his head regretfully for a moment, then his fist lashed out. The blow was supposed to be a surprise, but the wanderer had been trained by the greatest warrior of all time, had been blessed—and cursed—and so to him, the punch seemed to come as if through water. Still, his hands were bound tightly, the chair itself secured to the floor by chains, and so he could do nothing but grunt, his head rocking, as the punch struck home.

The man sighed, rising. "I swear, some folks just ain't got no appreciation for the arts. That makes me mad, don't it make you mad, Jack?"

"Mad," Jack agreed.

"Oh well," Walter said, shrugging, the knife still in his hand. "I s'pose it's about time we got started anyhow. You know how it is, when you got a job to do you'd best get on to doin' it. Won't do itself."

"Be a shame if it did," Jack said.

Walter grinned. "Well. S'pose that's true enough. See," he said, turning back to the wanderer, "in case you're wonderin' at all of this, like the fire poker Jack's got in his hands there, well, the two of us, we've been at this for a time. Done a few of these, you see? And experience shows that the poker, the heat, well, it helps to...prolong matters. Not indefinitely, but I imagine that, on your end, it'll feel just about exactly like that. Still," he went on, "if it's any consolation, you'll do well to know that you'll have company in the afterlife. See, our employers, those fellas we were tellin' you about? They're beginnin' to tire of the game, and I think they're startin' to figure they've got just about all of you. Why, you're the first one we've seen in...how long's it been now, Jack?"

"Six, seven days," the man said. "More, maybe."

"See there?" Walter asked, turning back to the wanderer. "A week or more. That's a long time since they had their last recruit, ain't it? Yeah, I'd say that well's pretty much runnin' dry."

The wanderer didn't care about that, not at the moment. "What did you do with my horse?"

The man frowned. "What horse? That big white bastard? Oh, don't you worry—we brought him along. He's in the stables—not that you'll ever see him again."

"I wouldn't bet on that," the wanderer said quietly, a small smile coming to his face.

Walter frowned, clearly not liking his tone. He moved toward him and abruptly brought the knife forward in a slash, and the wanderer cried out as the sharpened steel tore through his tunic and traced a crimson line across his chest.

"Now," the man said. "I don't like that, that attitude. See, fella, your mistake is thinkin' that you're anythin' more than a normal man. You'll break, you'll beg, just like the rest, but I'm gonna make sure you suffer for it." The man punctuated this remark by hauling off and punching the wanderer in the stomach with his free hand.

The wanderer grunted, bending over the blow as much as he could, his head hanging. Then, slowly, he began to laugh. A quiet, rasping sound, and he heard an angry hiss from his captor as he did.

"You think something's *funny?*" the man demanded.

"Kinda," the wanderer said.

"Care to enlighten us?" the man said.

"Rather not."

The man struck him again then, foregoing the knife he held in his anger, and the wanderer accepted the blow as he did the next, and the next, waiting. The blows hurt, it was true, but if there were any two things he had been given ample opportunity to practice in his life, it was waiting and pain. And so he waited as the man rained blow after blow down on him.

Then, there was the unmistakable sound of a loud neigh, and Walter paused, frowning. "What's that?" he asked, turning to his companion, panting the words, his knuckles bloody and scratched.

"Sounded like a horse," the other man said.

"I *know* it sounded like a damn horse, Jack," Walter snapped, "what I mean is, why don't you go see about it?"

"No need," the wanderer said. The two men turned to him, and he favored them with a bloody grin. "*Veikr,*" he shouted, "*I am here. To me.*"

The two men shared a look, and Walter opened his mouth, clearly preparing to say something, likely a taunt, but he never got the chance. Before he could, the wall suddenly exploded in a shower of wooden splinters as if struck by the fist of some giant god—or, in this case, by the hooves of a horse far greater in size and strength than any other of its kind walking the face of the world.

It had been early afternoon when the wanderer had entered the tavern asking after the Perishables, but in the time since his capture night had come on in full. Veikr, though, standing proud and tall in the hole where the section of wall he'd just demolished had once been, seemed to shine with white brilliance in the light of the room's lanterns.

"What the fuck is that!?" Walter shouted, stumbling away, in shock.

"*Veikr,*" the wanderer said, motioning at the metal hoops through which the chains fastening his chair to the ground were held. "*Sla.*"

The horse responded immediately, moving forward and stomping hard on the hoops. Once, twice, and on the third time the metal gave way, and the wanderer was able to stand. With a growl, he called on his strength, greater than that of any mortal man, and in a moment broke free of the bonds holding him, leaving the chair to fall to the floor.

"What...what the fuck are you?" Walter stammered.

"Maybe you were right," the wanderer said as he tossed the last of the ropes clinging to him away. "Maybe I am no better than a normal man. But *your* mistake was thinking that this, here—" he paused, glancing at Veikr—"as a normal horse."

The man, Jack, recovered from his shock quicker than his companion, drawing a sword that had so far remained sheathed at his side and charging. The wanderer did not bother going for his own blade where it sat against the wall. Instead, he waited for the man to come at him, raising the sword over his head and bringing it down in a vicious, two-handed arc.

The wanderer stepped to the side, catching the man's wrist, but instead of trying to stop his momentum, he added to it, forcing the man off balance and allowing him to rip the blade free. Then, stepping behind his attacker, he turned and plunged the blade into his back, up and at an angle so that it struck his heart.

The man died in that instant, and the wanderer pulled the blade free, letting him fall.

"What...what *are* you?" Walter said again, his voice shocked as he stared at his dead ally. He'd managed to draw his sword at some point, but it would do him no more good than it had his companion.

"What am I?" the wanderer said, walking toward him. Walter cried out, swiping at him with his blade, and the wanderer batted it aside contemptuously before driving his sword into the man's stomach, tearing it up higher and higher into his chest. The wanderer thought of Scofield, of Felden Ruitt, of the woman whose husband had been taken from her, of the tailor with his livelihood casually tossed into the street by the same people who were meant to protect him. "What *am* I?" he growled. "I'm *angry*."

The man, Walter, screamed as he ripped the blade free, but the scream cut off a moment later as the wanderer brought the blade around, severing his head from his body.

He stood there for a moment, looking at the two dead men, the bloody sword held down at his side, shedding crimson droplets onto the ground. Then he tossed the blade away. He went to the wall and retrieved his own sword, as well as the cursed blade. He glanced around, noting his other belongings, coin purse and the locket, sitting on the table. He was reaching for them when suddenly he hesitated, thinking, his eyes on the locket.

How long could a man be haunted by his own volition? How long until he could no longer countenance the voices of the ghosts, even should those voices speak wisdom as they did, from time to time. It seemed so possible then, in that moment, to let it all go. Perhaps the blade, too. It seemed more possible than it ever had before, and for a moment, he wondered. What if the world did end? Certainly, his had already, had ended a hundred years ago and more, and he not even able to attend the funeral which had marked its passing, it and the passing of the Twelve. The Twelve Eternals who had become, if not his family, then at least the closest to it since he had abandoned his own for the cause.

He could do it. True, the world might well end, but he had thought of saving the world for a hundred years—he could think of it no more. He had given and given until there was no more to give, until he himself was little more than a tattered ghost, frayed around the edges. A ghost which, it seemed, was destined to spend eternity walking circles around the face of the world. He was dust and rags and little else, his will, his *strength* as faded as the boots he wore, their leather cracked and sun-bleached from days, weeks, years spent on the road.

Whatever guilt he might have felt at the idea of giving it all up, of by his actions, damning the entire world, was a weak, unclear thing, faded in his mind the way the writing of a much-read note might fade with time.

Veikr snorted softly beside him. Telling him to hurry or sensing, in some way, the direction of his thoughts? In the end, the wanderer told himself that it did not matter, it could not. For in this, only he could choose. The sword was his burden, and he was the only one who might let it loose. Finally, he sighed, moving forward and pocketing the coin purse. Then, after a moment, he lifted the amulet, pulling the leather thong around his neck and feeling the familiar weight of the locket against his chest.

He did not do it for the world, for the world, he suspected, was long past saving. Neither did he do it for the hundreds of thousands of people crowding the face of the land, all with their own hopes and dreams. Such a thought was too big, those multitudes, in their great numbers, losing their identities, so that their faces were just a blur.

No, the reason he took the locket, the reason why he moved to Veikr and began securing the cursed blade was not to save the world or to save all its people—it was only to save three of them. The man, Dekker, Ella, and Sarah, she of the gentle laugh, her most of all. She who had patted Veikr's muzzle and called him "Beautiful" and "Sweet boy."

He would go on because, while the world might not be worth saving, that girl and her parents were. He moved to Veikr's front, resting his hand gently on the horse's side. "Thank you, old friend," he said.

Veikr gave a self-satisfied shake of his head, and the wanderer smiled. "Come—best we get out of here and quickly."

CHAPTER SEVEN

The wanderer's face and body hurt from where the man, Walter, had beaten him, and the cut across his chest, though shallow, throbbed with pain, yet he forced himself onward through the street. After all, it would not do to be linked to the two dead men, not at all. They might not have called their employers by name, but then they hadn't needed to. Whoever they worked for wasn't important—what was important was that the wanderer knew who *their* employer worked for—Soldier. Or at least the creature who now wore his face, used his identity, and ruled his kingdom.

In time, he passed through an archway and came to the poor district. There was no sign to mark it as such, but then there did not need to be one, for the transition could not have been more jarring. One moment, he was walking down a clean, well-maintained road, and less than five minutes later he was standing on cracked cobblestones, the shops and homes flanking the street simple, crude affairs, some with broken windows or half-collapsed roofs.

But those things were the least of the change. Another, more obvious sign that he had moved into the poor district was the lack of guards patrolling around him and, of course, the faceless watchers marking his progress from alleyways and windows as he ventured further in.

Despite the dangers in such a place—of which there were many—the wanderer found himself feeling more relaxed here than he had in the richer, more guard-patrolled area of the city. Part of this was the fact that, from what he'd seen since coming to the city, many of those guards were corrupt. Mostly, though, it was because the dangers of the poor district were ones he understood, the same way that, should he step into the wilderness, he might do so with the understanding that underneath the boughs of those gently swaying trees lurked predators. Predators that, if given the opportunity, would attack, not because they were cruel as the guards at the gate had been, but simply to survive.

He continued down the seemingly deserted road until two shadows separated themselves from an alleyway he passed, beginning to follow him at a distance. The wanderer might not begrudge the lion its hunt, but neither did that mean that he would volunteer to be its next meal. He turned, releasing Veikr's reins and casually drawing his blade. He stood there, regarding the shaded figures, their features indistinct in the darkness.

He waited, then, for what would come. The two figures stopped, watching him, reassessing the same way that the lion, discovering that what he had at first taken for an easy meal was something altogether different, might. In the end, the two figures glided back into the alleyway from which they'd come. The wanderer sheathed his blade once more and continued on.

They moved further into the poor district, the wanderer walking beside Veikr, marveling at the abandoned, destitute state of the district which had clearly been forgotten by the city's leadership. They'd traveled for another half hour when a young child stumbled out of a nearby alleyway, running in their direction, whimpering in desperation.

The thing was well done, the child practiced, looking frightened and shooting terrified glances behind him. The wanderer had seen such things before, and so he was not surprised when the child, in his panicked haste, bumped into him. Neither was he surprised when one of the young boy's small hands quested for his coin purse.

The wanderer let it, just as he let the hand pull away as the child stumbled, tucking the pouch into his own ragged, filthy linen tunic as he fell.

"S-sorry, mister," the boy stammered. "I—sorry."

The wanderer offered him his hand, and the child took it. A moment later, he pulled him to his feet. "Okay?" the wanderer asked.

"F-fine," the child said, doing a far finer job at his role than most actors the wanderer had seen performing in mummer's shows.

"Good. I wonder, can you tell me the directions to a tavern called The Spilled Tankard?"

The child didn't answer with words, instead pointing his fingers down the main thoroughfare.

"Thanks," the wanderer said.

The child nodded, hurrying away into the darkness, carrying the wanderer's coin purse with him. The wanderer let him go. After all, not all those creatures which roamed the forest were lions. There were smaller, more pitiful creatures too, but even they had to eat. He hadn't had much coin left in the purse anyway, but it would be enough to buy the child a warm meal, perhaps enough for him to find some shelter, at least for the night.

The wanderer turned and started down the street once more, walking around a pile of rubble where the cobbled street had cracked and been left in disrepair. There were many such heaps, grown over with grass, obstacles that would make bringing a carriage down the lane impossible, but then he doubted that mattered. After all, the citizens of this part of the city weren't likely to spend what little money they managed to gain hiring a carriage.

He passed several more decrepit homes and businesses many of which were permanently closed. In time, he came to a building with a man sitting out front propped against the wall, his eyes closed in sleep. Or, at least, appearing to be.

The sign above the tavern marked it as The Spilled Tankard. Finally, it seemed, he had arrived. The wanderer, eager to get his task done and get out of the city, did not hesitate. He left Veikr in the small lawn in front of the building, confident that the horse could more than handle any would-be thief who tried to steal him, then moved to the door. He glanced at the man sitting beside it, not sleeping, not really, but only pretending at it, then he swung the door open and stepped inside.

A gray haze of pipe smoke lingered in the air of the common room, parting like a curtain as the wanderer stepped through the door and closed it softly behind him. The tavern itself was packed, with men and women crowding the tables, talking and laughing. Here, at least, the spirit of the city of Celes seemed alive and well, a far cry from the quiet fear the wanderer had sensed when going through the richer parts of the city. Perhaps that had something to do with the lack of guards, but he doubted it. Instead, he thought that the people frequenting a tavern of the poor district—farmers and day laborers and more than a few prostitutes, based on their dress—were used to things being bad, had made their peace with it long ago.

The wanderer made his way to the bar and sat in one of the few available stools.

"Welcome, stranger." This from an older, skinny man standing behind the bar. The man had short gray hair, his cheeks and chin lined with white stubble.

"Thanks."

The barkeep let off wiping at the counter. "Don't think I've seen you in these parts before. First time in Celes?"

"First time in a long time, anyway."

The man gave a soft grunt. "A traveler of the world then, eh?"

"Something like that."

The man nodded amiably. "So, what'll it be? An ale, perhaps? Or would you like a bath? Got a small well outback, reckon we can set you up given a little time."

The wanderer hesitated at that. An ale sounded good, a bath better, but he remembered all too clearly the youth spiriting away his coin purse into the night and winced.

The barkeep must have taken his hesitation differently, for he held up a hand as if to say he meant no harm. "Believe me, fella, I don't judge. A man gets a little dirt on him, well, that's a good thing. You ask me, dirt gets a bad shake. Some of the most important things can't be done without a man gets a little dirt on his hands. Why, it seems to me that if a man finishes the day as clean as he started it then he's done somethin' wrong. Or," he went on, shrugging, "maybe it's just that he ain't done nothin' at all."

"Or that he's had a bath," the wanderer said, smiling. There was something relaxing about the barkeep's friendly demeanor that made him think it was unlikely that this barkeep, at least, would tie him to a chair and set about trying to torture him. Still, he told himself that the night was early yet.

The barkeep grinned. "Sure, or that he's had a bath. Anyway, what can I do for ya?"

Normally, the wanderer might have taken his time, felt the man out, but he was tired, and he wanted to get out of the city as soon as possible. Besides, he had never been much for subtlety—Charmer had often told him as much, and he'd never argued with her. So he only met the man's eyes. "I've come seeking the leader of the Perishables."

The barkeep hid his reaction almost perfectly. Almost but not quite. There was a slight widening to his eyes, one that most people would have missed. But then, the wanderer's training had not only been in combat. He had been taught many things over the years, by many masters, and one of those was to observe details, to catch the things others missed.

The barkeep recovered in a moment, frowning thoughtfully and scratching at his stubbled chin. "Perishables," he said. "Seems I've heard of them before. Some sort of club or somethin' ain't it? The kind that does a lot of talkin' about the government, holdin' signs and shoutin' in the streets, that sort of thing?"

"Something like that," the wanderer said.

The older man grunted. "Well. I'm afraid I can't help you there."

The wanderer opened his mouth, about to answer, when suddenly a hand fell on his shoulder roughly, and he turned to see a big man looming over him. Broad shoulders, a thick neck, and the mashed-in nose common among those who made their living—and often their deaths—fighting.

"The fuck you think you're doin'?" the mountain of muscle growled.

"Sitting, mostly," the wanderer said, not surprised for he had expected something like this. "And asking to speak to the leader of the Perishables. Do you know him?"

The man bared his teeth. "What if I do?"

"Then you'd save me a lot of time. Assuming you would point him out."

"And who are you, then?"

"They call me Ungr," the wanderer responded. *At least, when they call me anything.*

"Ungr," the man said. "That's a damn fool's name."

"I won't disagree."

"So, *Ungr*," the big man said, "why is it you've come here lookin' for the leader of a damn rebellion?" He waved his big arm to indicate the people in the common room, many of whom had turned to watch the scene play out. "We look like rebels to you?"

"I don't know," the wanderer said. "Is there a uniform?"

The man growled, clearly angry. "You made a mistake, comin' here. Thinkin' that Eternal prick in the castle'll keep you safe."

That was funny considering that the wanderer had spent the last hundred years evading the prick in question, as well as his eleven companions, but the big man obviously didn't appreciate the smile that came to his face.

"I say somethin' funny?" he demanded.

"You have no idea."

"Tell you what," the big man said, "how about you get the fuck out of here while you still can? You hang around, I can promise you, you won't be laughin'."

"I believe you," the wanderer said, "but I can't do that. I came here to speak to the leader of the Perishables, and I mean to."

The big man let out an angry growl, jerking him up by the front of his tunic. The wanderer allowed it.

"Well how about this," the man growled through clenched teeth, "say I'm the Perishable leader. Now, what have you got to say?"

"You're not, though."

The man's brows drew together. "What?" he demanded.

"The leader of the Perishables has managed to keep his group alive for several years," the wanderer explained. "Far longer than other such groups that have come before him, ones which usually fade—or, more likely, are destroyed—within weeks of declaring themselves. That makes him clever. He has also not chosen violence, trying to march on the castle or rouse an army for the task—that makes him wise. No offense, but you don't strike me as a man possessed of an overabundance of either wisdom or cleverness."

The man roared at that, bringing his free arm around in a punch that would have probably knocked the wanderer directly into unconsciousness, if not the afterlife, had it landed. Which, of course, it did not. The wanderer leaned his head back so that the blow hissed in front of his face, missing by inches, then he brought the ridge of his hand into the big man's throat. Not as hard as he could have, but hard enough.

136

The big man abruptly dropped him, bringing both his hands to his throat, his eyes bulging in their sockets as he wheezed and gasped.

"Easy," the wanderer said, "just take it easy, breathe, you'll be okay." He guided the big man into the stool beside him.

"As I said," the wanderer said to the gasping man, "I've come in search of the Perishable leader, and you're not him. Now, just relax—you'll feel better in a minute."

The man continued to wheeze until, finally, he regained some mastery of himself. Then he turned to the wanderer, his face flushing with fury. "You son of a bi—"

"Hank," a voice said, "don't."

The big man's fist froze in mid-air, and he and the wanderer turned to look at the barkeep.

The man shook his head. "Look," he said, "if this fella here is lookin' for the Perishable's leader, well, that ain't got nothin' to do with us, does it?"

The big man winced. "S'pose it don't."

"Well," the wanderer said, staring at the barkeep, "I'm not looking anymore."

The older man raised an eyebrow. "Sorry?"

"I think I've found what I'm looking for. A barkeep." He smiled. "Clever. Hiding in plain sight."

He suddenly became aware of a rustling and the creaking of many chairs being moved at once, and he turned to see that every single person in the tavern's common room had risen to their feet. They were all, as one, staring at him, as if only waiting for a command before charging him.

The moment stretched, the tension building, until the barkeep waved a dismissive hand. "Go on, the lot of you. Back to your meals. Go on, Hank. Have a seat—I'll bring you a drink out in a minute."

The big man shot the wanderer another angry look then rose and moved to one of the tables as ordered. A moment later, the people in the common room sat again, and the wanderer raised an eyebrow at the barkeep who sighed, giving him a tired smile. "How did you know?"

The wanderer shrugged. "Nothing you did. That one, though..." He nodded his head at Hank's back. "Well, a man doesn't get a nose like that from being too agreeable, yet when you told him to stand down he didn't hesitate."

The gray-haired man grunted. Then, after a moment, offered his hand. "The name's Clint."

The wanderer took the offered hand. "Ungr."

"So you said," the barkeep said, tossing away the rag he'd been using to wipe the counter down. "Ungr. A strange sounding name, from the old tongue unless I miss my guess. Means 'Youngest,' doesn't it?"

The wanderer couldn't help but be impressed. "It does. And here I thought everyone had forgotten the old words, yet recently I've met two who know them."

"That so?" the barkeep said. "Well, seems I ain't the only one likes to study the old texts. I'd like to meet this friend of yours."

"That'd be hard."

"Oh?"

"Yeah," the wanderer said. "He's dead."

The barkeep winced at that. "Sorry to hear that," he said in a voice that sounded genuine. Then his eyes traveled to the two scabbarded swords at the wanderer's back. "Hope it ain't goin' around."

"It's always going around."

Clint grunted. "Well, that's true enough, damn shame that it is." He studied the wanderer's face, scratched and bloodied from his run-in with the two men earlier in the evening. "Looks like you come pretty close to catchin' it yourself."

"You have no idea," the wanderer said honestly. "Seems I've made a bit of a habit of it."

The man, Clint, grinned. "I like you—you got a sense of humor, and the world bein' what it is, I reckon that's one of the few recourses left to honest men, though not the only one. Now," he said, his grin vanishing, his eyes sparking, "why don't you tell me, Ungr, what it is that you want—that'll go a long way to determining if you ever walk back out that door you walked into."

The gray-haired man was far smaller than Hank, his words far more tamed, but the wanderer had lived his life close to danger, and he recognized that here was a man, smaller or not, that was far more dangerous than the thug Hank could ever hope to be. "I haven't come looking for trouble, if that's what you're worried about."

"The thought had crossed my mind," the barkeep admitted.

"I was sent here," the wanderer said.

"Sent?" Clint asked.

"By a young man, Scofield, by name."

The barkeep's eyes widened at that. "Scofield." He winced. "I see. Well, I hope he ain't in no trouble. Scofield's a good lad. Gets into trouble, sometimes, but that's only on account of he's passionate about the cause and, you ask me, we could do with a lot more passion in this world, even if it does cause trouble from time to time. Anyway, is the boy alright?"

"No," the wanderer said, surprised at the sudden surge of grief he felt. "No, he isn't. He's dead."

The barkeep's jaw tensed at that, and his eyes traveled once more to the swords at the wanderer's back.

"Not by my hand," the wanderer said. "He ran into some trouble in a little village, Fulwell. I tried to help him, told him to get out of town, while he could, but..." He trailed off, suddenly finding it difficult to finish.

The barkeep let out a ragged sigh at that, looking as if he'd aged decades in a matter of moments. "I see. Well, now, that's a shame. A damned shame." He cleared his throat, running a hand across his eyes where tears had begun to gather. "Always did have a way of runnin' into trouble, that lad. That was just Scofield. But he was a good boy...a good man." He took in a slow breath, as if preparing himself, then met the wanderer's eyes. "How'd it happen?"

"A corrupt constable, his nephew, some few other hired hands."

"Damn Fulwell," the man said, shaking his head angrily. "I told Sco not to go back there. Some folks, like a lot of the folks livin' here in Celes, don't see the world's troubles. Others pretend they don't. The worst kind, though, are those as *do* see them, but instead of settin' out to right what's wrong, they take it as an opportunity. That bastard constable in Fulwell, he's one of those." He shook his head, his throat working. "Tell me, what happened to those as did for the lad?"

"Dead," the wanderer said.

The man's eyes widened at that. "The constable, too?"

"Yes. And that *was* by my hand."

The man stared, surprised, for a moment, then slowly nodded. "Well. That's good. Can't say as the bastards don't deserve it, though them bein' dead don't bring the lad back, does it?"

"No, no it doesn't."

Clint heaved another heavy sigh. "Well. What's done is done, they say. Still, all that don't explain why you come here."

"Scofield, before he...well, *before,* he asked me to deliver a message to the leader of the Perishables; he said I could find you here."

"A message, is it? And what'd that be then?"

The wanderer reached into his tunic to withdraw the rolled parchment and became aware, as he did, that the common room, which had resorted back to conversation, suddenly grew deathly silent. He held up his free hand to show he meant no harm and slowly retrieved the note Scofield had entrusted him with, offering it to the barkeep.

The gray-haired man watched him for a moment then took the parchment gently, as if it was a snake that might bite him if he weren't careful. He unrolled it slowly, skimming the contents, his eyes going wide as he did. Watching him, the wanderer could practically see the man's thoughts, see him examining it from every angle, searching for the best possible way to use the information the note contained.

"It's a mistake," the wanderer said.

The man looked up from the note. "What's that?"

"What you're thinking—it's a mistake."

Clint blinked. "It's a wise man that can tell what another thinks just from the lookin'."

"I read the note," the wanderer said. "Information like that, well, it'd be a fool who didn't understand what use you might mean to put it to."

"You're new to the city, aren't you, Ungr?"

The wanderer frowned. "Yes."

The barkeep nodded. "Then you cannot understand what we face. Things are bad here, Ungr. Very bad."

"Things are bad everywhere."

The man grunted at that. He glanced around the room then spoke in a quiet whisper. "You're thinkin', maybe, that we mean to kill him. Soldier, that is. But you're wrong—we just mean to talk to him. Talk to him in a way he can't ignore."

"Better if you tried to kill him," the wanderer said. "You'd fail there, too, but at least you'd fail doing something worthwhile."

The barkeep blinked. "You sound like you want him dead."

"There are few things I want more," he said, thinking of the other Eternals, of how he had watched them die, one by one, before grabbing the enemy king's sword and fleeing into the night, the wounded Sage hanging from Veikr's saddle only to die later that night from her wounds.

"I think maybe you mean that," Clint said. "But for a man wants him dead so bad, you seem to be awful against anyone tryin' to take a stand."

"There isn't much point in standing if you can only be knocked down."

The barkeep considered that, grunting. "I think maybe you're wrong there, Ungr. I think maybe standing matters most when a man is only likely to be knocked down for his troubles. Likely, Scofield would have agreed with as much."

"But he can't agree with anything," the wanderer said, surprised by the anger in his voice. "He's dead. Just like you and all the rest of the Perishables will be, if you keep going down the road you're walking. That's the only way it ends."

"Maybe," Clint admitted, "but then, a man can die in a lot of ways before his death finally claims him. That's a truth that, by the look of you, I'd say you've learned time and again."

There was no arguing that, so the wanderer didn't try. "Unless you want a lot more corpses on your hands, you'll let it go. You have no idea what you're messing with. Better to keep playing at being a barkeep, that and that only."

Clint scratched at his stubble. "You make some good points, Ungr, and I won't pretend news of the lad ain't a blow, 'cause it is. But you're wrong about one thing. I ain't 'playin' at bein' a barkeep. I am one. Was one long before all the rest of this got started. Thing is, a man can only hear so many stories about the sufferin' of others until he decides he's got to try to do somethin' about it."

The wanderer grunted. "And yet you still tend the bar. Seems to me, a man of your position, you could have someone else do it."

"And it seems to *me* that a man of my position shouldn't," the barkeep countered. "You ask me, Ungr, if a man means to lead, he ought to first learn how to follow, and if he means to be served, he ought first learn how to serve."

The wanderer stared at the man, thinking he understood a bit better the source of that passion that had so enlivened the young Scofield. But then, in the end, that passion had served no purpose but to see the man dead and so what was the good of it?

"He'll crush you," the wanderer said, deciding to try one more time. "You and all the rest. Scofield's death will only be the beginning. You don't know who you're dealing with—you don't know what he's capable of."

"And I take it you do?"

"The only ones who know better are the dead."

"I see. Still, we've made it this far, haven't we? As you said, further than anyone else has. Far enough to think that, if we go on a bit more, things might change, we might make the world a better place."

"The world doesn't *want* to be a better place, Clint," the wanderer said. "Take it from someone who knows. It's more than happy being exactly what it is, and if you can't even change a person who doesn't want it, how could you ever change the world? Anyway, you've survived this long because of being clever, subtle, but even a clever bug gets squished when the boot comes down—it's what bugs *do*. An ant, scurrying about the ground, might also go unsquished, but it's only because it hasn't become a problem, is easy to ignore. Let that same ant bite—or try to do something with that information in the note you're carrying—that changes. And you are very, very close to being squished, Clint."

The barkeep frowned. "Kept away from the boot this long."

The wanderer gritted his teeth, thinking of the way Scofield had looked as he lay in the burning stables, dying. "Damnit, you're not *listening*," he hissed, aware that the others in the common room had cut off their conversation again but this time not caring. "Have you been missing any of your agents lately? Besides Scofield, I mean? Anybody late to report?"

Clint's frown deepened. "One, a man by the name of Shane. Good man, if a little strange. Though, strange in these times, I reckon is just what we need."

"He wear a hat?" the wanderer pressed.

The barkeep raised an eyebrow. "Yeah, sure. But what—"

"An old brown cap? So faded anybody who didn't have some sort of attachment to it would have thrown it out long ago?"

"Damn if I ain't startin' to think you really can read a man's mind," Clint said. "How do you know that?"

"It's not reading your mind—I saw it. Saw what was left of Shane, too." Which wasn't exactly the truth, as he hadn't seen the body, but he figured near enough as to make no difference. "You see, I went into a tavern near the northern gate, asked after this place. Next thing I knew, I was strapped to a chair, having a conversation with a few men that worked for Soldier."

"A conversation," Clint repeated.

"Sure," the wanderer said, gesturing to his battered face, "where did you think all this came from? Thought maybe I just fell out of bed?"

"And I don't guess there's any point in askin' how that conversation ended."

"Abruptly."

"Well, I'll look into what you said, about Shane, I mean. But I don't see what the rest of it has to do with—"

"They told me some things, while we were talking."

"Told you some things," the barkeep repeated slowly.

"Sure. A man winds up strapped to a chair, the folks not tied down tend to think of it as a pretty safe space. Point is, Clint," he said, leaning in, "they *know* about this place. Maybe they don't know who you are—maybe they do. I don't think it really matters because they know that you're here, do you understand? They have known it for some time, in fact."

"But if they know," the man said, "if that's true, then why wouldn't they have 'squished' us, as you say?"

"Why does any man not squish a bug?" the wanderer countered. "Because he simply can't be bothered. But make no mistake, Clint, they are coming. Probably not today, maybe not tomorrow, but soon. And when they come, all your grand ideas of changing the world, all your passion and resolve and determination won't save you."

The barkeep sighed, rubbing at his temples. "I need a drink. Want one?"

The wanderer winced. "I can't—"

"On the house," the barkeep said. "The least I can do, considerin' that you helped Scofield."

Not that it did any good, the wanderer thought, just as he thought that his attempts here would prove equally useless. "I'll take an ale," he said.

While Clint poured the drinks, the wanderer glanced behind him at the common room. Most of the people seated there were casting glances in his direction. Some of those glances were scared, some angry, including a particularly nasty sneer from the man, Hank, but mostly he saw that they were challenging, determined.

"Don't mind them," Clint said, drawing his attention as the barkeep set a foaming glass of ale in front of him. "They thought you were the enemy, that's all. They're all good people."

"Good people die just like the bad ones."

Clint sighed, walking around the bar and taking a seat beside the wanderer, taking a long pull of his own ale. "Maybe everythin' you're sayin' is true, Ungr. But what are we supposed to do, then? Just quit? Just sit back and watch while corrupt officials take over our villages and towns? While an honest man or woman can't travel the roads without fearing bandits that have gone unchecked and unchallenged by the leader who's supposed to be lookin' after their well being?"

"You'd live longer," the wanderer said simply.

"Cowerin' and pretendin' nothing's happenin'. That don't sound much like livin' to me, Ungr, nor to these good folks here. It's *why* they found their way here in the first place. Maybe we'll all die and maybe we won't, but if there's even a chance of change, of makin' things better, then I don't see how we can't take it."

There isn't a chance, the wanderer thought, but he decided to leave it. He had said his piece—either the man would listen or he would not. It, like so much else, was beyond his control.

"Anyway," Clint went on, "you don't mind my sayin' so, Ungr, but I'm a bit surprised to hear you counseling caution."

"Oh?"

The barkeep shrugged. "Well. By the look of you, I'd think you were a man well-accustomed to violence. I can't imagine what makes a man carry two swords instead of one, but whatever one won't handle, I certainly wouldn't want any part of."

Mention of the swords made the wanderer reach back and check that the cursed blade was still kept hidden by the cloth he'd wrapped around it. "Being accustomed to a thing is far different than courting it," he said.

"Maybe," Clint admitted, "but then, I get the feelin' that you've been in a few scraps. Maybe more'n a few. True?"

"True."

"So, it stands to reason then, that you've found somethin' worth fightin' for at one time or another."

The wanderer sighed. "You don't mean to stop."

It wasn't really a question, but the barkeep chose to treat it as one. "No, no I don't. Wouldn't do that to all these folks here, folks who've given up more'n you can imagine just for the chance of makin' the world better'n the one we was born into."

"And if they weren't here?"

The barkeep laughed. "Fine, you got me. Even if they weren't, still I guess I'd keep at it."

"But *why?*" the wanderer said.

Clint considered that, then shrugged. "Maybe I'm just an old fool with grand ideas. But it seems to me that all the good things that've ever happened in the world, Ungr, happened because someone or another decided they wanted to make it a bit better."

"The same could be said for the bad things."

"S'pose that's true," Clint agreed. "But then, I can't just sit back and see sufferin' and do nothin' about it, not anymore. I did for a long time, but you swallow enough pain and sadness, well, you're liable to choke on it. Guess it's as simple as it just don't sit right with me, the way folks are suffering."

"Sits better than a sword in the gut would."

The barkeep laughed. "Maybe, but all things are temporary, Ungr. Even pain."

Speak for yourself, the wanderer thought. After all, he'd spent the last hundred years in one pain or another and with no end in sight. He drank the rest of his ale in one long pull, then set the empty glass down on the counter before rising to his feet. "Good luck, Clint," he said, offering the man his hand.

The barkeep took it, giving it a firm shake. "And you, Ungr. Here's to hopin' that the road ahead of you treats you better than that behind, eh?"

"We can always hope," the wanderer said without much conviction.

"You know, you're welcome to stay here for the night," Clint offered. "Free of charge, of course."

"Thanks," the wanderer said, "but it's past time I left."

"As you say," the barkeep agreed. "Only, you don't mind my askin', where will you go? Where that won't be the same as this?"

The wanderer shrugged. "The same place I always go. Away."

He turned, glancing around at the people in the room. He wished that he could help them, somehow, could save them from the pain that awaited them. But he could not help them—he could not save them. He could not save Felden Ruitt or Scofield. He could not even save himself.

With a sigh, he started toward the door. As he did, it opened, and for a brief moment he thought that he had been too late leaving the city after all. His hand was halfway to his sword when the door revealed not angry city guardsmen or an army or some creature out of nightmare, but instead a youth, little more than a boy, really, who ran past him without so much as a glance, hurrying over to the barkeep.

The boy spoke in hushed whispers, low enough that, from the distance, another man wouldn't have been able to hear, but the wanderer was not like other men, and he could hear it well enough.

"Sir," the boy said breathlessly.

"What is it, lad?" Clint asked.

"There's a problem with the supplies," the youth continued as the wanderer walked to the door and grabbed the handle, swinging it open. "The merchant is trying to charge double."

"*Double?*" Clint asked. "That snake, he's already been paid."

"Yes, sir," the boy said, as the wanderer began to step out of the door, "but he says now he wants double; Dekker said that he's threatening to turn us in otherwise."

The wanderer froze, one foot out of the door, his entire body tensing. *Dekker.* A coincidence. It had to be. After all, there had to be more than one person walking the world with such a name besides Felden Ruitt's son-in-law. And if not a coincidence, then likely the wanderer had just heard wrong. Only...he had not.

He hesitated there for a moment, one foot out the door, grasping the door handle in preparation to close it, and so he did, but not until he had stepped back into the tavern. "What name did you say, boy?"

Some of the wanderer's sudden anxiety must have been communicated through his tone for everyone in the common room turned as one to regard him, including the boy in question and Clint. "Sorry, Ungr," Clint said, "what was that?"

"I said," the wanderer said, walking closer, a tenseness in his movement that caused half a dozen people to begin to stand from their tables until Clint waved them down, "what name did you say?" he repeated, staring at the boy.

The boy fidgeted nervously, glancing at Clint. The old man watched the wanderer for a moment then gave the boy a nod. "F-forgive me, sir," the boy said, "b-but, do you mean 'Dekker'?"

"And this Dekker," the wanderer said, "what does he look like?"

The youth glanced uncertainly at Clint again, and the barkeep, his eyes never leaving the wanderer, gave him a pat. "That's a good lad. Go on, Wyatt. Go get yourself somethin' to eat in the kitchen. We'll speak more directly."

The boy hesitated, glancing between Clint and the wanderer. "Go on now, boy," Clint said again and this time the youth did, seeming all too relieved to be given permission to leave.

"You don't mind my askin', Ungr," Clint said when he was gone, "what business of yours is Dekker?"

"Maybe none," the wanderer said. "Only, I met him. Recently."

"And he's still alive? S'pose you must be slippin'." The barkeep smiled to show that he didn't mean it. "Anyway," he went on, walking closer, "this Dekker. He a friend of yours?"

"I don't know if he'd say as much, but I'd be proud to call him that."

"I see," Clint said. "Well, the Dekker the boy's talkin' of is a big fella, one of the biggest I've ever met, that's for sure. Good man, one of the best. Got a wife, Ella, and a daughter by the name of—"

"Sarah."

Clint blinked, grinning. "Well, damn that's right. Small world, ain't it?"

Too small, the wanderer thought. "And Dekker, he's part of..." The wanderer waved his hand vaguely at the common room and the people in it. "This?"

147

Clint laughed. "S'pose you'd say that. Another fool who dreams of a better life."

The wanderer gritted his teeth as visions of Felden Ruitt lying dead flashed in his mind. "Where is he?" he grated.

The barkeep frowned then. "You sure Dekker's a friend of yours?"

"I don't mean him any harm," the wanderer said. "You have my word. Now, will you tell me where he is?"

"And if I do?" Clint asked. "What then, Ungr?"

"I'll help." The words were out of his mouth before he'd even thought of them, and while they might have been foolish, and he was confident the ghosts would have plenty to say on the matter, he found that, just then, he didn't care.

"Help," Clint repeated. "You mean the sort of help that would be riskin' your life? The sort of help that, likelier than not, might get a man...what was it you said? Squished?"

The wanderer said nothing, and the barkeep watched him for several seconds, studying him intently. Finally, he gave a nod. "I'll tell you, Ungr. Because I have a feelin' about you and because I think that maybe you need *to* help as much as Dekker needs to *be* helped. As I said, I've a feelin', but I've been wrong before. Understand that you'll have to prove just how good you are with those swords you carry if any harm comes to Dekker or his family because of you."

It already has, the wanderer thought, but he said nothing, only watched the man.

Clint waited another moment, as if he might second guess himself, then finally he gave a soft sigh. "You'll find Dekker over on Brewer Street, at the shop of a weasel merchant named Valance."

The wanderer nodded, turning and starting toward the door. He was swinging it open when Clint spoke again, and he paused.

"Hey, and Ungr?"

The wanderer turned, glancing back at the man.

"Try not to get squished, huh?" the man said, a small smile on his face.

"I'll try," he said, then he stepped out of the tavern, closing the door behind him. But then, while he didn't know the thoughts of bugs or even if they *had* thoughts, somehow he doubted any of them started their day thinking they'd like to get squished. Instead, they, like men, spent the majority of their time trying not to and—more often than not—failing.

***

The wanderer retrieved Veikr from where he'd tied him and started through the city. Brewer Street, at least, was one he was familiar with, so it did not take him and his horse long to navigate their way there. This late at night, the street was largely deserted, the doors of the shops flanking it barred, their lights put out.

The wanderer did not know the location of this Valance's shop, for the last time he had come through Celes the man had not even been born yet. So instead he only led Veikr down the street, looking for any sign of a place still open.

It did not take him long to find it, partly because of the lantern hung at its front, one he saw from a distance but mostly because of the voice—a familiar one—that he heard raised in anger. And as he drew closer, he was able to make out what was being said.

"You can't do this!" Dekker roared from where he stood beside a conspicuously empty cart. *"You've already been paid, and now you're trying to double the price—it's ridiculous!"*

The merchant, a fat man with a long, oiled beard, might have normally been intimidated—as most would have—by the big man's obvious anger, but situated as he was between two men of nearly equal size to Dekker, both of whom were holding clubs, he looked comfortable enough. *"I* can do whatever I want," the merchant said smugly. "My prices go up, your prices go up. You don't like it, take it up with the Eternals—it's part of the Eternal Law, section five passage two paragraph one." His grin widened. "You know, in case you're interested."

"But people are counting on this food!" Dekker said. "They'll starve without it!"

The merchant snorted. "People. Revolutionists, you mean. And if they do starve," he went on, glancing at his two hired thugs, a grin on his face, "well. Maybe Perishables is just the perfect name for them."

"You son of a bi—" Dekker began, stepping forward then pausing as the two thugs moved in front of the fat man, brandishing their clubs.

"The price is double," the merchant said, folding his arms across his chest and effecting a bored manner and tone, "do you want it or not?"

"We don't have that much coi—"

"We want it."

Dekker, as well as the fat merchant and his two toughs, turned at the sound of the wanderer's voice, watching as he stepped into the circle of ruddy light cast by the lantern.

"And who by the Eternals is this?" the merchant demanded. "You know the deal, Dekker. You're to come alone."

"I *did* come alone," Dekker said, "I don't know this ba—" He cut off as the light fell on the wanderer's face. The big man's eyes went wide, and he blinked. "*Ungr?*" he said. "Is that you?"

"It's me," the wanderer confirmed.

"But...what...how—I don't understand," Dekker finally managed. "What are you doing in the city?"

"It's a long story," the wanderer said, "I'll tell you later."

"Okay, I'm bored with this," the merchant said. "Come back to me, Dekker, when you've got the coin, and you want your supplies." He shrugged. "Or not. A few dead revolutionists is no real trouble to me."

"Oh, we're ready for the supplies now," the wanderer said.

"Ungr," the big man said quietly, "I don't have any more coins."

The wanderer held up a hand, still watching the merchant.

"Oh?" the man asked, his eyes shining with obvious greed. "So where is it? Where's the coin then?"

"You already have it," the wanderer said.

The merchant frowned. "What?"

"An agreed upon price is an agreed upon price. You have been paid, so now you will hand over the product," he said, raising one hand to open the locket on his neck.

The merchant glanced between the two thugs with him, laughing. "Listen, whoever the fuck you are, I have already explained to your big bastard of a friend here that according to Eternal Law—"

"I heard you," the wanderer said. "And you're wrong—or misquoting the law intentionally, but surely you would not do that. After all, the first may be forgivable, but the second, as I imagine you know, most certainly is not. A misapplication of the Eternal

Law...well, that sort of thing is taken very seriously by the judges of Celes, isn't it?"

The merchant let out another laugh, but this one sounded far more forced, and his eyes shifted nervously in their sockets. "I've done no such thing, I—"

"But you have," the wanderer said. "You see, the section of the Law to which you refer is known as the Code of Commerce, and while it does state that merchant prices might be allowed to be raised in the event of natural disaster or low-yield years and other such problems, it also states that they may only be raised such that the difference in the increase in price to market and increase of price *at* market, are balanced. But even that isn't relevant to the current discussion. What *is* however, is that one of the foundational tenets of the Law is that no merchant shall raise the price of wares after an agreed upon price has been met, whether that agreed upon price was written into contract or merely verbal."

Thanks, Scholar, the wanderer thought, closing the locket once more.

The merchant shifted nervously, licking his lips, and the wanderer thought that he might cave after all. But then a slow, conniving grin spread across the fat man's face, and he glanced at the two big men beside him, as if just remembering they were there. "Maybe," he said, "but then the law is meant to protect the city's true citizens, not those who plot against its rightful ruler."

"Or those, one supposes," the wanderer said, "who make dealings with those who plot against its rightful ruler because they're greedy for profit."

The merchant's grin turned into an angry sneer. "Enough of this. Go on then," he said to the two men beside him. "Do what I pay you to do."

The two men turned back to the wanderer and Dekker, one of them giving a shrug as if to say that there were no hard feelings, but it was time he earned his pay.

"Not gonna draw that blade of yours, are ya?" Dekker asked quietly as the two men slowly came forward, raising their clubs. "Valance is an asshole, but the last thing we need is to kill someone—that'll bring the guards, guards that'll be asking a damn sight more questions than I'd like."

"No," the wanderer said, "the sword will remain in its scabbard. I'll take the one on the right."

Dekker grunted, his eyes traveling up and down the wanderer then moving to the man he'd indicated who was nearly twice his size. "Just hold him off long as you can," the big man said doubtfully. "I'll try to finish this bastard quick and come help."

"Sure."

Dekker gave him another doubtful look then moved to his man. The wanderer left him to it, directing his attention on the hired tough who moved up to stand in front of him, looming like some great mountain. "Sorry about this," the big man said.

"Me too," the wanderer agreed.

Then, as if he felt the need to explain himself, the big man went on. "Didn't always do this—but a man's got to make money somehow."

"Of course, though I'd think there'd be better ways."

The man shrugged, shifting his massive shoulders. "Well. You ready?"

"As I'll ever be."

The man nodded, then charged forward with a roar, swinging his club. The wanderer waited until the last moment, then lunged forward within the man's guard and brought a fist into his opponent's solar plexus. His own momentum, coupled with that of the charging tough, gave the blow considerable power, and he pulled away as the man stumbled, wheezing and gasping for breath, before falling to his knees, dropping his club beside him.

The wanderer knelt beside the man, a hand on his shoulder. "Just take it easy," he said to the gasping man. "Focus on your breathing, in and out, in and out. You'll be okay. Now, are we done?"

The big man, still struggling to get his breath back, turned his eyes on the wanderer, nodding.

"Good," the wanderer said, rising. He started away then paused, turning back. "What about a caravan guard?" he asked. "Or maybe you could work on the city's walls. A big fella like you, why you'd be indispensable."

The man nodded again, wheezing still. "Anyway, good luck, whatever you decide," the wanderer said, then he rose and started toward the merchant, pausing when he saw that Dekker was still fighting his man.

It was as if two giants had met. The tough no longer held his club, the weapon having apparently been knocked from his hands, and the men stood, blocking and trading blows. The wanderer watched as the tough swung a fist at Dekker's face. The big man dodged, but not quite fast enough, and he grunted as the man's knuckles scraped across his cheek, nowhere near as hard as it might have been, but hard enough that it would bruise.

It knocked Dekker off-balance, too, allowing the tough to land another blow on his stomach, to which Dekker grunted, stumbling away and just managing to catch himself on his wagon. He glanced over at the wanderer, saw him standing there, his own opponent still on his knees, still about the task of coaxing air back into his lungs.

"He tripped," the wanderer explained. "You alright?"

"Fine," the big man growled, then he stood up from the wagon. "Come on, then, you big bastard," he said. He started forward, and this time when the tough swung, Dekker ducked under the blow, pivoting and planting a large fist in the man's midsection. The breath exploded out of the street tough, but Dekker wasn't finished. He rose, striking the man in the side of the face with a hook. The man stumbled but did not fall. Not, at least, until Dekker hit him with a second hook from the other side, then he collapsed to the ground, unconscious or close enough as to make no difference.

Dekker rubbed at the side of his face where a bruise was already beginning to form. "Now then," he said with a growl as he turned to the merchant who was staring on, wide-eyed. "Where were we, Valance?"

"Fine, fine," the merchant said, holding his hands up and backing away nervously, letting out a whimper as he ran up against the wall of his shop. "Look, Dekker," he said, trying a nervous laugh, "y-you can't blame a man for trying to make a little extra, right? I-I mean, I've got a family to take care of—"

"You don't have a family, you damned worm," the big man growled. "You think we didn't do any looking into you?"

The merchant licked his lips. "Well, anyway, that is...I might, one day. But...but no offense, alright?"

"Not alright, Valance," the big man said. "Considerable offense. Now, enough of your damn blather. You're lucky I'm late as it is.

Otherwise, I might show you just how offended I am. The goods. Now."

"O-of course," the merchant said. "A-and, maybe, that is, how about I help you load it?"

"How about you do?"

The merchant nodded again, his head bobbing frantically, then he unlocked the door to his shop and disappeared inside. Dekker and the wanderer followed him to where the supplies waited in one corner of the shop. They began loading the goods onto the back of the wagon, foodstuffs mostly, with what appeared to be medicine as well.

They didn't talk as they worked and when they'd loaded the last box onto the waiting wagon, Dekker turned back to the merchant, who was standing there wringing his hands. "I'll be around to pick up the same order two weeks from now, understood?"

"O-of course," the merchant stammered. "I-I'll have it ready for you."

"Didn't doubt it for a minute," Dekker said, giving the man a humorless smile. "Now, best you get home, Valance. Startin' to get cold—hang around here much longer, you're liable to catch your death."

The merchant needed no more urging than that. He turned and hurriedly locked the door to his shop then scuttled off into the darkness like the bug fleeing the boot, leaving his two men where they were.

"Well, shit," Dekker said. "I appreciate the help, Ungr."

The wanderer shrugged. "Think nothing of it."

The big man sighed. "Well. Where are you stayin' for the night?"

The wanderer hesitated, thinking, and Dekker grunted. "Somehow, I figured as much. Look, why don't you ride on back to the house with me, eh? Maybe we can get some food in you anyway. The least I can do after your help."

The wanderer winced. "Thanks, but that's not why I've come. In fact, I mean to leave the city tonight. I just wanted to talk to you, about the Peri—"

"Not here," the big man said quickly, glancing around the empty street. "Besides, we've already lingered too long—come on back to the house. We'll talk." Left with no other option, the wanderer walked back to Veikr and climbed onto the horse's back, following the wagon as Dekker made his way through the city.

They continued on until, in time, Dekker slowed in front of a simple wooden gate beyond which lay a small lawn and a nice, if also small, home. Dekker clucked at the mule, leading the wagon through the gate and pulling it off to the side where a one-stall stable stood. He pulled the mule in and unhitched it, then put it into the stall. "You can stable your horse here," he said, nodding his head at the single stall in which the donkey stood. "If, that is, you don't think he'd mind."

"This one?" the wanderer asked, glancing at Veikr. "Oh, he'll be fine."

The big man nodded and soon they had Veikr unsaddled and standing in the stall, he and the donkey regarding each other placidly. "Go on then," the wanderer said. "Make a friend."

He turned back to find Dekker raising an eyebrow. "Talk to your horse a lot, do you?"

The wanderer shrugged. "Easier than talking to most people."

The big man grunted, idly rubbing at his cheek where the man had struck him. "Won't argue with you there. Now, you mind helpin' me get this wagon unloaded?"

"Sure."

Dekker moved to the back of the wagon, hefting several of the boxes, and the wanderer grabbed his own burden. He expected the man to take them into the house but instead he moved to a back part of the stable, glancing at the wanderer before setting them down in the corner.

"Not going to bring them into the house?" the wanderer asked.

The big man met his eyes. "I never bring my work into my home, Ungr."

The wanderer nodded, and then they continued on the task in silence. When it was done, Dekker grabbed a rag that hung from a post, wiping his hands before tossing it back. "Alright. Best we go on and get in the house. If I'm much longer, Ella's liable to send a search party."

The big man led the way, and the wanderer followed. Inside, the house was dark. "Just a second," Dekker said quietly, and the wanderer stood, listening to the sound of him moving in the darkness. There was a clatter as something fell, and the big man hissed. "Damnit."

Another few seconds passed, and then the big man spoke again. "There we are." Orange light suddenly bloomed, revealing a main room similar in size to the one the wanderer had seen at their old house. And though the furnishings were simple and plain, they were also obviously well-cared for.

"Now then—" Dekker began.

"Who's there?"

A woman's voice, and they both turned to see Ella, Dekker's wife, standing in the doorway that must have led to their bedroom, a fire poker in hand.

Dekker made a sound somewhere between a grunt and a laugh. "Just me, love. Or, well, not just me. Anyway, you can put the fire poker down."

The woman frowned at her husband. "Maybe I don't want to, you being over an hour late and all."

The big man's mouth split into a wide grin at that. "Sorry, El. Me and a couple of the lads stopped by a tavern after work for a drink and guess who I ran into?"

She followed his gaze to the wanderer, blinking. "Ungr?" she said. "Is that you?"

"Yes ma'am. I hope you'll forgive my intrusion."

"Of course, of course," the woman said, doing her best to smile but he thought he could see the grimace hidden beneath it, a grimace no doubt brought on by the fact that his presence reminded her of her recently deceased father.

There was an awkward silence then as the three of them stood there for a few moments, then Ella seemed to gather herself, shaking her head. "Anyway, you must be hungry. Are you? Hungry, I mean?"

"I really wouldn't want to put you to any trou—"

"No trouble at all, not at all," the woman said quickly, clearly eager for the escape of having something to do. "Dinner's already cold," she turned a frown on her husband, "it's what happens when you show up late. But I think I can at least offer you some bread and a little stew, if that'd be alright?"

"That'd be fine," the wanderer said.

"Good," she said, slightly too quickly, "that's good." She moved to the small kitchen area of the room and began putting together a plate. The wanderer glanced at Dekker who met his gaze with a meaningful stare of his own.

Soon, Ella had finished her brief preparations and they were all sitting down at the table. No sooner had they done so then Ella made a hissing sound. "By the Eternals, Dek, what happened to your face?"

The big man winced, bringing his hand quickly to his face guiltily. "Oh, this? That—it's nothing, El. I, well, the thing is..." He gave a soft, self-deprecating laugh. "Might be I had a bit too much to drink, at the tavern. Anyway, I was walkin' out the door and ran into the doorjamb, if you can believe it." He gave another laugh, shaking his head. "I swear they moved the bastard on me somehow."

"You ran into a door," his wife said.

"Sure," Dekker said. "Anyway, if you think this is bad, you should see the door, right, Ungr?"

The wanderer thought of the man who Dekker had fought and the fact that it was completely possible that the "door" was still lying unconscious in front of the fat merchant's shop. "Your husband definitely fared better between the two of them," he said.

"See there?" Dekker said.

His wife watched him for another moment then sighed, shaking her head. "My husband—the door killer."

"Oh, it wasn't killed," the wanderer said, "but I would say unconscious, at least." He was aware of Dekker staring daggers at him, but the big man's wife only laughed.

"That's funny," she said. "So, Ungr, what has become of you since...well, since the last time we saw you?"

It was the wanderer's time to shift uncomfortably. "Oh, not much. Just...well. Nothing really."

"I...see"

Another awkward silence followed, this time interrupted by the big man. "Anyway, where's my little princess?"

"Your little princess is asleep," Ella said. "Do you have any idea what time it is?"

"Uh...late?"

"True enough," his wife said in a scolding tone but smiling when she said it. "Anyway, how was your day at work, dear? How were your deliveries?"

The big man glanced at the wanderer, clearing his throat. "Oh, not bad, not bad. You know, I just, well, it's a job, anyway, isn't it?"

Ella rolled her eyes. "My husband, so eloquent of a speaker. I swear, you men. Ask you something as simple as what you've been up to or how your day's gone, and you freeze as if you've found yourself in the middle of a test you haven't prepared for. Sometimes I wonder what the use of you is at all," she said, smiling.

"Sure," Dekker said, "until you need something off the top of the cabinet, then it's 'oh my wonderful husband this' and 'oh my wonderful husband that.'"

"You are aware, I assume," his wife said, arching an eyebrow, "that there is a new invention called a ladder."

Dekker cleared his throat. "Well...sure."

The conversation slowly faded, and they ate in companionable silence, though a silence, the wanderer couldn't help noting, that was not quite as peaceful, as welcoming as it had been the first time he'd eaten with the family. It was as if some part of that peace had been taken away—which, of course, it had been, when Felden Ruitt had been killed by the Unseen.

Still, despite that absence, the wanderer found that here, among this family, among the warmth of their obvious love for each other, he felt more at peace than he had since...well. Since the last time he had been around them. Often, over the last one hundred years spent in his exile, the wanderer had wondered at what it was all for, what was the point of his struggle. And here, he decided, was the answer.

The food, despite Ella's warnings, was good, flavorful and filling, and when they finished, she smiled. "Full at least?" she asked.

"Full," the wanderer said.

"Good," she said. "Now, Ungr. You will be staying with us for the night."

The wanderer winced. "Forgive me, ma'am, but I don't—"

"Please," she said, waving her hand. "First, my mother was ma'am—for me, Ella will do fine or, if you insist on butchering my name as my husband does, El. Either is better than ma'am."

"Yes, ma'am—sorry, Ella."

She smiled. "Secondly, it wasn't a question. It is late, and you look just about as tired as I feel. Dekker will find you somewhere to stay."

Her husband didn't say anything and she glanced over at him, raising an eyebrow. Dekker cleared his throat. "Right, sorry, dear. Of course."

"Good," she said, "then it's settled. Now, I'm off to bed. I—"

She didn't get a chance to finish before another door opened, and the small girl, Sarah, stood inside of it, her blond ringlets a mess from sleep, rubbing at her eyes. "Mommy?" she said. "I thought I heard—" She cut off as she saw Dekker and then let out a squeal of delight, charging toward her father who lifted her up into a tight hug.

"Hello there, Sarah Bug," the big man laughed.

"I'm not a bug," she protested, "I'm a *princess.*"

"A bug princess," her father said, and then began to tickle her, and she giggled wildly as he did.

The wanderer glanced over at Ella and saw the woman watching her husband and daughter with a small, loving smile on her face.

After a time, Dekker let off his tickling and sat the girl down on his lap. Her eyes went wide as she noted the wanderer. "Ungr?" she said. "Is that you?"

"Yes, lassy," Dekker said, "that's Un—"

"Does that mean that Veikr's here?" the little girl interrupted, her voice bursting with excitement as she leapt up from her father's lap.

Dekker heaved a theatrical sigh. "Oh, she loves her father well enough, just so long as there isn't a mangy horse around."

"Veikr isn't mangy!" the girl said. "But is he, is he here?"

Dekker sighed again. "In the stables, lass, but you really need to—"

"Can I see him? Please, please, Daddy, can I see him?"

Dekker winced helplessly, glancing at his wife.

"It isn't up to us, young one," Ella said. "Veikr is not our horse, after all."

The girl turned to the wanderer then, and as her childlike, excited gaze fell on him he felt at once nervous and somehow a part of things, a part of the world in a way that a hundred years of traveling it hadn't been able to make him feel. "Can I see him, Ungr?" the young girl asked. "Please, can I?"

The wanderer cleared his throat. "Of course, he would be just as excited to see you. That is if it's alright with your parents."

"Well," Ella said, smiling at Dekker, "it's alright with me."

The big man sighed again. "Sometimes, a man's got to wonder what he done to be cursed with such a wife and daughter."

"Oh, dear," Ella said, "you couldn't do anything to deserve us. I suppose you're just lucky."

He laughed at that, a great, big laugh, bringing a hand to his belly. "True enough, true enough. Well, why not? It isn't as if little girls need their sleep, is it? Come on then, lass. Let's go see a horse about a horse."

The little girl squealed with excitement as Dekker rose. "You coming?" he asked his wife.

"Oh, I suppose," she said. "If I don't, you're liable to get lost and I won't see you again until next week."

Husband and wife rose, walking to the door hand-in-hand. The wanderer came to his feet, feeling at once like an outsider and privileged for being a part of the moment.

They all walked outside, the small girl leading, dragging at her mother and father.

When they were on the porch, the girl pulling at Ella, Dekker's wife turned to Dekker and the wanderer. "I'll take her. You two, feel free to sit down and relax," she said, nodding her head at a couple of chairs on the small porch.

"Come on, Mommy, hurry up!" Sarah squealed.

"But—you don't think, I mean, the horse is safe, ain't he?" Dekker asked.

"Of course he's safe," Ella said.

"Awfully big though," the big man said, scratching his chin.

The woman rolled her eyes. "The big ones are often the softest, isn't that right, Ungr?"

"Yes, ma'a—sorry, yes, Ella. And it will do Veikr good to see her."

"See?" she said to her husband. "Just relax. She'll be fine."

"Mommy!"

"I'm coming, I'm coming," Ella said, then turned to the wanderer. "Keep an eye on my wayward husband, would you?"

"Of course," the wanderer said. She asked the question lightly, but he found that, while he answered it immediately, he did not *mean* it lightly.

Dekker waved a hand at one of the chairs, and the two of them sat, watching as the woman led her daughter to the stables and inside where, even from here, the wanderer could hear Veikr neighing with pleasure. For a time, they sat in silence, listening to the sounds of the little girl's giggles, the mother's laughs, and the horse's pleased neighs. As they sat there, the wanderer reflected that, when a man spent all his time fighting, it was sometimes very easy to forget what he was fighting *for*. Now, though, because of this family, he remembered. But the world was full of dangers—that and little else—and he found his thoughts turning dark as he glanced at the big man, smiling wistfully as he watched his family.

"That's the happiest I've seen her since...well, since Felden," Dekker said, though whether he meant his daughter or his wife, the wanderer didn't know, thought that likely the man meant both.

"They don't know," the wanderer said.

Dekker's smile slowly faded, and he turned to the wanderer, a look of challenge on his face. "I told you—I don't take my work home."

"But why are you here in the first place?" the wanderer asked. "Why come to the city at all?"

The big man winced. "Well, after what happened to Felden..." He shrugged, shaking his head. "They were in a bad way—we all were. Always loved livin' in the woods, never thought that'd change, but...without Felden there...I guess. I guess it just started to feel empty. Lonely. You know the feelin'?"

"I know it."

The big man nodded. "I think maybe you do. Anyway, we decided to come here, to the city. I've been coming here fairly regular anyway over the years, and I thought being around other people, around other kids her age, might do Sarah some good. Shit," he said, shaking his head, "I thought maybe it'd do us all some good."

"And did it?"

The big man considered that, scratching his chin. "Yeah. Yeah, I think maybe it did. Seein' you—or, well, your horse, I think that did even more."

The wanderer gave a small smile. "He has that effect. Now, about this rebellion, Dekker, and the Perishables—"

"Come to join?" the big man said, nodding. "Well. Can't say we couldn't use you—particularly how damn good you are with that sword of yours. The Eternals know you ain't no slouch in a fight."

"I didn't come to join," the wanderer said honestly. "I came to talk you into leaving them."

The big man frowned, his brows drawing together. "Leavin'? Why would I do such a thing as that?"

The wanderer sighed. "Because they're all going to die, Dekker. And if you're with them, you'll die too."

The big man's eyes narrowed. "You can't know that."

"You're wrong," the wanderer said. "I do know that. You don't know what you've set yourselves against, not any of you."

"And you do?"

"Yes."

The big man studied him for several seconds. "Who are you, Ungr? Who are you really?"

The wanderer considered for a moment then finally shrugged. "I'm a man who doesn't want to see your family get hurt."

"Anymore."

"What?"

"You mean you're a man who doesn't want our family to get hurt any*more*," Dekker said. His eyes flashed in the moonlight and, for a moment, the wanderer was suddenly convinced that the big man meant to charge him. In the end, though, Dekker only shifted in his seat, stretching his legs out and crossing one ankle over the other. "After all," the big man went on, turning away from him and choosing to regard the star-filled sky instead, "we've already been hurt, haven't we? You ought to know as you were there to see it."

The wanderer winced. "I...I am sorry. About Felden. It was never my intent to cause your family harm."

"My da used to say, Ungr, that there's often a wide gap between what a man intends to do and what he actually does. After all, everybody wakes up in the mornin' with good intentions, but good intentions don't change nothin'."

"You're right," the wanderer said, his mouth suddenly terribly dry, "they don't."

The big man studied him for several seconds then, finally, sighed, seeming to deflate as he did. "I'm sorry about that, Ungr. Maybe I ain't bein' fair to you, and likely you don't deserve it. Certainly, Felden wouldn't have countenanced my behavior. It's just that...well. The Eternals know I bitched enough about my father-in-law while he was here, but the fact is, I miss the old bastard. My wife, El, she tries to hide her own thoughts on the matter so as not to upset Sarah, but she misses him too, I can tell. Some nights since, I wake up in the dead of night to her crying. Soft, quiet like, tryin' to keep me from hearin', tryin' to keep her grief to herself. I've tried to talk to her about it but..." He trailed off, shaking his head in frustration. "As for Sarah, well. She's been quiet lately, Ungr, real quiet, holdin' it all in like her mother, or tryin' to anyway, and I worry what's gonna happen when she finds out she can't. I guess that's just about all I think about."

The wanderer said nothing then, for he could think of nothing to say. He wanted to. He wanted to, if not take away the man's grief, then to at least share it, but he did not know the words, so he only sat in silence.

After a few moments, Dekker gave a short, humorless laugh. "S'pose maybe I ought to be thankin' you. After all, without you, well, that thing, it would have killed us all, maybe."

"Maybe. I'm sure you would have taken it."

"Could I have?"

There was such a note of meaning in the big man's voice that the wanderer pulled his gaze down from where he, too, had been studying the sky and saw that the man was no longer staring upward but was instead looking intently at him.

The wanderer hesitated for a moment then, finally, shook his head. "No."

Dekker nodded as if he'd expected as much. "I didn't think so. What was it then?"

"I do not know their real name, or even if they have one. I know them only by the way they hunt, the way they kill, and so I call them Unseen."

The big man grunted, nodding slowly as he absorbed this information, and for a time they were silent again. When the big man finally spoke, it was not to ask more questions, as the wanderer had expected. "Once, when I was a kid," Dekker said, "no more'n eight or nine, I guess, me and some of the other boys of my village went out to a nearby creek to fish. It was winter, and it had been rainin' a lot. The water was cold, the creek up, rushin' a lot faster'n it normally did. Well, we got around to tauntin' each other, darin' each other to jump in, you know, the way boys'll do."

"Yes."

"Well. Nobody else'd do it, but I did. Didn't even really hesitate, to be honest. I remember that feelin'," he went on, his eyes getting a distant look, "jumpin' in the water, and it closin' over me, slammin' shut like a door that didn't mean to be opened. Guess that moment was about the first time I had the inklin' that maybe I wasn't invincible after all. Anyway, after a lot of thrashin' I made it to the shore, if barely. I just lay there for a while, too tired to even so much as move after fightin' the water as I did. I guess I lay in bed sick for about a week after that."

The wanderer nodded slowly, thinking of his own time as a kid what felt like so long ago and past that, when he had thought that he would live forever. When they are young, everybody thinks themselves the heroes of their own stories and the world no more than the setting for their heroics, just as they thought that those stories could only end happily. It wasn't until a man got older that he came to realize that in the real world, there were no heroes, only victims, and that few indeed were the stories that ended in anything but tears.

"I guess I've always been like that," Dekker went on, his deep voice cutting into the wanderer's reminiscence. "Brave, sure, but stupid too. Too stupid to understand just how deep the water is, how cold. But brave. Brave or not, though, I don't mind tellin' you, Ungr, that I spent some days after that thing attacked us havin' nightmares about it. Ain't ever seen anythin' like it in all my life and never thought to. It's as if the monsters I imagined as a child are real after all. Damn ugly thing it was, an abomination, I guess. Probably a priest would have better words than that."

"I think you're doing fine."

Dekker grunted. "Don't know if it was worse, seein' it, or worse to be hit by nothin', sent flyin' through the air like I got struck by a runaway carriage, watchin' some invisible *thing* tear into my father-in-law."

"It is always better to see," the wanderer said. "Being blind to danger will not stop its coming. Better to see. To *know.*"

Dekker nodded slowly. "You believe that?"

"I do." He sat up in his chair, meeting the big man's eyes. "It's why I came here. Listen, Dekker, about this...the Perishables. I came to ask you to—"

"What was it, Ungr?"

The wanderer blinked. "Sorry?"

"You call it 'Unseen,' and I guess that's about as good a description as any," the big man said. "But what *was* it? I been thinkin' about that in the days since, and I can't figure it. At first, I thought maybe it was some sort of animal, some creature of the deep wood. I ain't ever seen nothin' like it, but my ma had plenty of stories she used to tell, once upon a time, of bogeys and faeries in the wood. I thought maybe it was somethin' like that, only it didn't look like no animal to me. What it looked like, more than anything, was a man. A twisted one, sure, like maybe the gods, when they were puttin' him together, ran out of matchin' parts and decided to use what they had on hand, but still a man."

The wanderer hesitated, unsure of how much he should tell the man, for while he believed that, as a rule, it was better for a man to know the truth, the truth sometimes came at a high cost.

Dekker must have seen him considering this, for the big man grunted. "I need to know, Ungr. It's a big world, I know that much, full of shit I don't know and don't understand, but I got to try." He paused, glancing in the direction of the stables where a warm orange lantern light was spilling out of the doorway. "It's my job."

The wanderer winced, then nodded. "Very well. Well, you are right in thinking it similar in aspect to a man, for it was once. A man who has been twisted by dark magics and experiments, forged the way raw steel might be forged, to be made into something else, something with only one purpose."

"One purpose," Dekker repeated. "And what's its purpose then?"

The wanderer met the big man's eyes. "I think you know."

"I see. And I'm guessin' you've seen that sort of thing before?"

The wanderer nodded. "And more besides."

"I ain't clever, Ungr," Dekker said, "I leave that to my wife—the Eternals know she's better at it than me. But that thing, it didn't happen upon us by accident."

"No."

"It came for somethin'. Or someone."

"Yes."

Dekker considered, scratching at his chin, maybe trying to decide the best way to figure out what he wanted to know. Maybe trying to decide if he wanted to know at all. Finally, the question he settled on was not the one the wanderer had expected. "And who is it then?"

"What?"

"A dog gets sicked on somethin' or someone, there's usually a master who did the sickin'. So what I'm askin' you, Ungr, is who sent it?"

"Better if you didn't know."

"Maybe," Dekker said. "Best if I didn't see it in the first place. But I *did* see it, Ungr," the man said, "me, and my wife, my *daughter.*" He finished the last in an emotional growl. "I'm a fool, Ungr, but I'm not so big a fool as to think I can protect my daughter from everythin'. That isn't to say I don't mean to try, and I can't protect her if I don't even know what—or *who*—I'm protecting her from."

The wanderer nodded slowly. "It won't be easy to believe."

Dekker barked a humorless laugh. "Neither is it easy to believe that an invisible creature broke in through the wall as if it were made of paper and killed Felden. Why don't you give me a try."

"Very well," the wanderer said. "If you ask me who sent it, I will tell you. Soldier."

Dekker waited, watching him, as if the wanderer might say no. When he did not, the big man grunted. "And by Soldier, you mean—"

"The man—or creature—who currently rules the kingdom of Aldea, yes."

"I don't mean to lecture you, Ungr, but jokes are supposed to be funny." Dekker watched the wanderer for another minute then frowned. "But you're not joking."

"No."

Dekker grunted again. "So, if I'm to believe you, then Soldier, the man who has ruled our kingdom for several hundred years, who, along with the other Eternals, is believed to be more of a god than a man, has suddenly turned evil and has begun...what? Experimenting on people?"

166

"Something like that."

"And he's sending these experiments after you?"

"Yes."

The big man didn't call him a fool or grow angry with misplaced loyalty as the wanderer would have expected him to. Instead, he nodded slowly. "Why?"

"Why what?"

"Why is he sending these things after you?"

The wanderer winced, suddenly very aware of the cursed blade sheathed beside his own where it hung at his back. "Because I have something that he wants."

"I see," the big man said. "And if he gets it? Will he be satisfied? Will he stop making these creatures?"

"No. He'll only do it better."

"Huh."

They were silent for some time then as the big man likely tried to make peace with the idea. The wanderer understood, for he had been trying to do the same thing for a hundred years and more.

"Listen, Dekker," the wanderer said finally, "that's why I came here. I heard you were in town and wanted to speak to you. This rebellion, these Perishables...they're doomed. I came to talk you into leaving before something bad..." He paused, thinking of Felden Ruitt, lying dead on the floor of the family's home. "Before something *worse* happens," he finished.

Dekker frowned. "So you're tellin' me, Ungr, that our leader is corrupt, and you want me, knowin' that, to sit back and do nothin'?"

"Yes."

"Why?"

Just then, there was a loud, childish giggle from the stable, and the wanderer turned to regard the distant building. The big man followed his gaze then grunted. "I see. And if I told you that I wouldn't quit?"

The wanderer winced. "Please, Dekker. Think of your daughter. If you think it has been bad so far...you have no idea how bad it can get."

The big man seemed to consider that, taking his time, enough that the wanderer began to hope that he had gotten through to him. Finally, though, Dekker shook his head. "No, Ungr. I appreciate the warning, but I can't quit."

"But, your daugh—"

"Tell me, Ungr," Dekker said. "You ever have kids?"

The wanderer thought of her again, standing in the wood beside their tree, as beautiful as the sunrise. He thought, also, of the life he had abandoned to become what he now was. "No," he said, his voice a low, throaty croak.

"I didn't think so," the big man said, apparently unaware of the emotional storm his words had breathed into life. "If you did, you wouldn't say for me to think of my child. You would know that any father—any *real* father—thinks of little else. My job, Ungr, my most *important* job, is to protect my daughter."

"But Dekker, that's exactly what I mea—"

"Sometimes," the big man went on, "that means rousting monsters out of closets where they don't belong. Sometimes that means puttin' food on the table or standin' between her and as much of the world as I can. Other times, though, it means teachin' her to protect herself, you see? And to do that, sometimes there's a bit of risk. When Sarah was first learnin' to walk, El and I were a nervous mess, terrified she'd fall, hurt herself. But she had to learn—I can't learn it for her—and my job, then was to let her try, let her *fail* if she had to. It was a risk, but it was one that was worth it because it made her better able to get around in the world without me. Now, what we're doin', me and the other Perishables, well, that's important work, too. Sure, there's risk, but there's also a chance, a chance to make the world better, *safer* for my daughter."

The wanderer rubbed at his temples where a headache was beginning to form. "Look, Dekker, I know you said that Felden's death was...difficult, but there are better ways to make your peace with it than this. Safer ways."

The big man grunted. "So, what then? You're thinkin' that after Felden's death, after seein' what I saw, I went lookin' for some sort of meanin', came to town and found it with the Perishables?"

"Didn't you?"

Dekker shook his head slowly. "Fact is, Ungr, I been a part of the Perishables long before you ever came to our home. I come to town from time to time, always told El it was to trade, sell some of the food out of our fields, and that's true. But it wasn't only for that."

"I see," the wanderer said, surprised. "But it makes no difference, Dekker. What you're doing, you and the others, it's dangerous."

The big man shrugged. "Life's dangerous, Ungr. That can't stop a man from livin' it. Anyway, if what you're sayin' is true—and I don't doubt it...maybe I should, but as I said, I've never been all that clever. Anyway, if it's all true, then that's just more reason for me to stick. A man can't stand guard over his daughter's bed forever, makin' sure the monsters don't come out of the closet. But if he goes into the closet, if he beats the monster, well, then they can both sleep easier."

"And if the monster beats him?" the wanderer asked quietly.

Dekker smiled. "That's why a man brings back up, isn't it? Like the other Perishables."

The wanderer winced, thinking of the men and women—farmers and day laborers, not warriors—that he'd seen in The *Spilled Tankard*. He doubted if more than a handful of them knew how to hold a sword, let alone how to use it. Still, he saw that the big man would not be swayed, so he sighed. "I wish you luck, Dekker. All of you."

"But you still think we're being fools."

The wanderer considered that for a moment then finally shook his head. "No. Not fools. There's nothing foolish about wanting to make the world a better place." *It's only foolish,* he thought, *to believe it's actually possible.*

The big man nodded, a small smirk on his face as if he could hear the wanderer's thoughts. He said nothing, though, and they sat in a companionable silence, the wanderer enjoying the slight breeze on his face and hands as they listened to the giggles of a little girl and her mother and, of course, the unmistakably happy neighs of a very-satisfied horse.

In time, the mother and daughter walked back out of the stables, hand in hand.

"So, how was it, princess?" Dekker asked, grinning. "Everything you hoped and dreamed?"

Ella laughed as she glanced at the heavy-lidded eyes of her daughter who was clearly struggling to keep them open. "Dreaming is right—I'd say our princess is ready for her beauty sleep."

"Well, thank the Eter—" The man cut off, frowning. "Thank goodness for that. She's startin' to look a little scruffy around the edges. Keep goin' this way, lass, folks'll try to put *you* in a stable."

The little girl giggled sleepily, and Dekker grinned, rising from the chair and scooping her up. "Come on then, lass. Let's get you to bed." He started toward the door then turned and glanced back at the wanderer. "You're stayin' the night then?"

The wanderer glanced at the woman, Ella, who was watching him with one arched eyebrow as if daring him to say the wrong thing and smiled. "I guess I'd better."

The big man nodded, glancing at his wife. "Coming, love?"

She smiled. "Of course, just...give me a few moments, will you? I need to get our guest settled."

"Of course," her husband said, "but don't take too long, eh? This little one will be wantin' a story, and I'd really hate to have to do the voice of the princess again. My throat was sore for a week."

Ella grinned. "But you did it so well, dear, and I'm afraid some sacrifices must be made for such art." Dekker rolled his eyes, glancing at the wanderer. "See what I got to put up with?"

"A tragedy," the wanderer said dryly.

The big man barked a laugh then turned and walked into the house.

Ella shook her head, still smiling, as she stared after her husband for a moment before turning back to the wanderer. "There's a loft in the stables. A long way from a room in a castle, but it's warm at least. I'll show you to it."

"If it's good enough for my horse, then it's good enough for me," the wanderer said.

She nodded at that, and then turned, without another word, and started toward the stables. The wanderer followed.

Ella led him into the stables, still holding the lantern she'd lit before. The wanderer walked past the stall Veikr and the mule shared and saw that his horse was fast asleep, looking just about as contented with life as any horse could. Sarah, apparently, had not been the only one exhausted from the excitement of their reunion.

Ella led him to the back of the stable where a ladder was situated leading to the loft. "As I said," Ella said apologetically, "it isn't much, but there's hay to keep warm, and I'll bring some blankets out to you."

"Thank you," the wanderer said, "for your hospitality."

She smiled. "Of course. I'll go get you those blankets." She started away then turned back. She stood there for a moment, unmoving, silent. Then, "I love my husband, Ungr."

The wanderer, unsure of what was expected of him, nodded. "Of course."

"Him and Sarah, they're my world. All that I have, all that I *need*. I love them both with a love that can sometimes drive me crazy. But what that love doesn't do is make me blind."

The wanderer said nothing, only watched her, waiting for what would come.

"I'm not so blind, for instance," she said, "to believe my husband when he tells me that the bruise on his face came from running into a door. Neither am I so blind that I cannot see the marks on your face from where it looks like somebody mistook you for a training dummy."

"What are you asking me?" the wanderer said.

She considered that, and the question seemed to be right there, on the tip of her tongue. In the end, though, she only shook her head. "I'm not asking you anything," she said, "not really. I won't ask you about that thing that...attacked my dad. Neither will I ask you where those scrapes and cuts really came from. But if I did...would you tell me the truth?"

The wanderer considered that, then slowly nodded his head. "Yes."

"Then I won't ask," she said. "I only wanted you to know. My husband, he hides some things from me. I let him do it—or at least let him imagine that he does it—because I love him, and I know he does what he does only because he wants to protect me, protect *us*. And I let him to continue doing those things he does because I believe that the world will never change, will never get *better*, if good men do nothing. Do you understand?"

"I...think so."

She nodded. "And what do you believe, Ungr?"

He took his time, thinking over the question. He had known the answer once, and it had been that answer, that knowing, that had set his feet upon the path he had chosen, the path which had taken him here, away from what might have been, away from the woman he had loved. Now, though, the answer, if still there was one, eluded him, and he shook his head. "I don't know."

She stared at him with such compassion in her eyes then that he felt it almost like a physical weight pressing on him. "I am sorry," she said. "It seems to me that a person ought to know what they believe in. Otherwise, what's the point of anything?"

There was a sudden lump in the wanderer's throat, and he realized that he could not find the words to answer.

"I didn't mean to pry," she said, "nor did I mean to poke at old wounds, so if I did, I apologize."

"No apology is necessary," the wanderer said, trying a small smile. "After all, you're not the one that gave the wounds."

"Maybe not," she said, "but I'm sorry just the same. I guess all I wanted to know...wanted to *ask,* is if you would...look after him. My husband, I mean."

The wanderer, who had been planning on leaving in the morning, planning on getting the cursed blade as far away from Soldier as possible while he still could, hesitated.

Seeing him hesitate, Ella held up her hand. "You don't have to answer now. Just...think on it. Will you do that?"

"I will."

She smiled. "Thank you. I'll go see about those blankets."

She turned and retreated out of the stables, moving faster than she needed to, and the wanderer looked after her, thinking. He had set out, a hundred years ago, with the cursed blade in his possession, with the intention of saving the world. Had set out, in truth, long before that, when he had first sought the Eternals, when he had thought to join their ranks. Now, he knew that the best way of doing that, of keeping the world safe, was to leave the city. But what point, he wondered, in saving the world, if a man neglected to save the people in it?

It was this thought which followed him into sleep, which lingered even as he dreamed of the man, the boy he had once been, of all that boy had stood to gain. And of all that boy had lost.

CHAPTER EIGHT

He woke to the sound of screaming.

He was on his feet in a moment, tossing aside the blankets Ella had brought him as fear surged through him with the force of a lightning strike.

Not again, he thought. *Please, not again.*

He grabbed the two swords from where he'd laid them before he slept, not wasting any time with the ladder. Instead, he leapt from the loft roof, hitting the hay-laden floor of the stables in a roll and coming to his feet. He spared a glance to see Veikr standing in his stall, a tenseness in the horse's posture that spoke of his own anxiety.

Then he was running. He shoved the stable door open and sprinted outside. It was still dark, the moon high in the sky, and he drew his sword from its sheath, scanning the yard.

"Dekker!"

There was the scream again, and the wanderer's eyes locked on the source of those screams, a young boy, the same one, he realized after a moment, as he had seen back at The Spilled Tankard, and his fear increased.

The door to the house swung open and the big man, Dekker, stepped out, finishing the process of pulling on his boots even as he did.

"Billy?" Dekker asked, as he started down the steps. "You got any idea what time it is, lad?"

"S-sorry, Dekker," the kid blurted, "b-but it's the tavern."

The big man walked up to the boy as did the wanderer, and the big man acknowledged his presence with a troubled nod before turning back to the youth. "What is it, Billy? What about the tavern?"

"Th-the guards," the boy stammered, tears in his eyes. "Th-they're attacking it."

"Attacking it?" Dekker asked as if he couldn't believe the boy's words.

"Y-yes sir," the youth said, nodding his head frantically. "They came, dozens of them, and they set fire to the tavern while most people were sleeping. Some men tried to get out, but they're attacking anyone that comes outside. They're killing them, Dekker! Not asking them any questions or nothing! Clint sent me to get you and the rest of the men. I was only able to escape because of the window at the back, too small for any of the others, but Dekker, if we don't do something' they're all going to burn, they're going to—"

"Easy, lad," Dekker said, pulling the boy into a hug and glancing at the wanderer with a troubled look. "Easy there. Nobody's going to burn, alright? We'll get them."

"Dekker?" A worried, woman's voice, and the big man turned, along with the wanderer, to regard Dekker's wife, Ella, standing in the doorway of their house, dressed in her night clothes, her eyes big and wide in the moonlight. "What is it?"

"Nothing, El," the big man said, "everything's fine. You just go on back to bed."

"Don't you lie to me, Dekker," she said.

The big man winced, nodding. "There's a bit of trouble at a tavern I frequent. Needs lookin' into, but I'll be back before you know it."

The woman opened her mouth, clearly meaning to argue, but the wanderer, knowing that time was of the essence, spoke first. "I'll go with him," he said. They all turned to him then, and he shrugged. "You know what they say—two sets of hands are better than one."

"You thought of what I asked?" Ella said quietly.

"I did."

"And?"

"I'm going with him," the wanderer said, not ready to commit to anything more and not willing to commit to any less.

She nodded and that, and Dekker frowned. "Well, let's go then. And El? Maybe let Sarah sleep in the bed with you tonight, keep you company 'til I return."

The woman was clever, and the wanderer could see in her eyes that she understood well what her husband meant, that should things come to the worst, it would be best if she had the young girl close. She nodded. "Be careful," she said.

"Always," Dekker growled, and then he was turning to the wanderer. "That horse of yours, reckon he could carry two?"

Or a dozen, if need be, the wanderer thought, but he nodded. "Yes."

They raced to the stables, quickly strapping on Veikr's saddle and then they were riding out into the night, Ella watching them, her face worried and pale in the moonlight.

"I'll be wantin' to know what you and my wife talked about," Dekker said as they rode.

"Later," the wanderer said.

"Later," the man agreed.

***

So late at night, the streets of Celes were, if not empty, then as close as they likely ever came. This gave Veikr the opportunity to make use of his speed, unmatched among his kind, and so it did not take them long to reach their destination. They turned a corner and there, in the distance, the wanderer could make out the tavern. There was no mistaking it as the building, at least parts of it, were on fire.

Two men dressed in uniforms marking them as city guardsmen stood at the door, swords in their hands, and the wanderer noted at least three forms lying unmoving at their feet. Men or women, it seemed, who had sought to escape the blaze and had only found death waiting for them.

"*Bastards,*" Dekker growled, his voice deep and angry.

The wanderer didn't waste time agreeing. Instead, he surveyed the area. More guardsmen waited in a semi-circle in the street, facing the building, their weapons drawn. Among them, he noted two men holding not swords but crossbows.

In another place, such a spectacle might have drawn a crowd, but the people of the poor quarter had apparently decided that this was one of those times when the less a person knew the better chances they had of keeping breathing.

The guardsmen were intent on the building and so did not notice the horse and the two men, though likely they would not have noticed anyway as Veikr had navigated them to the shadowed opening of an alleyway.

The wanderer continued to look over the scene, scanning the buildings. His gaze moved to the rooftops and that was when he saw them. Two crossbowmen positioned on the top of what appeared to be a shoemaker's shop across the street from the burning tavern.

"I'll show those bastards," Dekker said, dismounting from Veikr and taking with him the pitchfork he had grabbed from the stables before they left.

"Wait," the wanderer said.

"*Wait?*" Dekker demanded. "What do you mean, *wait?* Can't you hear them screaming, Ungr? The bastards are burning them alive!"

"Remember the water you jumped in as a child?"

"Of course I remember but what does that have to do with anything?" the man snapped.

"Everything," the wanderer said. "If you go now, Dekker, this time you won't make it out. The water *will* swallow you, and you will leave Ella without a husband, Sarah without a father."

"So what then?" Dekker demanded. "How do I help them?"

"You can't," the wanderer said simply, dismounting himself and drawing his sword. "But I can. Wait here—when I give you the signal, go and fetch your people."

"What signal?" Dekker demanded.

"You'll know it," the wanderer said, and then he was sprinting through the shadows, not in the direction of the burning tavern but instead toward the shoemaker's shop across the street.

He reached it and tried the door, unsurprised to find it locked. He called on his considerable strength, giving the door a kick in the place where the latch would sit. The wood snapped, and the door swung open.

The wanderer quickly stepped inside, closed it behind him, and waited, listening for any sound of someone approaching. At first, there was nothing, and he was just beginning to think that the two crossbowmen had not seen a need to leave a guard when he heard it. The soft, almost imperceptible sound of breathing, of a sword leaving its scabbard.

Then light bloomed in the darkness, revealing a man in the uniform of the city guardsmen standing there, a sneer on his face, lantern in one hand, sword in the other. "You should not have come here," the man said.

"Maybe," the wanderer said, "but it's too late now. For both of us." He knew that time was of the essence, so he did not waste it, lunging forward. The man managed to let out a surprised cry, raising his sword halfway. That and that only before the wanderer's blade took him in the chest, piercing through the flesh and into his heart.

It was over that quickly, and the wanderer pulled the blade free, allowing the corpse to collapse to the floor at his feet. Then he was scanning the shop, his gaze roaming over shelves of boots and shoes until it settled on a ladder behind the counter. He took the rungs two at a time. There was a wooden hatch at the top, and he threw it open, climbing onto the roof.

The nearest crossbowman must have heard the sound of the trap door opening, but it did not save him. He spun, his crossbow taking aim on the wanderer but didn't manage to fire a shot before the wanderer closed the distance and plunged his blade into the man's midsection. The guardsman screamed, dropping his weapon, but went silent a moment later as the wanderer dragged the blade upward.

Knowing that the other crossbowman could not have helped but note his companion's scream, the wanderer spun, leaping to the side and hearing the whistle of a crossbow bolt as it flew past, missing him by inches.

The crossbowman, his eyes wide and wild in the darkness, cursed as he tried to reload his weapon, fumbling the bolt as he did. He was reaching to snatch it up when the wanderer came upon him. The man had time to look up and let out a gasp of shock before the wanderer's sword severed his head from his body in a bloody fountain.

The wanderer sheathed his sword and retrieved the crossbow and bolts from the dead man then regarded the guardsmen standing in the street once more. The first bolt took one of the crossbowmen in the neck, and the man collapsed to the ground.

With shouts of surprise, the guards nearest the unfortunate man spun, trying to discover the source of the bolt that had taken their friend and noticed him in another moment. The second crossbowman, responding to his companions' shouts, spun at the last moment, so the bolt that had been meant for his upper back instead took him in the shoulder, enough to make him drop his weapon but not enough to kill him.

The guards shouted in anger and six of them charged toward the shoemaker's shop, meaning to attack the wanderer. He saved them the trouble, discarding the crossbow and leaping off the roof and onto the wooden awning situated above the shop's door then down into the street. He rolled to absorb the shock and came to his feet, drawing his sword.

The half a dozen guards, which had been roaring and charging toward the shop, hesitated at this, spreading out in a semi-circle in front of him.

"Who the fuck are you?" one growled.

"Does it matter?" the wanderer asked. "You came for death, and so you have found it."

He noted the other guards in the street giving up their positions, moving toward him, and he frowned. Six would have been difficult, improbable. Twelve was impossible. Still, there was nothing to be done.

The first man charged him, forcing the wanderer to parry a wide, overhand strike, and then it was started.

They came on fast, their steel flashing, and instead of countering and finishing the first man, the wanderer was forced to parry wildly, backing away as he did.

He wasn't sure how long it went on, him forced on the defensive, unable to do anything but bide time, avoiding the questing steel of the soldiers as they pressed in all around him. At least, mostly. He sported several thin cuts on his arms and one on his chest where he had been too slow to react to the whirlwind of blows coming at him.

Had it not been for his countless years of training, he would have been dead in seconds. As it was, he thought that he would still die, only slower. But as there was no choice, the wanderer did what he had done for the last one hundred years—he fought to survive.

He managed a glancing blow to one of his attackers, a cut across the man's arm, far from fatal, and the man stumbled away only to be replaced by another. As the fight dragged on, the wanderer felt his movements slowing, his body tiring from the frantic parrying and dodging.

He felt more than saw a blade coming at him from behind, and he knocked a sword away from his front, spinning and knowing even as he did that he would not be quick enough.

He was surprised, then, when he did not feel the hot agony of the blade finding purchase in his flesh and instead turned to see a man standing before him, not a guardsman this one, but Dekker, and at his feet lay sprawled the guardsman who had attacked him. Dead or unconscious, the wanderer did not care which.

And then other men and women charged into the guardsmen, several of which the wanderer recognized from the tavern when he'd visited it earlier. He watched as the big man, Hank, smashed his fist into the jaw of a nearby guardsman sending him reeling.

Their numbers seemed to continue to grow until, in moments, it was the guardsmen who were outnumbered, several falling to makeshift weapons—chairs and ale steins, mostly—before the few that remained turned and fled into the night.

The wanderer, his body aching from a dozen small cuts, stood panting heavily, watching them. Those who had fought with him did much the same, at least those who did not lay sprawled in the street among the dead guardsmen, unmoving and likely never to move again.

Someone let out a ragged cheer, and then all of them were shouting and cheering, clapping loudly as they turned to the wanderer. As he only stood, saying nothing, their cheers began to falter then stopped altogether.

"Why do you cheer?" the wanderer asked honestly.

There was a hesitation from the crowd at that and then someone shouted from the back. "Because we won!"

There were several shouts of approval at this, and the wanderer waited for them to die down before he spoke again. "And what did you win?" he asked. He glanced meaningfully at the dead men scattered among the guardsmen. "Does this look like victory to you? That taste in your mouth—it is not victory. It's blood."

There were several confused murmurs at this, and then the big man from the tavern, Hank, stepped forward. "Fuck off, you prick," he said. "What do you know of it? We sent those guardsmen runnin' didn't we?"

"You did," the wanderer agreed. "And where do you imagine they will run to?"

The man frowned at that. "What the fuck do I care?"

"I imagine you'll care a great deal when they bring more of their companions back next time, a dozen, maybe a hundred. Or maybe they'll bring something altogether worse."

"I'm just about tired of your damned mouth," the big man growled, starting forward, but Dekker stepped in front of the wanderer, holding up a hand.

"Don't you take another step, Hank," Dekker growled. "Not unless you want to contend with me."

The big man looked shocked, his gaze traveling between Dekker and the wanderer. "What are you sayin', Dek? You tellin' me that you'd take this, this *bastard's* side over me and your people?"

"What I'm saying," Dekker said, "is that this *bastard* just saved your lives. *All* of our lives," he went on, then glanced at the wanderer.

"Like shit he did," Hank growled.

"Oh?" Dekker asked. "Did you see those crossbowmen up on the roof of ol' Henry's shop, Hank?" he pressed, gesturing at the rooftop where the wanderer had killed the crossbowmen.

The big man frowned, his eyes narrowing, but he said nothing. "What about you, Clark?" Dekker asked another man. "You see them?"

The man in question, an older man with salt and pepper hair, frowned, looking at the roof.

"Me neither," Dekker said, then turned and gestured at the wanderer, "but *he* saw them, and a good thing too. If he hadn't, I'd have a crossbow bolt in my back, and you all'd be burning along with that tavern there." He nodded his head at the building, well and truly engulfed in flames now.

Hank growled angrily, then opened his mouth to speak but before he could another voice spoke from the crowd. "Let it go, Hank."

They all turned, the crowd parting as the man, Clint, stepped through the opening. The old man's shirt was singed, his face and clothes filthy with smoke, but he smiled as he turned to regard the wanderer. "Ungr," he said, nodding his head. "Thanks."

"Don't thank me," the wanderer said. "I haven't saved you—nothing can." He turned to regard Dekker. "A man who chooses to leap into the roiling waters might escape once, if he's lucky. Perhaps more than once. But sooner or later, he will drown. It is the only way it ends."

"Might be you saved us," Hank muttered, frowning like he'd like nothing more than to punch Ungr in the face, "but far as pep talks go, you're pretty well shit."

There was some scattered, nervous laughter at that, but Clint turned to Dekker. "Dek," he said, offering his hand. "Good to see you."

Dekker grinned. "Wouldn't have missed it for the world. So what now, boss?"

Clint's smile slowly faded as he looked around the street at the dead men, his gaze moving toward the front of the building where three more lay dead and then to the building itself, burning in the darkness. "That's the question, isn't it," he said thoughtfully, and in his voice the wanderer could hear the grief for those who had fallen.

He thought, watching the Perishables leader's eyes dance with unshed tears, that here was a good man. Dekker, too. Not that it mattered. Good men died just like the rest—often times easier. The wanderer knew this, for he had seen it. Far too many times.

"I might know a place," a timid voice said, and they all turned to regard a man who appeared to be in his early twenties. Unlike the rest gathered there, the man was wearing expensive, fine clothes that marked him as either the son of a rich merchant or a nobleman. At least, his clothes *had* been fine. Now, his dark blue tunic and white trousers were stained with soot, his blond ponytail messy and filthy with ash.

Clint winced. "Will?"

The young man's throat worked. "Well, as you are aware, my family owns an estate in the city. We could go there. It is gated and—"

Hank snorted. "Bullshit. I'll be damned if I'm goin' to spend the night in some spoiled nobleman's home, havin' his parents, the lord and lady, starin' down their noses at us. And how long will it be, do you reckon, before the lord or lady choose to tell the guards they've got near fifty commoners litterin' their perfectly-kept grounds?"

"Oh, I wouldn't say fifty commoners, Hank," Dekker said. "After all, you're just about as uncommon as they come."

There was some scattered laughter at that, and the big man frowned. "I'm just sayi—"

"I know what you're saying, Hank," Clint said, "and you are wrong to say it. Will may be a nobleman, but that is nothing to hold against him. He can no more control the life into which he was born as we can and, even if he could, what then? Who among us would refuse an offer of a better life? And yet Will, instead of living in luxury as he might have, instead of allowing the suffering of others to be something he heard about and no more, has risked all of that to help. He doesn't deserve your enmity, Hank—he deserves your respect. *All* of our respect."

The big man turned red at that, his eyes studying the street. "Sorry," he muttered.

"I-it's no problem at all," the young man said, then turned to Clint. "So...will you come?"

"Hank might have been rude," Clint said, shaking his head, "but he's right about this much, at least, Will. Our bein' there would raise questions with your mother and father, and the answers to those questions would put not only us, but them in danger as well. No, we can't do that. Better if we find another way."

"Yes, sir," Will said, nodding, "but...forgive me for asking...what other way?"

Clint winced again, glancing at Dekker.

The big man shrugged. "He's got a point, Clint."

"Besides," the young nobleman went on, a note of eagerness in his voice, "we can use my family's guest house. It's rarely ever used now, only once or twice a year when my uncle and his new wife visit, and that won't be anytime soon as they just left last month. It's perfect. My parents are out of town for a week and, anyway, I can keep the servants from coming to clean if—"

"Servants," Hank muttered, shaking his head.

"Hank," Clint said in a warning tone, "enough."

"Anyway, I think...I think it could work," the youth said. "At least, until you figure out what we should do."

The older man hesitated, scratching at the gray stubble on his chin before finally, nodding. "Okay, Will. If you're sure."

"I am," the young man said, nodding excitedly, and the wanderer didn't think he had ever seen a man sign his own death warrant with such enthusiasm, but he didn't bother saying as much. It wasn't as if anyone would listen if he did.

"And what of you, Ungr?" Clint asked, turning to look at the wanderer. "I can't thank you enough for what you did here—if it weren't for you, as Dekker said, we'd all be dead. But it ain't safe for any of us out in the streets and now, considerin' what you did, I'd say that includes you. Especially since some of those guards that escaped might well have marked any man here."

The wanderer hesitated, unsure, and Dekker spoke. "He'll stay with me and my family tonight," the big man said.

"You mean you don't mean to come sip fine wine and get fed grapes with the rest of us, Dek?" Hank asked.

Dekker sighed, shaking his head. "I'll bring my family tomorrow mornin'."

Clint considered that. "You sure?" he asked. "It's unlikely that the guardsmen will come back tonight, at least, but it isn't impossible. After all, I didn't think they'd make a move this soon and..." He paused, glancing at the wanderer. "Well, I was wrong. If any of those that ran recognized you..." He trailed off, not finishing, but then he didn't need to. They all knew what was at stake. If they didn't, all they needed to do was glance around at the corpses in the street, and they would be reminded quickly enough.

Dekker shook his head slowly. "Better done durin' the day. Any movement in the poor quarter after all this, well, I can guarantee it'll be marked, and the last thing I want is to lead them right to you all. No, the mornin's better. Easier to blend in with the rest of the crowds. Besides, if any of the guards do decide to pay me a visit, well..." He paused, looking at the wanderer. "I think I'll be okay."

Clint nodded. "If you're sure."

"I am."

"Okay then," the leader of the Perishables said, gesturing to the street. "It's your show, Will. Lead on."

The men started forward and Clint turned back as they did, offering his hand to the wanderer who gave it a shake, then to Dekker. "We'll expect you tomorrow?"

"You got it."

The wanderer and Dekker stood as the men filed past. Then, the big man cleared his throat, turning to the wanderer. "Thanks," he said. "I acted a fool, and if it hadn't been for you, Sarah'd be growin' up without a da. She don't deserve that."

"No," the wanderer said, "she doesn't."

The big man met his eyes and nodded. "Anyway. You ready?"

The wanderer glanced around at the corpse-filled street. How many dead there? A dozen? Twenty? Too many, and that was all that anyone need know of it. Still, there was nothing he could do for them, and so, as he had many times before, the wanderer leapt onto Veikr's back and, once Dekker was situated, rode into the night, leaving the dead behind him.

CHAPTER NINE

They had barely ridden up into Dekker's small lawn when the big man's wife came rushing out of the door. "Oh, Dekker!" she said. "I was so afraid."

Dekker dismounted from Veikr's back as she sprinted toward him and his feet had barely touched the ground before she pulled him into a tight embrace. "I'm okay, love," the big man said as she buried her face in his neck. "Everything's alright. Why, I got my guardian angel right here, haven't I?"

Ella looked up from where her chin was on her husband's shoulder, meeting the wanderer's gaze with tears brimming with tears. "*Thank you,*" she mouthed, and the wanderer smiled, inclining his head.

Finally, the embrace ended, and Ella met her husband's gaze. "So, will you tell me what happened?"

Dekker fidgeted. "Well, see, it was nothin' really, El. Just a barfight. The boy, Bill, panicked is all and—"

'You listen to me, Dekker," Ella interrupted, "it was all well enough for me to pretend I had no idea what was going on before you started being in danger." Dekker opened his mouth preparing to speak, but she held up a hand, forestalling him. "Now, though, we're past that. If what you're doing has a chance of leaving me sleeping in a cold bed all alone, then you're going to tell me—all of it. Do you understand?"

Dekker turned to look to the wanderer as if for help, but the wanderer only smiled, giving a small shrug.

"Well?" Ella demanded, her eyes not leaving her husband. "Do you?"

Dekker winced, clearing his throat. "I understand, dear."

"Good," she said. "Now, come on inside. We'll get something on that bruise of yours—you know, the one where the *door* hit you, and then we'll talk. Once that's done, we'll get some sleep. With any luck, we might be able to manage some before sunrise."

The big man grunted. "You comin'?" he asked, turning to look at the wanderer.

The wanderer smiled, shaking his head. "The barn's good enough for me and Veikr. You go on."

The big man nodded. "Alright then."

"Goodnight, Ungr," Ella said.

"Goodnight."

The wanderer stood, watching, as the woman led the big man toward the house, one hand gripping his so tightly her knuckles were white, the other on his shoulder, as if she was afraid that, should she let go, even for a moment, he might float away.

Then, when the door closed behind them, he turned back to his horse. "A good family," he said.

Veikr tossed his mane at that, and the wanderer patted his muzzle. "I know," he said softly. "You want to stay. But you know we cannot. Staying, we only put them in danger—and not *just* them. The entire city. Now come, we will stay the night but in the morning we will—we *must*—leave."

He was not sure whether his words were for the horse, himself, or both, but either way he knew that they were true ones. He would do far more harm than good, should he stay. He knew this and yet the knowing of it did not stop the ache, born of loneliness, which began to form in his chest at the thought of leaving the family behind, of once more wandering the world alone.

He realized he had not moved and cleared his throat. "Come," he said again, and then he and Veikr walked toward the stables.

He unsaddled his horse and put him back into the stall once more. Once Veikr was taken care of, the wanderer climbed the ladder to the loft and lay among the hay. He lay there, but he did not sleep. Sleep was beyond him, in that moment, for his thoughts were too sharp, cutting, as he thought of continuing his unending journey again. And even had they not been, still he would not have slept. Twice, he had been lulled to gentle sleep by the peace being near the family provided and twice that sleep had been interrupted with violence.

So the wanderer only lay there, listening to the soft, sleeping sounds of the horse and donkey, listening to the sounds of the night, foreboding in its stillness. For sometimes, he knew, a man might see a storm approach, might mark it by the dark, angry clouds roiling toward him, by the distant crash of thunder. He might see it in curtains of hard rain as they came on, sweeping across the land. And in seeing this, the man might take steps to protect himself and those things for which he cared, might find shelter and prepare to wait it out. These storms were dangerous, but they were also predictable and so in their predictability lost much of their menace.

The worst storms of a man's life, though, did not announce themselves and their coming. Instead, they came upon him quietly, slipping into the silent moments where he believed himself safe. They came not as rampaging warriors but as thieves, as assassins, not seeking to destroy but seeking to rob him of all that mattered, so that in the end, he would destroy himself.

And so the wanderer lay in the stillness, in the silence, contemplating storms, thinking of those men and women taking shelter in the nobleman's home, of the family lying less than a hundred feet away, and wondered what shape this new storm might take.

***

The sun dawned red.

The wanderer, from his place in the stables' loft, watched as that red glow leaked its way in through the crack in the stable doors, slowly growing like a pool of spreading blood. Many might have discounted such a sign, claiming that omens and portents were only for the very old or the very young, but the Eternal had lived long, and he knew that dismissing a thing did not change it.

So he watched, a sense of foreboding growing within him, as that pool spread across the stable floor, making its way toward where Veikr still slept. He considered opening his locket and asking Oracle what she thought of it. He had spent some time training with her, as he had all the Eternals, but her lessons had been some of the most difficult for him, for she claimed that he had no natural aptitude for differentiating true signs from the many false ones the world provided. Saying things like "to tighten his grip, a man must first let go," or "to find a thing, a man must first lose it." The sort of things that didn't make sense to him even now, more than a hundred years later. In the end, she had done what she could, and he had done what *he* could, yet she had claimed that he would always be a hammer, and to hammers, everything must be a nail.

He stared at the growing puddle of crimson light on the floor. A false sign or a true one? The Oracle would know. His hand drifted to the locket hanging from his neck, but he hesitated. The ghosts, following his recent activity, would be restless, angry. How much scolding would he have to endure before finally speaking to the Oracle, likely only to learn that it was no more than a false sign? Perhaps, he told himself, when a man was not good at seeing signs, he should endeavor not to.

The thought, though, did little to quiet the anxiety in him. He rose, pulling on his boots and strapping his swords over his back. He climbed down the ladder then, waking Veikr, resaddling the horse and packing his meager belongings once more. He started to lead Veikr out of the stables then, at the doors, hesitated as he realized something.

He did not want to go.

For many years—all his life, it sometimes seemed—the wanderer had traveled alone, and he did not wish to do it any longer. And yet, now, as always, what he wished accounted for nothing. If he stayed, he would only put himself, the family, and the world in danger. He did not want to go.

And so he must.

And better to do it now, he thought, while the family still slept, than to remain and only make it more difficult. Veikr snorted softly beside him, as if aware of his thoughts, and the wanderer grunted. "I know," he said, "but don't fret. Life is a journey, remember, and as Oracle was so fond of saying, there is no knowing where that journey might take us. Perhaps we will see them again."

But the truth was that he did not think so and thought that maybe that was for the best. After all, was it not better for a man, destined to lose something of value, to have never possessed it in the first place? For through that possession he felt its absence all the more keenly, the way some amputees were said to still feel their phantom limbs.

"Come," he said, his voice rough. "We must be off."

He swung the door to the stables open, leading the horse out before closing them again. He did not look at the house where the family lay sleeping—did not dare to look. So he was more than a little surprised when a voice hailed him from the porch.

"Mornin'."

The wanderer turned, along with Veikr, to see Dekker sitting on the porch, his feet propped up in the second chair, a piece of long grass in his mouth.

"Good morning," the wanderer said.

"Damn strange sunrise, ain't it?" the big man asked.

The wanderer turned and looked up at the sun, seeming to glow red. "Yes."

The big man laughed. "That's the thing about you, ain't it, Ungr? You just talk too damn much. So," he went on, glancing at Veikr. "Planning on getting an early start of it?"

The wanderer, for reasons he could not explain, felt a stab of guilt at that. "I thought it might be best."

"Gettin' out while the gettin's good, eh?"

"Something like that."

Dekker nodded slowly. "Suppose you might be wonderin' what's roused me from my bed this early in the day."

"Suppose I might," the wanderer agreed.

The big man grunted. "Would you believe that I wake up about every mornin', round this time, just to watch the sunrise?"

The wanderer watched him for a moment then slowly shook his head. "No, I don't believe I would."

Dekker laughed at that. "Well, you got me there. Can't remember the last time I sat and watched the sunrise, and if they all look like that, I don't see as I've been missin' much."

"So if not to watch the sunrise," the wanderer said, "why are you awake?"

The big man scratched his chin. "Well, that's the question, ain't it? See, thing is, Ungr, I figured you might plan on gettin' an early start, and I thought it'd be a shame if I wasn't awake to say goodbye, to tell you thanks one more time for savin' my ass back there at the tavern."

"It's nothing," the wanderer said.

"Huh," the big man said. "Well, suppose you are wrong sometimes after all. Whatever it was, Ungr, what you did, what you kept me *from* doing, it certainly wasn't nothin'." He glanced back up at the sky then sighed. "It's a shit sunrise, sure, but I can't say I ain't glad that I'm here to see it."

Suddenly, the door opened, and Ella walked out. And behind her, a sleepy young girl, rubbing at her eyes. But her tiredness vanished in a moment as she saw Veikr, and she let out an excited shout before running at the horse and beginning to pet his muzzle. Veikr stood there, contentedly enjoying the treatment, and glanced sidelong at the wanderer as if to say he could learn a thing or two.

"Damn," Dekker said, "what are you two doin' awake?"

Ella glanced at him, raising an eyebrow archly. "I could ask you the same thing."

"Me?" the big man asked innocently. "Oh, I just came out to see the sunrise, that's all, make sure it's still there."

"Uh-huh," his wife said doubtfully before turning back to the wanderer. "You mean to leave already?"

"I thought it best."

"Without even saying goodbye?" the woman pressed.

It took an effort not to fidget, and the wanderer was well aware of Dekker grinning out of the corner of his eye. "I...sorry."

The girl paused in her petting of Veikr to glance back at her mother. "They don't have to leave, though, do they, Momma? Please, say they don't."

Ella shook her head. "Of course, not, sweetie." She glanced at the wanderer. "You're welcome to stay, you know. You and Veikr," she said, bowing her head at the horse with a smile, "as long as you like. Isn't that right, Dek?" she finished, glancing at her husband.

"That's right, love," Dekker said, meeting the wanderer's eyes, "but I don't think that they will."

The wanderer hesitated then, the three of them looking at him, feeling the weight of their hopeful gazes on them, a sort of comforting pressure. He could stay. How long had it been since he had been welcomed? Wanted?

And so what if I did stay? part of him demanded, a childlike, selfish part. *What would be the harm? What could it hurt?*

And then another voice, not that of the ghosts, but sounding like them. *You know what it could hurt,* the voice said. *Everything. It could hurt everything.*

He winced. "Thank you," he said, meaning it, "but...I really must go."

"But...but you'll come back?" the girl said hopefully.

"Yes," he said, telling the lie not just for the girl but for himself as well. "One day, I will come back."

She smiled at that, smiled past the tears in her eyes as she desperately petted the horse.

"Come on then, lass," her father said, clearly struggling to make his voice sound light. "Let's see about getting you some breakfast."

"Do I have to, Da?" she pouted.

"Yeah, princess," Dekker said, "I think you'd better."

The girl gave one more desperate pat to Veikr then hugged him tightly. "I love you," she said.

The horse neighed softly, as if in response, and then the young girl ran to the porch where her mother and father waited. The wanderer looked at the three of them standing there, and suddenly felt as if he owed them some explanation, a reason. But knowing it could do them no good—it could only hurt, so he cleared his throat where he felt a lump gathering. "I'm sorry," he said.

The girl, tearing up in earnest now, suddenly fled into the house. Ella and Dekker shared a troubled look. "I'd better go see to her," the woman said. She turned back to the wanderer. "Good luck, Ungr," she said. "And thank you again...for everything." Then, before he could respond, she turned and disappeared into the house.

The wanderer stared at the door, feeling cruel and not knowing what he could do about it.

"Don't worry about her, Ungr," Dekker said. "She'll be alright." He paused, meeting the wanderer's eyes. "Will you? Be alright, I mean?"

The wanderer considered that then shook his head. "I don't know. But I'll try. Goodbye, Dekker."

"Goodbye, Ungr. And safe travels."

The wanderer, knowing that his travels would be anything but safe, inclined his head, then turned and led his horse out into the city.

CHAPTER TEN

The wanderer allowed Veikr to guide them through the city, for his thoughts were elsewhere. Specifically, they were on the family and, by extension, those men and women who, along with Clint, were now sheltering in the nobleman's estate.

Had Soldier—the *real* Soldier—been there, he might have ordered him to clear his mind of distractions. Oracle, had she been present, might have told him to empty his mind, that it might be filled. Leader, always practical, would have told him to focus on the task at hand, to focus on moving forward. But they were not there. They were trapped inside the locket, and the locket was closed. And so the advice that they might have given went unsaid, went unheard.

And the wanderer went on through the city, barely paying any attention to those few he passed, men and women looking to get an early start on the day. He was distracted, emotional, and so, like the deer wandering innocently, naively, into the tall grass, he was unaware of those predators which lurked within it.

At least, that was, until they turned down an alleyway, and Veikr pulled to an abrupt stop, his nervous neigh jerking the wanderer from his thoughts. He looked up and saw that they were about halfway down an alleyway. At the alleyway's opposite end stood a figure. He appeared to be a man of average build. The man said nothing, only stood there, and the wanderer frowned, regarding the figure in silence.

There was something odd about the man, the way he stood so still, as if he were not a man at all but some statue sculpted to appear as one. There was something else about the man that bothered the wanderer, but at first, he couldn't place it. Then he did.

The morning was warm, unseasonably so, yet the stranger, whoever he was, wore a long-sleeved tunic and long trousers which covered every inch of him. He wore a mask, hiding his face, with a cloak and hood pulled over his hair so that not a single part of his skin showed. But what struck the wanderer the most was the man's gaze showing beneath his hood. It was a cold, dead gaze, flat and empty and devoid of all human life, all human emotion.

"*Shit,*" he hissed.

He gave Veikr's reins a pull, turning the horse in the other direction only to find that another figure stood in that entrance of the alleyway as well.

Fool, he cursed himself inwardly. *This is what comes of allowing yourself to be distracted.* As Soldier might have said, a blade is only useful so long as it remains sharp.

He considered trying to charge through the man. Surely, anyone gazing upon the scene, would have thought that the giant horse upon which he rode would have had no difficulty in riding over the figure waiting at the other end of the alleyway. But then, they would have been wrong.

"*Damn,*" the wanderer said. He looked around for any means of escape, but there was nothing, not even so much as a locked shop door or a window he might crawl through and even had there been, he would not have left Veikr.

Slowly, he dismounted. The figures remained still as he did, seemingly in no hurry. Veikr snorted and gave his head an angry shake, but the wanderer patted him. "No, boy," he said. "You remain. And...should the worst happen, escape. If you can."

The figures continued to watch, wordlessly, as he drew his blade. Then, slowly, they started forward, like two ends of a trap snapping together to kill whatever unfortunate fool had wandered into it.

The wanderer knew that, should he allow both those ends to close, should he allow them to both come upon him at once, he was doomed. So instead, he did the only thing he could. He charged the nearest.

The figure continued toward him, undaunted by his charge. As the wanderer drew near it, the figure reached out, as if meaning to grab hold of him, but the wanderer, now at a sprint, fell to his knees, sliding past it and bringing his sword around as he did. The blade bit deep, cleaving through the figure's midsection, then striking something—its spine, perhaps—with a brutal impact and the wanderer just managed to keep hold of his sword as he turned his slide into a roll, coming to his feet at the end of the alleyway.

He turned, looking over his shoulder at the figure, still facing the other end. Wanting it, *willing* it to fall. But the figure, despite the fact that it had been cleaved through, did not fall. Instead, it turned slowly to face him, and even as it did the wanderer saw that the great, bloodless chasm the sword had carved began to heal, flesh seeming to grow within it. In moments, there was no proof that he had struck the creature at all save a ragged tear in its tunic.

"Shit," he said again.

The wanderer had encountered such creatures before, in his travels, but always he had been able to outrun them, for while they seemed to heal from nearly any wound, and while they were possessed of a strength far greater than normal men, they were not particularly fast.

Now, he stood at the end of the alley, both creatures on the opposite side of him, and so he *could* run, but to do so would mean leaving Veikr, his horse, his friend these last one hundred years, to the mercy of creatures which had none.

The ghosts would have told him to go—he knew this—but then the ghosts did not love Veikr the way he did, for they were beyond such conceits as love and hate. In their perpetual pseudo-life, they felt only emotionless practicality. The wanderer had thought himself much the same over the years, had come to believe that he, too, was becoming little more than a ghost, an empty shell, like some automaton who felt no joy or pain or grief, who only existed for its purpose and that only.

Since meeting the family, though, he had discovered that he had been wrong. He was not a ghost—he was a man. He was a part of the world.

And he did not run.

Instead, he started back toward the creature, his sword held down at his side. It waited, watching him with its empty eyes, and he wondered what it thought, wondered if it thought anything. The creature had been a man once, and though the enemy's attentions had stripped away its humanity, he wondered if scraps of that humanity still clung to it.

It does not matter, he told himself. *It is what it is, and you are what you are. You are a blade, and a blade is made for one thing and one thing only—to cut.*

And so he did. The wanderer charged forward again, lunging at the creature's heart, a fatal blow. The creature tried to intercept the blade with its hands, but it was too slow, and the wanderer felt a great relief as the steel sank deep into its chest, piercing its heart.

That relief faded in another moment, though, when the creature did not collapse as it might have. Instead, it grasped the blade with one hand, unaware or uncaring about the sharp steel cutting into its flesh. The wanderer thought that it meant to jerk the blade free, but he was wrong, and by the time he had realized his mistake the creature had already pulled the blade deeper into itself, dragging him along with it.

The creature's other fist swung in an almost casual gesture, and the wanderer turned, ducking his head so that the blow hit him in the shoulder instead of the face. A good thing, as it turned out, for the blow was shockingly powerful, and he cried out as incredible pain ran up his arm as if he had been struck with a smith's mallet. He stumbled away, his arm already numb, and his sword was left piercing the creature's chest, as he shuffled backward, his teeth clenched in agony.

The creature stared at the blade in its chest as if it were a puzzle it was trying to work out, then it drew it out, continuing to hold it by the blade instead of opting to use the handle. It tossed the blade to the alley floor as if it were a trinket of no use and, more importantly, no danger. The wanderer heard Veikr neigh and shot a quick look past his adversary to see that the other figure had reached his horse. Veikr spun, lashing out with his back legs in a kick that would have broken any mortal man. The kick sent the creature flying back down the alleyway where it struck the ground hard, and the wanderer held his breath as it lay, unmoving, hoping.

But those hopes were to be dashed a moment later as the creature began to climb its way to its feet, its chest, caved in by the horse's powerful blow, already beginning to reform.

The wanderer wanted to help his mount, but he knew that to try would only doom them both. For now, the horse was on his own. His own opponent walked toward him, taking its time, in no hurry, and the wanderer's mind raced, looking for some way, if not to victory, then at least escape.

It was ironic, perhaps, considering that these creatures worked for the thing that had replaced Soldier, that he might hear his old mentor's words in his head now. *If you're in trouble, Youngest,* he had said, *then the quickest way out is always the same—forward.*

"Okay then," the wanderer said quietly. "Okay." He charged the creature again, only this time, leaping into the air at the last moment and putting both of his feet forward. The creature might have been strong, might have been able to heal from nearly any wound, but that did nothing to keep the force with which he struck it from knocking it from its feet.

Instead of leaping away, the wanderer grabbed hold of the creature's front as it fell, so that when it struck the alley floor, he was knelt atop it. Forced back by the power of his kick, the creature slid across the ground, and as it reached for him the wanderer rolled away, scooping up his sword and coming to his feet.

The creature, apparently unperturbed, started to rise, and with a shout of anger, the wanderer brought his sword down, one-handed, into the back of its neck as it sat up. No blood fountained out, but the creature's head was severed cleanly from its body, and the body itself collapsed to the alley floor, unmoving.

The wanderer stood panting for breath as he regarded it, his hurt arm throbbing painfully. Then, deciding that the creature would not heal from this wound, at least, he looked up just in time to see Veikr aiming another kick at his own opponent.

This time, though, the creature sidestepped the powerful blow, planting a fist in the horse's flank. Veikr cried out as his entire, muscular body, was rocked to the side, striking the alley wall hard before half-collapsing.

"*Veikr!*" the wanderer shouted. And then, hurt or not, tired or not, he was running, sprinting toward the creature who was calmly walking toward the horse, intent on finishing the job.

It never got the chance, for then the wanderer was there, just as the creature was reaching out toward his horse. He didn't have a good angle on its neck, so he did the next best thing he could think of, burying his sword in its stomach. He didn't stop there, though. Instead, he continued to charge forward, roaring as he poured every ounce of energy into the blow, not having a plan beyond getting the creature as far away from Veikr as he could.

He drove it farther down the alleyway at the point of his sword, but then the creature planted its feet, and he could push it no further. The creature grasped the sword in both hands, clearly intent on pulling it free. Instead of fighting it, the wanderer released his hold on the blade and grabbed the creature by the back of its hooded head, then made use of his own, not inconsiderable strength, and smashed the creature's face into the stone alley wall.

Powered by the wanderer's strength, the creature's face met the wall of stone, struck it, and then went *into* it in a shower of stone and a cloud of dust. The wanderer pulled it back to see that its features were twisted and broken but even then beginning to mend. The creature, if it felt any pain, did not show it. Instead it reached for him, but before it could grab him, he buried its face in the wall again. Again and again and again, roaring in anger. He kept at it until on the fifth time, the creature's head buried into the wall and then stayed there, the creature unmoving, hanging limply.

He was panting hard when it was finished, struggling to catch his breath. His left arm hung numb at his side, and the muscles of his right ached and burned from the exertion. He heard a pained whinny and turned to see that Veikr had climbed to his feet but that there was a tenseness to his posture that showed he was in pain.

The wanderer shuffled toward the horse, panting its muzzle. "Okay, boy?"

The horse gave a soft neigh as if to say that it had been better, and the wanderer grunted. "Sure, that'd make two of us." He started to mount then an idea struck him, and he froze. Now that the danger was past, and he was able to think things over, he did. The creatures had sought him, had come for him, and that was bad. What was worse, though, was that Soldier was apparently willing to use his monstrosities even inside the city itself.

The wanderer brought his hand to the locket hanging from his neck. He hesitated for only a moment before opening it.

At once, a storm of disapproving words erupted from the ghosts.

Normally, he had always shown the ghosts respect, shown them what he had thought their due for who they had been. Now, though, they were wasting valuable time, and he was angry. "*Quiet,*" he hissed and, to his surprise, they grew silent.

"Oracle," he said, a growing sense of disquiet rising with him, "can you sense anything about them? Where they came from? Why they are let loose in the city?"

Not...not from here, Youngest, the old woman's voice spoke. *To do such a thing would require a Sojourn, and you are wounded, hurting. It would not be wise to—*

"*Do it,*" the wanderer hissed, his thoughts on Dekker and his wife, on their child.

A brief hesitation from the old woman ghost. *Very well,* she said after a moment.

The wanderer closed his eyes, focusing on concentrating past the pain of his arm, the weariness of his body, and most of all, his fear. He pushed it all away. At first, they did not want to go. They sat like great boxes in front of the door, the one that must be opened. Growling with anger, he concentrated harder, shoving them aside and clearing the door, which he threw open.

An old woman stood on the other side, looking like someone's favorite grandmother in a simple linen dress, a gray shawl over her shoulders. The only remarkable thing about her appearance was her eyes, eyes that appeared to have no pupils but were instead completely white. "Come in," the wanderer said. "Quickly."

The old woman did as was asked, stepping into his body, his mind.

The wanderer had suffered the strangeness of Sojourns before over the last hundred years, allowing the ghosts to take control of his faculties, but never before had he been hurting, physically and emotionally, as much as he was now. He had thought he had grown accustomed to that strange pain, the feeling of being invaded, but he was wrong, and he gasped for breath as her entering felt to him like being plunged into a freezing lake.

Under the grip of the pain, the vision of the room and the open door, representing his mind, faltered, began to blur.

You must hold on, Youngest, she said. *Only a little while now.*

Straining against himself, feeling as if he might *lose* himself, the wanderer did as she said. The old woman, using his body, shuffled toward the corpse of the second creature, still hanging with its head embedded in the wall, and then touched it.

The wanderer felt a great jolt of shock as she connected with the creature, with what remained of its life essence. For a second, nothing happened—then suddenly, knowledge began to pour into his mind. Bits and pieces, mostly, random and making no sense. There was the image of a woman, smiling. A mother, perhaps? A wife? Then another image of a baby rocking in its cradle. The man's child? Or the man himself? There was no way to know and no time to think of it for the images came in rapid succession, one after the other. Then, suddenly, the wanderer was confronted with another image, one which sent a lightning-crack of fear into his heart.

It was the image of a home, but not just any home. A nobleman's estate, one with a wrought-iron gate outside of it. He did not need to wonder at whose home it was, for the instant he saw it, he knew. It was the nobleman Will's home, the same place to which Dekker would travel with his family today, if he had not gone there already.

"*Out,*" he hissed.
Very well, very well, the ghost said, obviously reluctant, as they always were, to abandon a living body, *only, if we look deeper, perhaps—*

"*Out!*" the wanderer roared, and then he was grabbing her by her shawl, forcing her out of the door and slamming it shut.

Back in control of his own body, he shuffled toward Veikr, forced to keep one hand on the alley wall while his mind became acclimated to his body once more. "They are in danger, Veikr," he said, "the girl, her family. Far greater danger than they can imagine, do you understand?"

The horse snorted as if to say he did, and the wanderer nodded. "Can you walk?"

Veikr tossed his head, and the wanderer nodded. "If you can walk, then you can run. Come, Weakest, show me the error of your name."

He began to climb into the saddle, then paused at a voice.
Youngest.

It was Leader, a voice that would have once caused him to freeze in whatever he was doing to listen and even now, rushed as he was, scared as he was, he found himself stopping, one foot in the stirrups.

You know that to go to them would be to endanger everything, everyone. Them as well. You must not do this, Youngest. You cannot do this.

The wanderer hesitated there. He thought of Felden Ruitt, lying in a pool of his own spreading blood. He thought, too, of the girl's giggling, of Dekker's loud, carefree laugh, and Ella's quiet, contented smile. He thought of her asking him to look after her husband.

"You're wrong, Leader," he said finally. "I can do nothing else."

He snapped the locket closed, and then he was in the saddle. Hurting or not, wounded or not, he had never seen Veikr run faster than he did then, galloping through the city, leaving those few who were up at this hour to stare after them in shock and wonder.

CHAPTER ELEVEN

A thousand fears ran through the wanderer's mind as he and Veikr careened through the city. That he would not get there in time, that he would arrive only to find the dead, those well beyond saving. But despite his many worries, when they arrived at the gate, he discovered nothing troubling.

Nothing, at least, save for how empty the street was. Even at this hour, he had seen people in the city, if not many, but the street upon which the noble's home was situated was completely empty. It was as if, on some level, the people of the city sensed what was coming. They did not know the specifics of what was coming, perhaps, but guided by some subconscious instinct engrained in men over centuries, they had avoided the street.

There was a guard at the gate, this one not wearing the uniform of a city guardsman but instead a uniform which marked him as the family's personal guard.

"Hello," the man said, smiling far more affably than any city guardsman might in the wanderer's experience, "how might I help you, sir?"

"I need to be let in," the wanderer said tiredly. "Now."

The man's smile slowly faded at that. "Forgive me, sir, but the family is not accepting visitors right now. Perhaps, if you come back la—"

"Listen to me," the wanderer hissed. "I know well who shelters beyond these gates, and I must speak with them. If you do not believe me, only go and ask, tell them that Ungr is here. But be quick about it, for there is little time."

The man frowned for another moment then nodded. "Just a moment, please, sir." Then the guard unlocked the gate, stepping through before closing it again, eyeing the wanderer one final time. Then he turned and walked into the grounds, moving past several expertly-shaped sculptures of men and women, likely the ancestors of the noble family, down a cobbled lane and turning not to head to the main house but to a large, if not as large as the first, house to the side of the property.

The wanderer watched him, willing him to move faster, to hurry, and then the man was beyond his sight, and he was left standing beside Veikr, the horse shifting anxiously beside him.

"Easy," the wanderer said, the word both for the horse as well as himself, "just take it easy. We are not too late."

The guard returned a few minutes later, not walking now but jogging. "Forgive me, sir," he said as he hurriedly set about the task of opening the gate, "I did not know who you were."

You still don't, the wanderer thought, *no one does. Even I am no longer sure.*

The gate swung open, and the guard motioned toward the house. "Please, sir, this way. I can escort you if—"

"Thank you, but that won't be necessary," the wanderer said as he moved past him, guiding Veikr down the cobbled path toward the waiting house. *Please,* he thought, *please don't let them be here, let Dekker have decided to stay with his family at their home, please.*

The door opened before he'd reached it, and the wanderer's heart sank as Dekker stepped outside, followed by Clint, the leader of the Perishables, and Will, the young nobleman.

"Ungr," Dekker said, grinning. "Decided you couldn't stay away, eh? Must be the charm my wife's always claimin' I don't have. Anyway, what's all the hurry about?"

"You're already here," the wanderer said, trying to get his head around it. "Listen, Dekker, it isn't safe here, you have to get your family and—" He cut off as another figure stepped out of the door, the young girl, Sarah.

"Daddy, what is it, what's—" she froze as she saw Veikr, her eyes going wide, and she squealed in delight as she rushed toward the weary horse. "What's wrong with him?" she asked after a moment, looking up at the wanderer.

"He's had a long morning," the wanderer said. *We both have.* "He'll be okay."

Dekker glanced at his daughter and at the wanderer's face then winced. "I'm sure Veikr could use some rest. Will, I wonder if you wouldn't show him to your stables, maybe see that he has something to eat? My Sarah can go with you, keep the horse company."

"O-of course, Dekker," the young nobleman said, bobbing his head and stepping forward. The wanderer let the nobleman take his horse's reins.

"I'll be along directly," he told Veikr, and the horse only plodded on wearily as he was led to the stables, the little girl flitting around him like an excited bee.

"Alright, Ungr," Dekker said, not smiling now, "what's all this about?"

"They're coming for you," the wanderer said, not daring to waste any time, "all of you," he finished, looking at Clint.

"But that can't be," Dekker said. "We only just got here, they couldn't know where we are, could they?"

"How do you know this, Ungr?" Clint asked.

"Does it matter?" the wanderer said. "I told you, they're coming. They'll be here soon—for all I know, they might already be on their way. You have to get out of here, all of you."

"But *how* do you know?" Clint pressed. "Did you hear it from one of the Eternal's men?"

The wanderer winced. "Something like that, yes."

"I see," the Perishables leader said, nodding thoughtfully. "And this man, can we speak to him?"

The wanderer tensed, feeling time slipping away. "No, you can't. Not unless you can speak to the dead."

"Ah," Clint said. "Well, perhaps you're right, Ungr. Perhaps they are coming, but then they have come for us before, haven't they? And yet, they were beaten. Anyway, it seems to me that if they *are* coming, we will be much safer here in William's gated estate than we would be out in the street where they might come upon us from anywhere."

The wanderer gritted his teeth, forcing himself to remain calm. "You do not understand," he said. "What comes is something far beyond you, far beyond normal guardsmen who you might best and send fleeing in fear. What comes does not *feel* fear, and it will not flee. Neither will it stop, not until you and all the others are dead, do you see? You have to run, run *now* before it's too late."

"Say that you're right," Clint said, "say that we *do* run...where do you imagine we would run to, Ungr? We've got more'n fifty men and women here. Men and women with families, with children. They can't just up and leave the city, what would happen to their loved ones?"

"And what will happen to them if they stay?" the wanderer countered. "Look, it doesn't matter *where* you run, just that you do." He turned, looking to Dekker, pleading now. "You've got to get your family out of here. Please. Run wherever you want, only *run.*"

Dekker hesitated for several seconds then, looked up, clearly having come to a decision. "And what then, Ungr?" he asked quietly. "Will I just spend the rest of my life runnin'?"

"At least you'll *have* a life," the wanderer said.

The big man sighed heavily, shaking his head. "A man can only run for so long, Ungr. Sooner or later, he's got to find somethin' worth stickin' for, worth *standin'* for."

"Even if it kills him?" he asked.

The big man gave a slight shrug of his shoulders. "Maybe especially then. A man's got to find somethin' worth riskin' his life for to even be called a man, don't he? And my family, Ungr...I'd risk anything for them, so that they could have a better life. Anyway, call me a fool, but I believe, I have *faith* that no matter how dark this world can sometimes be, Ungr, light'll always win out."

"I cannot talk you out of it?" the wanderer asked, glancing between the two men. They did not answer, at least with words, but then they did not need to—their determined expressions were answer enough.

The wanderer considered the two men for several more seconds. Dekker said that a man had to find something he was willing to stick, to *stand* for. Another way of saying he had to *believe* in something. The wanderer had once been such a man, long ago, when he had first sought to join the illustrious ranks of the Eternals, intent on making the world better. That belief had faded over the years, eroded by time and despair and one tragedy after another.

After all, he *had* stood, hadn't he? He and the other Eternals, standing against the greatest threat the world had ever faced like the heroes out of some bard's tale. Only, unlike those heroes from the stories, they had lost, and the wanderer had watched as each of the Eternals, his friends, his family, had been cut down. Since then, he had spent his life running, moving from one place to another, not giving any thought to victory, only to staying ahead of his pursuers.

And as he stood there, looking at the two men, fools, perhaps, but brave ones, the wanderer came to a realization. He was tired of running. Perhaps, in the end, standing would mean death—there was no way of knowing that, for even Oracle could not predict such a thing. What he *did* know, though, was that running was its own kind of a death. A slow death, maybe, an erosion of his beliefs, of himself, until he was no more than a shell. A death that took years, decades, but a death just the same.

"Very well," he said after a time, "then I will stand with you."

"Really?" Dekker asked, sounding at once surprised and relieved. "But...I thought, well, from all you said, I thought you didn't think we had any chance."

"I don't," the wanderer said honestly, then gave a small smile. "But some things are worth standing for."

The big man grunted a laugh, clapping him on the back. "You're a good man, Ungr. You try to hide it, but you're a good man just the same."

A good man. The wanderer couldn't remember the last time he'd thought of himself in such a way. Not since running from the final battle, at least. A hundred years or more, a hundred years during which he had thought himself a coward, a failure, shouldering the guilt of that loss, the one which had put the entire world and all the people in it in great danger.

Once, when he was much younger, he had sought to be an Eternal, to make a difference, yes, but he could not deny that there had also been a part of him that had loved the idea of being adored, being respected, the way the Eternals were. Now, he realized that the respect of the world meant little when compared to the respect of a good man. "Thanks," he said.

Clint nodded slowly. "Well, then. Now that's settled, what d'you say we get inside. If things are goin' to get as bad as Ungr here says, I reckon it best we have a plan."

"A plan aside from dyin' horribly you mean?" Dekker asked.

"Right," Clint said, giving him a tight smile, "aside from that." He turned back to the wanderer. "I'd be mighty grateful, you'd join us."

The wanderer inclined his head.

The Perishables leader nodded, a thankful expression on his face. "Good," he said. "Then come—we will sit and eat. And plan."

***

The wanderer followed them inside the house into a large and ornately decorated foyer then through it into a large dining room, though dining "hall" might have been closer to the truth. One glance at the gold and silver furnishings, the paintings and sculptures adorning the wall, and it was clear that whatever else Will the nobleman was, he was most certainly rich.

There was a large table—nearly big enough to host a small army in the center of the room which was just as well, considering that, just then, it very nearly was. Men and women were seated around the table, chatting while they ate from various platters, grinning and laughing as if they were on vacation. Understandable, perhaps, the wanderer thought, considering that they were sitting in a far finer room eating a far finer meal than any of them had likely ever imagined.

Understandable, but considering what they faced, not forgivable.

Some of his feelings on the matter must have shown in his expression as he gazed out at the table, for Dekker clapped him on the back. "Easy, Ungr," he said quietly. "They're just trying to relax a little, that's all."

"Relax enough and you'll die," the wanderer said, automatically reciting another of Soldier's favorite sayings.

Dekker and Clint winced at that. "Why don't you come, have a seat?" Clint asked. "You can get something to eat—I'm sure you must be hungry. And we can talk about what's to be done."

The wanderer shook his head slowly. "Later—there's something I need to do first."

"Oh?" Clint asked. "Any way we can help?"

"Yes," the wanderer said, "just don't bother me. I'll be back."

He left the two men staring after him as he turned and walked back out of the room. Perhaps, he thought, he shouldn't have been so abrupt, but he had other things on his mind now than social niceties. Things like how he was going to keep them all alive for the next twenty-four hours.

He walked out of the manse, closing the door behind him then glanced around, making sure that he was alone. No one else walked among the grounds, and he could hear the muffled sounds of delight from the girl where she and the nobleman attended Veikr in the stables.

Alone, then, and this time, at least, glad of it.

He took a slow breath, preparing himself, then he opened the locket. As usual, a deluge of disapproval washed over him as all the ghosts talked at once.

"Quiet," he said, "there is no time."

But there is time yet, Youngest, Leader said. *You have made a bad decision here, but it is not too late to undo it. You might still yet leave. The creature impersonating Soldier knows you are in the city now which means that the enemy as a whole will know it, if they do not already. If you leave now—*

"I will not leave."

Then you will die, Youngest, Leader said, his voice sad.

"Then I will die."

And what of the world? What of those millions who will suffer because you chose death? Do you not think of them?

"I do not know them," the wanderer said honestly, glancing at the stables where he could hear the girl's laughter.

Ah. You think of the girl and her family. But even should they perish, Youngest, their lives mean nothing when compared to the life of the world, to the lives of everyone in it.

"You're wrong," the wanderer said, contradicting him, a thing he never would have done in the past. "They don't mean nothing— they mean everything, and I will not leave them. Now, enough talk. Tactician, I have need of you to see what might be done while there is still time yet to do it."

Even my expertise cannot help you in this, Youngest, Tactician said. The man had been a nobleman once, long ago, and though he had lived as an Eternal for centuries after his birth and had lived another century as a ghost in the locket, still he had not fully lost the arrogance to which he had been born. Yet arrogant or not, the wanderer knew that he was his only chance.

"It is your choice, of course," the wanderer said. "Only know that I and those others with me will fight this battle with or without your help."

What battle? Tactician demanded. *You have no defensive fortifications, Youngest, save a wrought-iron gate and fence that looks ready to collapse should the wind pick up. You have no heavy cavalry to create a breach in the lines, and no footmen to take advantage of it even if you did. You have no army at all, Youngest. This will not be a battle—this will be a massacre. Those men and women, those fools, will die. They can only die.*

"Then I will die with them," the wanderer growled, angry now, letting his emotions get the better of him. He took a slow, deep breath, centering himself. "You can help or you can refuse—that is your choice. Just know that I remain, whatever choice you make, for I have already made mine."

An angry hiss from the nobleman ghost, but no more than that and for several seconds, there was silence.

"Very we—" the wanderer began, cutting off as Leader spoke.

Lend him what aid you can, Tactician, the ghost said, a note of resignation in his normally confident tone.

Fine, Tactician said, *though I still call it folly.*

"Noted," the wanderer said. "Now, are you ready?"

You must first walk the grounds, Tactician said irritably, *let us see what we have to work with—pretty statues and mole droppings, likely.*

The wanderer did as asked, taking his time, walking around the perimeter of the fence, ignoring the guard who watched him curiously. He kept at it for nearly an hour, Tactician's steady stream of commentary—mostly derogatory—interrupted only as the wanderer asked questions to clarify one point or another. He was so involved in the discussion, in the preparation, that he did not notice Dekker walking up behind him until the big man spoke.

"Ungr."

He spun, his hand halfway to drawing his blade, and the big man grunted, taking a step back and holding up his hands. "Damn, you really are fast. Hey, sorry, I didn't mean to surprise you."

"My fault," the wanderer said. "What is it?"

"Well," the big man said, "you just sort of walked off kind of abruptly back there. I just thought I'd check, make sure everything was alright."

In fact, things weren't alright. The last hour had been an enlightening one listening to the Tactician, for whatever else the ghost was, he was an unrivaled genius when it came to military strategies and defensive tactics, viewing the fight to come and what they had to work with like a chess master might the board, seeing dozens, hundreds of moves and countermoves. But however he analyzed it, the result seemed to be the same—imminent death for him and all those involved. "Everything's fine," he lied.

The big man watched him carefully, as if he could see some of his thoughts on his face, then he nodded. "You're alone then?" he asked, glancing around.

"Why wouldn't I be?"

Dekker grunted, waving a hand. "Just thought I heard voices is all."

"Talking to myself, I guess."

"Hey, no judgement here," Dekker said, grinning. "Been doin' a bit of prayin' myself. Imagine that's what you were up to?"

"Say that I was," the wanderer said, and that, at least, was not a complete lie. After all, the Eternals had been revered as gods for centuries. They still were, in fact, though no one knew that those brilliant men and women they revered had been replaced by the cruelest, most dangerous creatures the world had ever faced. No one, at least, save him.

"Well, as I said," Dekker said, "I won't fault you for it." He watched the wanderer for a second. "You're still thinkin' I'm a fool for stayin', aren't you?"

The wanderer considered the question then shook his head. "No. Not a fool. You hope," he said. "And hope is a good thing. I had forgotten that, for a while."

"Remembered now, have you?" Dekker asked, grinning.

The wanderer found that, despite the last hour spent listening to Tactician telling him the thousands of ways they would die, that he was smiling as well. "I begin to," he said.

"Well, that's somethin'," Dekker said. "Now, do you have any tips on how we might survive what's comin'?"

"Aside from running, you mean?"

"Yeah," the big man laughed, "aside from that."

The wanderer nodded. "I think that I do, but first, I will need to speak to the nobleman, Will."

"Sure," Dekker said. "He came inside a little while ago, think he's eatin' with the rest."

"Show me to him."

The big man nodded, leading him without another word back into the large guest house where the others waited. The wanderer noted Ella, sitting with her young daughter off to one side, the girl apparently having returned from the stables while he was examining the grounds. The woman waved, and the wanderer waved back, then forced thoughts of the two out of his mind. He could afford no distractions, not now, when every minute squandered would be paid for in blood.

He followed Dekker to the nobleman who sat beside the Perishable leader, Clint, though just then Will was speaking with another man, grinning and laughing at some apparent joke.

"Your name is Will, isn't it?" the wanderer said without preamble.

The nobleman looked up, blinking, and the wanderer noted the drink-induced flush to his cheeks. "It is."

"Do not drink anymore, Will," the wanderer said. "Nor any of you," he went on, speaking loudly enough to be heard over the many conversations being had in the room, and everyone turned to him.

"What's this?" a familiar voice asked, and the wanderer glanced over, unsurprised to see that it was the big man, Hank, who'd spoken. "Tellin' us what to do?"

"Yes," the wanderer said, "I am."

There was a pregnant silence as the big man frowned at him, and Clint spoke. "He's right, Hank. All of you—no more drinking."

"That so?" Hank asked. "He the leader now or somethin', Clint? What's this all about?"

"It's about surviving," the wanderer answered. "Unless, of course, you'd rather be slaughtered to a man. Then, I suppose, drink as much as you like—it makes little difference to me."

Those few who had not set their glasses down paused then, their eyes going wide, and in another moment, no one in the room was still holding a drink in his or her hand.

"Good," the wanderer said, turning back to the nobleman. "Now, do you have any weapons here?"

"W-weapons?" the nobleman asked uncertainly.

"You know," the wanderer said, his face expressionless, "the sorts of things that those who come will be using to kill us with."

The nobleman winced, his face flushing further. "Um...well, there's a small armory, for the guards on duty here and those my father hires to protect his caravans from bandits. A few more, I guess, of my father's—swords and spears, mostly. He's a bit of a collector," the nobleman finished almost shyly.

"Good," the wanderer said. "Go and get them."

"S-sure," the nobleman said, "uh, which ones?"

"All of them."

"O-of course, anything else?"

"Do you have any wine?"

"Y-yes, sir," the nobleman said, "but I thought we weren't to drink anymo—"

"Not for drinking," the wanderer said. "Show me."

The young man glanced at Clint, and the leader of the Perishables nodded. "Do as he asks, Will."

"Of course," the nobleman said, "this way."

"I will return shortly," the wanderer told the older man. "When I do, I will tell you what can be done."

Then with that, the nobleman started away. *Alright, Alchemist,* the wanderer thought as he followed the young man, *you're up.*

CHAPTER TWELVE

By the time the preparations were finished—or, at least, as finished as they were likely to get—night was coming on.

The Perishables had returned to the guesthouse to prepare. The wanderer, who had made it a point to always be prepared, stood in the stables with Veikr, running his hand across the anxious horse's muzzle in hopes of calming him. In hopes, too, of calming himself.

You have done what you could, Youngest, Leader said, and the wanderer thought he detected a hint of grudging respect in the ghost's voice. *You have, in the space of hours, turned a nobleman's luxury home into a relatively formidable fortress.*

With no small help from me, Tactician put in.

Leader ignored the other ghost, speaking on. *Thanks to your efforts, those fifty some odd men and women might stand some small chance against the weight of the city guard that is likely to come upon them. But whether they are to win or lose, you know that you cannot help them, don't you?*

The wanderer frowned. He had been thinking of that, during the preparations, and Leader, of course, was right. The last thing Soldier knew, he had been leaving town. Likely, the creature thought he had fled the city. After all, the same thing had happened dozens, hundreds of times over the years. Soldier would not have expected him to come here. But should the wanderer fight, it would not be long before Soldier heard of it, and with the cursed blade as his possible prize, there was, the wanderer knew, nothing the creature would not do to see them all destroyed.

The wanderer would be forced, then, should the worst happen, to watch his friends die, to watch them die as he had watched his other friends, so long ago. To watch and, in the end, to flee.

If it helps, Youngest, Tactician said, in a voice that, while still possessed of the man's usual arrogance, also held a note of compassion, *commanders are squandered on the front line. Better that you remain in the back, so that you might direct the defense.*

"Yes," the wanderer said.

And should you win the day, Youngest, Leader said, *what will you do then?*

"I don't know."

I see. Will you remain, attempting to guard men who have set themselves against an evil they do not, cannot understand? One against which they can only fail?

"I don't know."

And what will you do, I wonder, Leader persisted, *should Soldier choose to send more than only guardsmen after you and your companions? What will you do should he send some of his...experiments?*

"*Then we will die,*" the wanderer hissed angrily, snapping the locket closed.

"Ungr?"

He turned from Veikr to see that Dekker had walked up to them. "Yes?"

"It's time," the big man said grimly. There was no need to ask him what time he meant, for the wanderer knew well enough. It was time for blood. Time for death. The only question was whose death it would be.

"Very well," he said. "Are the men in position?"

"They are."

"And your wife and daughter, are they—"

"Already in the cellar," the big man interrupted. "We are ready, Ungr."

At least as ready as we can be, the wanderer thought, but he nodded. "They are outside the gate?"

"Yeah. Marchin' in even as we speak."

The wanderer nodded. "Then I will go and speak to them."

"Speak?" Dekker asked confused. "Do you think it will help?"

The wanderer considered that for a moment then shook his head. "No, but that does not mean that we should not try."

He started away and Veikr let out an anxious snort. He turned back to the horse, patting its muzzle. "Not this time, friend," he said. "I'm afraid you'll have to wait this one out."

He turned to Dekker and gave a nod. "Let's go."

They stood outside the gate, a hundred men, at least, all wearing the uniforms of city guardsmen, many holding torches. Not that they needed them, for one of the steps the wanderer had taken was to have lanterns and torches placed throughout the property. After all, if a man could not see, how could he be expected to fight?

The wanderer chose his path carefully as he made his way across the darkness-laden trail. Approaching the gate, he walked past a dozen Perishables, the pitchforks and chair legs they carried as weapons a far cry from the swords of the guardsmen.

A man stood at the front of the rows of guardsmen, the insignia on his breast marking him as the commander. "*You know why we are here,*" the commander bellowed. "*We have come for those rebels who call themselves Perishables. I give you this chance and this chance only—open the gate and let us in, now, and you might be shown mercy. After all, our venerated leader is nothing if not merciful. If you refuse, then you will all die here tonight.*"

The wanderer came to stand in front of the gate, Dekker standing grimly beside him. He allowed the silence to descend for a moment, then he spoke. "I also, offer you a chance. Turn around now and leave this errand to others. For you do not know that creature whom you serve, not truly. I must believe that there are those among you who are innocent, who seek only to fulfill your duty. I ask you to please leave this. Leave it while you can, for the blood that will be spilled here tonight will not be ours alone."

The commander sneered. "You dare to ask these loyal men to forego their oath to their rightful ruler?"

"No," the wanderer said, "I ask them to forego their oath to a liar, a murderer, an impostor, and worse."

"How dare you blaspheme Soldier?" the man said, his face flushed with anger. "Enough. *Guards, break down the gate!*"

"Very well," the wanderer said as the men separated and half a dozen carrying a battering ram moved forward. "You have made your choice."

He turned and walked away, and Dekker followed. "What now?" the big man asked, an unmistakable note of nervousness in his voice.

"Now it begins," the wanderer said grimly.

And, indeed it did, for in another moment there came the tortured groan of metal as the battering ram struck the gate, again and then again. The craftsman who had fashioned the gate had done so with an eye toward its aesthetic properties, not intending it to be used as a true means of defense, and the wanderer knew it would not take long for them to break their way through.

He moved to stand beside the dozen or so Perishables, all of them looking nervous now or outright frightened. The wanderer understood. It was easy to be brave in a warm dining hall with your friends gathered close. It was quite another when it came time to bleed.

"Steady," he said softly. "You know what to do."

He turned back to the gate. Already, the metal frame had been bent and twisted by the battering ram's blows. Another strike, perhaps two, and the guards would be inside the grounds. The only consolation was that they would not be able to work their way over the fence, for in their preparations, he'd had the Perishables pile up the lawn's many statues and benches around the fence so that any man meaning to scale it as a point of ingress would be forced to clear the debris first.

"Think it'll work?" Dekker said. "The traps, I mean?"

"We're about to find out," the wanderer said.

Another blow, and the gate gave way with a tortured squeal of metal. The guards, perhaps eager to get the thing done—or more likely, eager to display their loyalty—rushed through the gate the moment it was down, charging at the meagerly-armed defenders, their swords drawn.

"Wait," the wanderer said quietly as several of those present began to fidget. "Just wait."

The men charged farther into the lane, toward the defenders, and then, when he judged that at least half of the hundred guardsmen were through, the wanderer looked up at a large oak near the gate where, unseen in the darkness, a man waited. *"Now!"* he roared.

There was a spark, then another, a muttered curse, and the wanderer had time to think that it would all fall apart because of something so simple as the man unable to light a rag. But then, when things did fall apart, more often than not, he knew that the cause was usually a simple one.

Just when he was beginning to despair, flame bloomed in the shadowed confines of the tree's canopy and a blazing bottle fell down. A dozen things could have gone wrong then. The man could have missed, the wind could have knocked the flame out, or many others. But, for once, at least, nothing did.

The flame fell, striking the oil-soaked ground and suddenly the grass blazed to life like some demon. A line of fire, suddenly as tall as a man, shot out as if eager to devour the guardsmen, cutting a line across them to the other side of the gate.

Men screamed in the middle of the press, crying out in agony and terror as they were set alight. More still were stampeded by their comrades, uncaring of their companions and wanting only to escape the burning flames.

But two dozen, at least were at the front, far enough in to avoid the flames, and they continued charging.

"Now," the wanderer said, *"retreat."*

He and the others turned and ran into the darkness, and the guards, roaring in anger, rushed after them.

When he was far enough away, the wanderer turned to watch their progress. Had they chosen to come in the day, instead of like thieves in the night, then the guards would have likely noticed the strange lumps in the ground where the turf had been torn up. But they had chosen darkness, and so they did not see what awaited them until the ground disappeared beneath their feet and they fell into pits prepared with large stakes.

They screamed then. Terrible, wailing cries of despair, of fear and pain, but the wanderer closed his heart to them. They had chosen, unwittingly or not, to serve the enemy, and so had chosen their fate.

"Oh gods be good," Dekker said as he stood beside the wanderer, his voice breathless as he gazed out at the burning men, listening to their screams as well as those of their companions, impaled on wooden stakes. "What have we done?"

"What we had to," the wanderer said. "And there is more to do yet. You must go and ready the others."

"O-of course," the big man said, wiping his hand across his mouth, his eyes as wide as dinner platters in the darkness, yet despite his words, he did not move.

"Dekker," the wanderer said.

"I-it's so terrible," the man said quietly, almost as if he was talking to himself.

"*Dekker,*" the wanderer snapped, and this time the man turned to him. "Those men, if given the chance, will kill you, and they will not stop there, do you understand?"

The man turned, unconsciously looking back at the house where his wife and daughter sheltered. "Yes," he croaked.

"Good," the wanderer said. "Now go—hurry. Those flames will not last long."

The big man rushed off into the night, and the wanderer stood with the ill-equipped Perishables, all of them staring in shock at the sight of the dying guardsmen as if they could not believe that, in a battle, men might die, or perhaps just how easily they did so.

In time, the screams quieted as many of those who had been caught in the flames or the pits breathed their last. Quieted, but did not stop altogether, for some men were wounded but still alive, at least for the time.

The flames began to die down, helped along by the guardsmen who used branches and some of the debris that had been stacked against the walls to put them out.

"*You will all be made to suffer for that!*" the commander roared from the other side of the flames, his voice choked with fury.

The wanderer glanced at the Perishables, their sickly faces of horror, and thought that they suffered already, but he turned away in another moment, back to the gate. Men make their choices, that's all, and the only thing that might be truer is that they all must live with them.

Once the flames were mostly put out, the remaining fifty or so guardsmen poured through the gate, though they slowed as they breached it, carefully picking their way among the pits and the terrible fates which had befallen their companions.

The wanderer and those others standing with him continued to retreat, backing away slowly, until they were against the noble's house, left with nowhere else to go.

The guardsmen came on grimly, their commander at their front, until they were all past the traps, standing in the center of the lawn, the guest house off to their right.

"Kill them all!" the commander roared.

Eager to avenge their fallen brethren, the guardsmen rushed forward, closing the distance between them and the ragged group of defenders quickly, so intent on their cornered quarry that they did not take note of the dozens of figures rising like phantoms from the dark grass to their right. Not, at least, until those figures, not armed with pitchforks and chair legs, these, but swords and spears, charged into their flank.

The wanderer saw Dekker at the front, wielding a massive two-handed axe with far more eagerness than skill and beside him, Clint, the old man carrying a spear. The guardsmen, alerted by the Perishables' shouts, spun to face them and so did not notice the other figures who rose on the other side of the lawn. These, too, charged into the guardsmen, along with those standing with the wanderer.

And then it was begun in earnest.

The Perishables had had no training in combat as the guardsmen had, and it showed. Despite the element of surprise, the wanderer saw several of them cut down in the first few minutes. The guardsmen also suffered casualties though, for while the Perishables might have lacked skill, eagerness they had in abundance.

The wanderer watched, his hands flexing anxiously.

You cannot help them, he told himself, *you know that.* Knew it right up until he saw Dekker stumble away from a sword strike, a jagged cut across his arm. The wanderer's sword was in his hand before he knew he intended to draw it, and then he was running, charging into the melee, his sword flashing in the darkness.

As always when he fought, the wanderer lost track of time, only focused on his feet beneath him, the sword in his hand, an extension of himself. After what might have been an hour or minutes, the thing was finished, the last guardsman cut down.

Less than two dozen Perishables remained standing. The guards all lay dead at their feet, and those survivors of the Perishables looked exhausted, several slumping to their knees, weary both in body and spirit.

As the wanderer sheathed his sword, Clint shuffled up to him. The old man bled from a wound on his head, thankfully not a deep one, and one of his arms hung limply at his sides.

Dekker came toward him also out of the darkness. The big man held his hand clasped against his upper arm, the sword he'd wielded nowhere in sight. For a time, the three of them stood silent, as did the other Perishables. There was no cheering, not now, as they all only stared at the devastation, at the dead, friend and enemy alike, taking in sights that the wanderer knew would haunt them all for the rest of their lives.

"It's...terrible, isn't it?" Dekker asked.

"Yes," the wanderer said. "In such a thing, there are no true winners."

"Thank you, Ungr," Clint panted. "I...I saw you, in the melee. You fought like...well. I've never seen anything like it."

The wanderer said nothing, for out of all the things of which a man might be proud, he did not think that his ability to kill other men should be one of them.

"*Who are they?*" a voice asked, drawing the three men's attention.

"*More guardsmen,*" another man growled, and the wanderer saw that it was Hank.

The wanderer followed their gazes to the gate where a dozen figures stood in long-sleeved tunics, masks about their faces, the hoods of their cloaks pulled down. They held no weapons, but that meant nothing, and a shock of fear went through the wanderer. "*No,*" he breathed. "*Not so many.*"

"*I'll show you bastards!*" Hank roared, and the big man charged toward the twelve.

"*Wait!*" the wanderer shouted, but the big man was beyond listening. He bellowed as he approached the nearest who only stood as the big man plunged the sword he held into its midsection.

There was a frozen moment in time as the figure only stood there, Hank staring at it, his posture revealing his shock. Then, the figure reached out, almost casually, grabbing hold of the big man's face and, with a brutal twist, snapped his neck. Hank fell dead at the figure's feet, and the figure proceeded to pull the blade out of its stomach, tossing it away.

"That...that's impossible," Dekker breathed.

"W-what kind of man could do such a thing?" Clint asked, understandable fear in the older man's voice.

"They are not men," the wanderer grated. "They are Revenants."

"What...what do we do?" the Perishable leader asked as those that remained of his men formed up into a ragged, terrified line.

The wanderer flexed his jaw. "Pull your men back."

"What?" Clint asked.

"Pull them back," the wanderer said again. "Against these, they can only die."

He drew his sword then, keeping the blade low and at an angle to the ground.

"What...what do you mean to do, Ungr?" Dekker asked.

He turned and looked at the big man. "What I have to." His gaze moved to Clint then, the old man looking unsure for the first time since he'd met him. "Should I fall, save those you can. You do not face guardsmen anymore. Do you understand?"

"Y...yes," the man said.

Clint shouted for the men to retreat, and they did so quickly, not attempting to hide their eagerness. As they moved past him, the wanderer stepped forward, walking until he was no more than a dozen feet in front of the nearest figures who only stood motionless, regarding him with their dead eyes.

He knew that he could not defeat so many. Two had nearly been more than he could stand. Against twelve, the outcome was not in doubt. He was simply not strong enough, not fast enough.

Not, at least, alone.

The thought seemed to come out of nowhere, but it was his own thought. If he fell, the others would die. He knew that. Not just Clint and the Perishables, but Dekker, too, his family. The creature masquerading as Soldier would not be satisfied until they were all dead, wiped from the face of the world as if they had never been.

But what a terrible choice it would be, he told himself.

Then: *What choice?*

He had watched his friends killed in front of him once. He would not do it again.

The wanderer reached over his shoulder and with his free hand clenched the handle of the cursed blade, a weapon of such power that he had been forced to flee with it, keeping it from the enemy and thereby saving the world. Or, at least, postponing its death.

Then, he did the unthinkable, a thing he had been striving to prevent for a hundred years.

He drew the cursed sword.

Power surged through him, *into* him like a firestorm threatening to scour everything in its path. The wanderer stood, trembling, gritting his teeth so hard his jaw ached and feeling as if he stood in the midst of some roaring storm. Just when he thought he could stand it no longer, the terrible force that had inundated him began to lessen.

"Come then," he growled at the creatures, the words sounding like a thundercrack in his head. "Let's get it done."

The creatures obliged, rushing forward, and he charged to meet them, bellowing his anger as he did.

The first he came upon stood, not even attempting to dodge his lunging blade before it tore into the figure's chest. The creatures had been twisted by the dark magics of the enemy, but the same alien power which had warped them was also coursing through the blade, through the wanderer himself, now. So as the cursed blade drove into the creature, it did not heal, not this time. Instead, it seemed to wither before the wanderer's eyes, as if the blade were draining what pseudo-life it possessed from it. With a growl, the wanderer pulled the blade free, and the dried, twisted husk that fell at his feet could hardly even be recognized as anything resembling a man.

They were all around him then, swinging their fists with blows that could kill in a single hit. The wanderer, imbued with supernatural strength and speed, fought better than he ever had, weaving in and out of their blows, using his normal steel to parry or knock the attacks off course enough to avoid being struck. Meanwhile, the cursed blade reaped a terrible harvest, sending one and then another of the creatures to the ground.

Something struck him in the back and magic blade or not, the blow felt as if he'd been kicked by Veikr. He went flying forward into two more of the Revenants, and then all three of them were on the ground. The wanderer tried to come to his feet but one of the creatures grabbed him by his jerkin, burying a fist in his stomach, and he cried out as several ribs cracked.

Then, roaring in agony, he let his regular steel drop from his hand. He grabbed the creature's wrist, pushing against its grip, not powerful enough to break free, but enough to afford him the space he needed to bring the cursed blade around, severing its head from its body.

He climbed his way to his feet, his left arm wrapped around his wounded ribs and saw that six of the figures remained. They did not hesitate as a normal man might at witnessing the fate that had befallen their comrades. Instead, they charged forward with no regard to their own safety. Wielding the blade in two hands, the wanderer waded into the creatures, aware of a terrible, burning pain in his hands where he gripped the cursed blade's handle.

The creatures were not built to dodge, to evade, but only to accept what blows came and destroy, so the job was easier than it might have been. Gritting his teeth against the terrible pain in his ribs and back, the wanderer scythed into them with the cursed blade, cutting down one, then another, shouting his fury as he did, fury built over a hundred years of fleeing.

A man has to stand for something, has to believe *in something.*

It seemed to go on forever, the ache in his arms a terrible pain, though nowhere near as bad as that in his ribs. Then, finally, there was only one left, not attacking him but only regarding him blankly. The wanderer stood, watching it, his breath rasping from his dry throat.

The creature continued to only stand there, and the wanderer stalked closer, burying his blade in its stomach. The Revenant grabbed him then, on either shoulder, leaned in close, and did something that sent a shiver of gooseflesh running over the wanderer's entire body.

It smiled.

Life suddenly came into the revenant's dead eyes as it bared its teeth, leaning closer still so that its face was only inches from the wanderer who could not break free of its grip.

"*I. See. You.*" the creature hissed.

The wanderer finally managed to jerk his way free, and the creature only stood there, still smiling, as his sword tore its head from its shoulders.

The headless body fell then, and the wanderer, seeing that there were none left, that this was the last, collapsed to his knees in front of it, exhausted and in terrible pain.

"*Ungr!*"

He looked up to see Dekker running toward him, the man falling to his knees beside him. "Eternals be good, I've never seen anything like that in all my life. You...you beat them."

"Yes," the wanderer croaked, looking at the cursed blade, still clenched in his fist where it sat against the blood-sodden ground. "But at what cost?"

"Come on," Dekker said worriedly, "we'll get you looked at. It's over now, Ungr. It's over."

The wanderer groaned as the big man pulled him to his feet with surprising gentleness, and he looked around at the dead things, the words the last had told him replaying over and over in his mind. "No, Decker," he said, swallowing hard. "The cursed blade has been free, the wandering sword found. This is not the end. It is only its beginning."

Now, dear reader, we have come to the end of *The Wandering Sword*. I hope that you enjoyed the read. Book two of The Last Eternal will be coming soon, so you don't have long to wait!

In the meantime, if you're looking for another book to dive into—don't worry. I've got you covered.

Want another story of an anti-hero in a grimdark setting where a jaded sellsword is forced into a fight he doesn't want between forces he doesn't understand?
Get started on the bestselling seven book series, *The Seven Virtues.*

Interested in a story where the gods choose their champions in a war with the darkness that will determine the fate of the world itself?
Dive into *The Nightfall Wars*, a complete six book, epic fantasy series.

Or how about something a little lighter? Do you like laughs with your sword slinging and magical mayhem? All the world's heroes are dead and so it is up to the antiheroes to save the day. An overweight swordsman, a mage who thinks magic is for sissies, an assassin who gets sick at the sight of the blood, and a man who can speak to animals…maybe.
The world needed heroes—it got them instead.
Start your journey with *The Antiheroes!*

If you've enjoyed The Wandering Sword, I'd appreciate it if you could take a moment to leave an honest review. They make a world of difference, and I'd love to hear your thoughts.

If you'd like to reach out and chat, you can email me at JacobPeppersAuthor@gmail.com or visit my website at *www.JacobPeppersAuthor.com*.
You can also give me a shout on Facebook or on Twitter. I'm looking forward to hearing from you!

Sign up for my VIP New Releases mailing list and get a free copy of *The Silent Blade: A Seven Virtues novella* as well as receive exclusive promotions and other bonuses!
Go to JacobPeppersAuthor.com to claim your free book!

Note from the Author

And so we have reached the end of *The Wandering Sword*. I hope you enjoyed the adventure, dear reader, and do not fret—we might have reached the end of this tale, but the larger one is just beginning. The cursed blade is drawn, the wanderer wanders no longer, and the true battle has only just begun.

This book was my, possibly poor but certainly heartfelt, fantasy homage to some of the classic westerns and western writers that I have enjoyed so much and was a joy to write. Which is why I can safely say that book two is well on its way, and you won't have to wait long!

Now then, I would like to take an opportunity to thank all of those who have made this book possible.

As always, first and foremost I want to thank my wife and two kids (soon to be three). I spend a lot of time in fantasy worlds, but you are what makes the real one not just bearable but incredible.

I would also like to thank my friends and family who manage convincing smiles of interest as I regale (read: badger) them with yet another plot point or character. Writing is difficult work, there's no doubt of that, but I can only imagine that being friends with a writer is just as hard and quite possibly worse.

Thank you, of course, to those amazing beta readers who always take time out of their days to read over what I have written and make it better. Like...a lot better. What can I say? You guys are awesome.

Lastly, thank you, dear reader. For showing up. It's a sad show that, when the curtains open, reveals an empty audience. Without you, this book is just words on a page—you are the one that makes it more than that. By being here, by watching the show. I can't thank you enough for that. All I can do is promise you that, if you keep showing up, so will I.

Happy Reading and until next time,
Jacob Peppers

About the Author

Jacob Peppers lives in Georgia with his wife, his son, Gabriel, newborn daughter, Norah, and three dogs. He is an avid reader and writer and when he's not exploring the worlds of others, he's creating his own. His short fiction has been published in various markets, and his short story, "The Lies of Autumn," was a finalist for the 2013 Eric Hoffer Award for Short Prose. He is the author of the bestselling epic fantasy series *The Seven Virtues* and *The Nightfall Wars.*

Made in the USA
Middletown, DE
14 December 2023

45534441R00129